A NEW TWIS

D0440254

For John Surrey, working at a time travel agency was not just a job . . . it was an adventure. The pay was good, and the perks were fantastic: One day, he'd be heading back to 1966, to watch a hot new band called the Doors play the Whiskey . . . another day, he'd visit 1940 and see what Humphrey Bogart looked like in living color.

But a paycheck always comes with a price. And John Surrey is about to embark on an assignment that gives new meaning to the term ''job stress'' . . .

TIMESHARE

TIMESHARE

JOSHUA DANN

ACE BOOKS, NEW YORK

If you purchased this book without a cover, you should be aware that this book is stolen property. It was reported as "unsold and destroyed" to the publisher, and neither the author nor the publisher has received any payment for this "stripped book."

This book is an Ace original edition,
and has never been previously published.

TIMESHARE

An Ace Book / published by arrangement with
the author

PRINTING HISTORY
Ace edition / July 1997

All rights reserved.
Copyright © 1997 by Joshua Dann.
Cover art by Victor Stabin.
This book may not be reproduced in whole or in part,
by mimeograph or any other means, without permission.
For information address: The Berkley Publishing Group,
200 Madison Avenue, New York, New York 10016.

The Putnam Berkley World Wide Web site address is
http://www.berkley.com

Make sure to check out *PB Plug*,
the science fiction/fantasy newsletter, at
http://www.pbplug.com

ISBN: 0-441-00457-1

ACE®
Ace Books are published by The Berkley Publishing Group,
200 Madison Avenue, New York, New York 10016.
ACE and the "A" design are trademarks
belonging to Charter Communications, Inc.

PRINTED IN THE UNITED STATES OF AMERICA

10 9 8 7 6 5 4 3 2 1

TIMESHARE

ONE

SO THERE I WAS, DANCING UP A STORM IN 1978, ARMS OVER my head like everybody else, fashioning the Y-M-C-A to the retro—sorry, *Disco*—beat of the still-popular Village People hit. The opening game of the World Series was on, and I was probably the only guy in the whole place not sneaking peeks at the TV, since I knew the Dodgers would take the first two games and then blow it, just like the year before.

It'd been a long time since I'd gone dancing, and I'd forgotten how much I enjoyed it. I'd danced the last five numbers with a cute brunette in tight designer jeans, a tube-top and peekaboo heels, and we seemed to be getting along; we'd finished the last three songs with her doing a dip into my arms.

I was at the Swashbuckler in Hermosa Beach, the Southern California regional headquarters of the 1970s. I'd been working far too hard lately, and I needed a break. That was why I had chosen 1978 for a night off. It was a mindless and highly enjoyable year, and what made it particularly charming was that everyone seemed to be aware of that even while it was happening. Unlike the time that I came from, it was a period where no one seemed to take anything seriously except having fun. Even sex, a subject causing much angst in my own present, was easily available and even more important, risk-free.

An incredibly moronic tune called "Disco Duck" segued in, and my partner showed not the slightest hint of fatigue. That was all right with me; once I get going on a dance floor, it's hard for me to stop. For the first time in quite awhile I was at peace, my mind at ease. I caught the eye of my dancing partner and was rewarded with, if not quite a smile, a look of approval. I had passed a test of some sort and my examiner was pleased.

At that very moment, of course, my Decacom began vibrating against my hip. I reached down and gave it two beeps, my personal code for *leave me alone*.

But duty called. I can't ignore a Decacom page. I am, after all, chief of security, and it goes with the territory. That's why I get the embarrassingly astronomical bucks. I smiled sadly to myself, gave the pretty girl a final spin, and pushed the button. Whereupon, I disappeared, leaving the poor girl to wonder if I had only been a strange illusion.

"Welcome home, John," called the wiseass voice of Terry Rappaport. I'd hired Terry, a disabled NYPD organized crime unit detective, a few months before. He'd become my right hand, and we had immediately hit it off in a teasing sort of way. He'd been shot when he finally badged the mob boss he had operated for more than two years, and now he walked with a cane.

"I'm still on the Department's health plan," he said as I finished the dance step I had begun thirty years before. "So I don't have to go on the company's health insurance now that I'm here for three months. What I want to know is, when do I get to go back into the 1970s for some serious nightlife?"

"Terry. This had better be awfully good. Did I say 'good?' No, what I meant to say was 'urgent.' Not just urgent, but a matter of life and death."

In our business, an emergency was always a matter of life and death. There were just too many dangers involved, and I had as much as begged Herself not to allow our clients to go On Tour without at least some loose supervision. But she wouldn't hear of it. "Our clients want privacy," she had stated. "Our success is due in large part to our discretion. That will be all, Mr. Surrey."

I had wanted to tell her that our success was due solely to the fact that we could give our clients something that no one else could, namely a vacation from this utterly depressing era we live in, and in doing so were responsible for their safety. But the money rolled in so fast we could hardly count it. My tax return for '06 looked like a sushi menu card after an office party. And that was just my declared income. I was growing filthy, disgustingly rich on investments I had made—well, you can guess where. Or *when*, to be more accurate. Anyway, let's just say that I had no shortage of Frequent Flyer mileage on Swissair.

"What's the deal, Terry?"

"We've got a code three in sector B12," he said. I finished dressing and and stepped out of the transport area, which we refer to as the Zoom Room.

"Damn it!" I said. That was beginning to happen more and more. A code three was something we hadn't even thought of when we started up, and now it was occurring with a worrisome regularity. A code three was a Tourist who didn't want to come back. "What's B12?"

"It's . . . 1949. Redondo Beach. Yuppie couple and two kids. The Haas family."

"Punch 'em up," I said. Terry hit a few buttons and the standard '00s family of four popped onto the screen. The pleasant, wussy-looking young dad with the horn-rims, the soupbowl-haired mom in khaki walking shorts, the two junior-surfer boys who were too hyper to stand still for a photograph.

I picked up the interdepartmental phone. "Get me wardrobe."

"This is wardrobe," a metallic voice announced. "Please enter your voice identification code now."

"Surrey, John. Pound-sign eight, two-six, alpha."

"Voice identification confirmed. Surrey, John, vice-president, security. Enter wardrobe request now."

"Sector B12, class B." Class B was a suit and tie. Our wardrobe selections ranged from underwear to tuxedos. That was another extra our clients were offered for the exorbitant fees they paid: no luggage or packing required. "Sector B12, class B. Thank you, Mr. Surrey. Your request will be forwarded to Armoire D in thirty seconds. Is there any adjustment to this request?"

"Yeah. No hat."

"Hats are required in sector B12, Mr. Surrey. We must look fashionable, after all."

"Oh, all right. Give me the damned hat."

"Thank you, Mr. Surrey. Enjoy your trip."

The baggy, Forties-style pants were a little tight around the waist. I'd either have to log in an adjustment to my measurements or do some more sit-ups. But lately I'd been so busy that I'd neglected my daily workouts. I'd have to watch that. Maybe I'd get back into training after I cleared up the problem in sector B12.

I stuck my hand in the small well inside Armoire D and withdrew a glass of water and a miniature paper cup full of pills from another recess in the back of the closet. Our medical teams gave our clients full physicals before allowing them to go On Tour; but the further back one went, the more attention had to be paid to vaccines, dietary supplements, and stomach pills to adjust to the foods of the target period. We had found out the hard way that the average diet of the '00s did not travel well. Early on we had sent an impossibly healthy couple back to 1939 for the *Gone With the Wind* sneak preview in Riverside: They saw the movie, stayed a few days at the Beverly Hills Hotel, and spent a week in the john upon their return. I didn't plan to stay in 1949 long enough for lunch, but it was better to be safe than nauseated.

I adjusted my tie and placed the hat at a rakish angle on my head. I hate hats and normally don't wear them, but I wanted to be as unobtrusive as possible.

Terry laughed at me and made the wa-wa sounds of a cheap 1940s nightclub saxophone. "She was the kind of dame who could make your mouth water by just crossing her legs," he narrated.

"Somebody was inside my skull playing a refrain of the Anvil Chorus," I replied. I checked my pockets for currency. I had five hundred dollars and a few coins. My wallet contained a California driver's license and a forged ID from Naval Intelligence which insured me of immunity should I become entangled in any legal problems. Then I checked my Decacom and Taser and stepped into the Zoom Room.

"All set, John?" Terry asked through the intercom.

"Ready to jive and thrive," I answered.

A salty breeze filled my nostrils as I appeared at the corner of Broadway and Sierra Vista, just a block or so from Veterans Park. It was late afternoon and some children were playing punchball on the quiet street. I recognized Jeremy and Ryan Haas. Although they were bigger than the other kids, they weren't any older—which I chalked up to the diet and exercise of their native era. They seemed to have made an easy transition into the half-century before they were born, but we had always found that children discover a common ground far easier than adults.

The company had leased a wooden bungalow for the Haases's Tour, and although small, it seemed ideal for a family on a budget vacation. It had six rooms, including a "modern" kitchen, and was an easy walk to the beach. Redondo was a quiet oceanfront town at the time; there were no freeways to help make it the crowded-bedroom community it would later become.

I walked up the creaky wooden steps and knocked on the door. She of the soupbowl opened the door, and I saw that her hair had grown out and reached almost to her shoulders. In the background was the sound of a manual typewriter clacking away.

"Yes?" Her smile melted into a look of abject terror. "Walt!" she called. "It's them!"

"No, Mrs. Haas, it's just me," I soothed. "There's no them. I just want to talk, clear up any misunderstanding we might have."

"What'd you say, hon . . . oh." Walt Haas, wearing Bermuda shorts and an open-necked sportshirt, appeared in the doorway. He put a protective arm around his wife's shoulders.

"Can I come in?" I asked politely. "I just want to talk to you folks."

"There's nothing to talk about," Mrs. Haas said firmly. "We're not going back."

"Julie . . ." Walt's voice trailed off. "Come on in, Mr . . ."

"Surrey, John Surrey. Thank you."

I followed them inside. The living room was simply appointed with comfortable, seaside furniture, wickers and light-colored wood. There was a freestanding, cathedral-style radio in one corner.

Walt motioned me into a chair and sat beside his wife on the couch.

"I don't know what to tell you people," I began, wincing inwardly at my own words. I sounded like a polite mob shark making a collection. "Look. Why don't you tell me what's on your minds."

Haas sighed, took off his Clark Kent glasses, and rubbed the bridge of his nose. "Mr. Surrey, it's simple. We love it here. We love it now. We want to stay."

"Why?" I asked, although I knew full well what their answer would be.

"Because it's so . . . nice!" Julie Haas exclaimed. "Back where we came from, everything was so awful! I couldn't stand it another minute!"

I looked into her sincere, fearful eyes and felt like a complete shitheel. "I can't let you stay. Can you understand my position?"

"Can you understand ours? Do you have children, Mr. Surrey?"

"No, ma'am. I'm not married. I haven't been that fortunate."

"I don't want my children growing up back there," she said defiantly. "What are you going to do? Make us go back? Drug us? Knock us out?"

Well, it had happened. But only with troublemakers. Decent people like the Haases usually changed their minds when tactfully made to face the prospect of being completely cut off from everything and everyone they had ever known. The finality of it all was usually frightening enough to snap them out of it.

"Do you have any relatives Up Front?" I asked.

"Where?" Haas asked.

"Sorry, shop jargon. That's what we in the business call . . . where we come from."

"No," Haas said. "None that we care about. Anyway, that's beside the point."

"All right, Mr. Haas," I said reasonably. "What *is* the point?"

Haas stood up and pointed out the window. "I've got two sons out there. Good kids. I don't mean just well-behaved and polite and decent students—I mean *good*. Perceptive. Non-malicious. Good-hearted."

"They seem like fine boys," I agreed.

"Right now, they go to parochial school. You know why? I'm not Catholic. My wife hasn't seen the inside of a church since her confirmation. But if we sent them to public school, they'd be dead, or on drugs, or getting the shit kicked out of them for their lunch money. Do you understand?"

"I'm beginning to."

"Oh, really? Well, guess again. You know what it costs? The good Sisters have us over a barrel, and they know it. Forget that tuition goes up every semester. Forget the 'incidentals' that cost us two hundred dollars here, five hundred dollars there. Forget that we each have to work forty 'volunteer' hours a semester or pay the difference. I'm using their college fund to send them to grammar school. By the time they're in high school, it'll be gone."

"What'll happen then?" Julie Haas said. "Public school? Great! They'll wind up in a gang—or in a drive-by shooting! I won't allow it!"

I sighed and turned to look out the window. An awkward girl was having trouble connecting with the red rubber ball.

The older Haas kid ran in from his position in the field and began to patiently instruct her in the intricacies of punchball. The girl looked up at him with adoring eyes; first love. The younger brother stood in the field offering encouragement, cheering her efforts.

The Haases were right; they were good kids. I could see that, even from the window. I turned to the parents. "Look, if it's a question of money, I could—"

"That's sweet of you, Mr. Surrey," Julie Haas said with a note of surprise in her voice. "But, no. Thank you."

"I don't mean charity. Certain investments . . ." I trailed off. Either they'd get the idea or not. Anyway, fatigue was beginning to settle over me like water finding its own level. I was time-lagged. My body clock was still in 1978, and I had been dancing all night. What I needed now was sleep, not more problems to solve.

"It's not just the money, Mr. Surrey," Walt Haas said. "Okay, so they get through high school. What's next?"

"College?" I suggested.

"Okay, college. And after that?"

"A life? A career?"

"Doing what? I'm an engineer, Mr. Surrey. I've even got a doctorate. Julie has an MBA. We make a combined salary of sixty thousand dollars. Not exactly poverty level, but not really enough for much of anything beyond the basics these days, is it? After taxes, after tuition for the kids, mortgage, insurance, food—what's left? We're even still paying off some of our college loans. We can't save anything. And it's not as though we have any toys, or any expensive habits. We go to a movie once in a while, that's it. This is our first vacation in years."

"Your company is a new one, Mr. Surrey," Julie said. "What did you do before you were hired?"

"I was a police officer. Detective, LAPD."

"Then you would know better than anyone what they're faced with."

"Mr. Surrey, Julie and I both work. Damned hard. And at jobs for which we are grossly overqualified, that we are profoundly lucky to have at all. That we could lose at any time. Then what would happen?''

"I just want my boys to have a chance, that's all," Julie said, beginning to cry. "Damn it! I'm sorry."

I tried a new tack. "Okay, you stay here. You're not on a movie set; there are real people here. There are still Jim Crow laws in the South—and not a hell of a lot of restaurants or hotels up north that allow blacks, either. It'll be five years until a polio vaccine is discovered. *Everybody* smokes. The McCarthy hearings are about to go into high gear. Next year, the Chinese are going to take a little hike across the Yalu River. This isn't Paradise. And what if I do let you stay? Your kids'll grow up; they'll be around when things start going down the tubes, even if you won't."

"We've timed it perfectly," Walt answered. "They'll just miss Vietnam. Maybe they'll have to do a year or so in the service before it starts, but they won't have to fight like my Dad did. And they'll have enough money to live someplace where things aren't so rotten, if it exists."

"At least they'll have a chance for some sort of life," Julie said. "They'll go to school when there are no drugs or gangs. We'll be living in a time when the economy won't make every little thing such a burden."

Walt looked down at his shoes. "Please, Mr. Surrey. Give them a chance, won't you?"

I had underestimated him. Perhaps he wasn't such a wimp after all. When begging is distasteful, it can take more balls than anything else.

I stood up slowly. "I was going to say," I chuckled awkwardly, "give me a little more time. But that's neither here nor there, is it?" I walked over to the couch and took both of their hands, a gesture that would have been patronizing at any other time. "I can't promise you anything, you understand."

Julie squeezed my hand. "It's enough that you try."

"You have no idea how much we appreciate this," Walt said.

"Like I said, no promises. But whatever happens, I want you to give me your word on something."

"Name it."

"Take my damned money. Even if it's not exactly what you had in mind."

TWO

"ANY TROUBLE?" TERRY ASKED.

"Oh, yeah, a real emergency, you asshole. They just wanted to stay another week. Somebody got their signals crossed."

"Whoops," Terry said. "And to think, it interrupted your night off."

"Ter, be a pal and put the Haases's request through billing for me? I'm bushed."

"Sure thing, kiddo. Want to go grab a beer?"

"Some other time, Terry. I've got to get some sleep."

"No problem. Be careful driving home."

I chuckled at his last remark. I had recently installed bulletproof windows in my eight-year-old Camaro. I also kept my old off-duty piece, a Glock 19, under the seat. It was illegal to own a handgun in Los Angeles, but if I got stopped by a cop it'd probably be someone I knew. And if I got chased by marauding car-jackers, I wasn't about to go gently into that good night.

I had been an L.A. cop for twelve years, eight of them as a detective. Most of those eight years had been spent on the Fugitive Squad, which I had found challenging and exciting. It had even held an element of glamour. But budget cuts forced the department to disband the squad, figuring that once a crook left the city, he was someone else's problem. The upshot was that if a crook blew town, he was home free. Other departments and the Feds all had more than enough on their plates; they were not about to do our work for us.

I was transferred to Juvenile, the absolute worst experience of my life. Although my marriage had been brief and childless, I had always loved kids. I guess that's because I had had a happy childhood, and I'm still such a kid in some ways. But in Juvey, all you ever see is tragedy—tragedy made all the worse because the victims are kids. As are many of the criminals, and it breaks your heart to write off a kid as hardcore by the time he's twelve.

The worst thing of all is to see a sad little face robbed forever of its innocence, exuberance, and wonder. It sickened me to see children exposed to all of the rotten things in life and none of the good things. Six months was all I could take.

I gave my résumé to a headhunter, and in less than week I was interviewed by Cornelia Hazelhof, the founder of Timeshares Unlimited. It was beyond me why a travel agency needed a security chief, but Ms. Hazelhof's roundabout seduction intrigued me, especially when I found out that it was my experience on the Fugitive Squad that put me in contention for the job.

Ms. Hazelhof was not your run-of-the-mill travel agent. In fact, she didn't know anymore about the travel industry than I did. What she did know about was science, particularly physics and computers. A former tennis star, she had won the Grand Slam and was well on her way to doing it again when a rotator cuff injury finished her career for good. But she had been barely twenty at the time, and had already made her parents wealthy after five years on the circuit. Fortunately for her, her megalomaniacal parents didn't piss all of her money away; a trust fund was put aside for her own use. Corny might have been weaned on a tennis racket, but she was no dumb jock. She was admitted to Cal-Tech, which she could afford in style, and showed the same fire in the classroom and lab that she had shown on the clay.

Although the job market for just about everything had been flatter than a bad punch line for decades, Corny was besieged by offers after she earned her doctorate. There hadn't ever been a tennis star who was also a post-doc. Corporations fought to get her on their letterheads. But Corny had her own ideas. In fact, if anyone took the time to study her tennis matches, they could see that every move she made was part of a grand strategy. She had treated tennis like an athletic version of chess: playing against an opponent's weaknesses, riling the temperamental ones, masquerading a strength as a deficiency. Given time, she would have been the greatest champion the tennis world had ever seen. Instead, she became the science world's most brilliant physicist.

She went to work for the government. That was all she would say: "I worked for the government for twenty-two years. Before that, I played a little tennis." I would imagine that the CIA or the Defense department were involved. But she never volunteered the truth, and I never pressed the issue. At any rate, she opted for the gold watch at the age of fifty-one and retired into a contented obscurity. She put her savings into a travel agency. She had nothing to do with its actual operations; her longtime companion, Felice, who had been the chief financial officer of a large super-market chain, took care of that. But the company's breadth of operations had to depend upon string-pulling and con-nections at the highest levels, which could only be the result of many years of favors and cultivation.

I liked Cornelia from the moment I met her. I had always enjoyed the company of intelligent, self-possessed women, the kind who don't take any crap from anyone but also don't hate you for just being a guy. Our relationship was a formal one—I called her Ma'am or Ms. Hazelhof and she referred to me as Mr. Surrey—but I admired her and I liked to think that she respected my ability. And—okay, sue me—I loved those tennis-legs. You can't bust me for look-ing, can you?

It was Felice who had screened me first. Felice was a petite woman of fifty who had hollow eyes that made her look like she was going to burst into tears at any moment. But she was far from being a timid little mouse. A former athlete like Corny, she had been a member of the U.S. gymnastics team at the 1976 Olympics. Read me off on another PC breach; I was by no means the only person in the world who fantasized about the goings-on in *that* boudoir.

The agency, located on Canon Drive in Beverly Hills, seemed to have no customers at all. There were a few empty desks with computer units, but there didn't seem to be any other employees. Felice kept me waiting while she studied my résumé, which I took to be a tactic because she wouldn't have called me in for the interview if she hadn't already seen it.

"Why do you want to leave the LAPD?" she asked me without looking up.

"My squad was disbanded," I replied. "I was transferred to Juvenile, which is now the most overworked squad in the detective division. I can't stand seeing anymore children victimized."

Felice looked up. "Do you have children?"

"I'm not married. No ma'am, I just don't want to see another child murdered, or abused, or even frightened."

"Hmmm. I see. Well, if you come to work for us, it won't be any bed of roses, but it also won't be as traumatic. It says here that you received the Medal of Valor, two citations for Meritorious Service, and numerous commendations. Are you a cowboy?"

"No, ma'am. I just did what the situations called for, what my training prepared me to do."

"Can you keep a secret?"

I leaned forward. "Ma'am, I won't do anything illegal or hurtful to anyone. I draw the line there."

She laughed, a brief, charming bubble. "No, no. What I meant was, much of the information you'll be privy to is proprietary. You won't be able to discuss what you do with anyone . . . in any detail, that is."

I digested that for a moment. "If you don't mind my asking, what does a travel agency need with a chief of security?"

Felice flashed a winning smile at me. "Wait, and all will be revealed. For the nonce, let's just say that we're opening new frontiers in travel. Frontiers in which *you* will be the pioneer." She lifted her phone and pushed a button. "Corny? Mr. Surrey is here."

You almost expected a fanfare to blare out when Herself entered the room. She never came in by simply opening the door. Instead, she would lightly fling the door open and then sweep in. A hangover, I guess, from her years as America's sweetheart on the courts.

She wore her blond hair back in the same ponytail that had adorned the covers of *Tennis* and *Sports Illustrated* many years before. Her piercing hazel eyes held that same challenge, the one that said, "Okay, try and con me. See how far you get." She still did an hour on the tennis court every day and it showed. The first time she looked at me, I knew my job-hunt was over. We'd get along just fine.

Corny sat in the chair opposite me and moved in closely. She may not have leaned toward men, but she clearly liked them and wasn't above enjoying a little display of flirtatious power. "So you're the famous John Surrey," she said, her voice cool.

"Famous?" I'd once placed third in the national police pistol championships, but that and ten cents . . .

"I saw you speak at a WorldKids benefit last year," she said. "I was impressed. And moved."

WorldKids was a glitzy charity headquartered in Beverly Hills. It was extremely effective in helping abused children, and I had found it worthy enough to donate my time to doing some volunteer work. It gave me the opportunity to rub shoulders with movie stars, and as a Juvey cop I brought with me more than a little credibility. But that was just something I did without thinking. Plenty of cops were involved in charity work. When giving of themselves to the community in a joint effort, cops and rich people could actually deal with each other without gagging.

"When I heard you were job-hunting, I practically jumped for joy."

"You mean, I'm hired? Just like that?"

"Just like that. Of course, it doesn't hurt that having J. S. Devon working for us would also be quite an honor."

Shit! How the hell . . . "How the hell?"

"Enough of our friends have kids, Mr. Surrey. How many copies of *Danny Dreamer* have we bought over the years, Felice?"

"God," said Felice, rolling her weepy eyes good-naturedly. "I'm surprised Mr. Surrey needs a job at all."

"We haven't seen Danny in quite a while, Mr. Surrey. When is he coming back?"

Okay, I confess. I'm also J. S. Devon.

I started writing *Danny Dreamer* stories while still a probationary officer. My sister had just had her first child. So I made up this bighearted, but slightly wiseass, little boy named Danny who always daydreamed, but when he returned from a flight of fancy was too knowledgeable about his experience to have not really done it. He flew planes, quarterbacked in the Super Bowl, gave medical aid to kids in Africa. Danny's long-suffering teacher, Mrs. Welch, was always trying to trap him and, to the delight of his classmates—and secretly, Mrs. Welch herself—never succeeded.

"Oh, so you've been off flying an F-16, have you? Well, Danny, why don't you share your experience with the rest of the class, who had to be satisfied with boring old spelling?"

Danny, who was crazy about Mrs. Welch, always ignored her sarcasm. *"The best thing about it, Mrs. Welch, is that when you cut the throttle to pull a tight turn against an opponent, you can firewall the A.B. and it'll come right back on again when you need it. We intercepted some Navy F-18s right out of the merge . . ."*

My sister, almost as big a wiseass as Danny himself, paid me the high compliment that started my literary career: "Hey," she said, "you really ought to write that shit down."

So I did. The nom de plume was *really* imaginative. The
J. and S. were my initials, and Devon was short for Devonshire Division in Northridge, where I had been working
patrol duty at the time. If I had waited, my pen name could
have just as easily been J. S. Rampart or J. S. Newton. I
wasn't the first L.A. cop to write a book—not by a long
shot—but I was possibly the first ever to write children's
stories, and I didn't feel like taking any crap for it at roll
call, especially since I was a rookie and therefore could
have been fired if a sergeant's kid took it the wrong way.

Danny was pretty good to me. He bought me a condo in
Studio City, a Cessna 172, a Porsche (later stolen right out
of the parking lot at Rampart Division), some nifty duds,
tuition for my sister's kids, and a sybaritic vacation or two.
You may recall that "Dream something for me, Danny"
became a pretty popular catchphrase for awhile. But I dried
up on the kid when I was assigned to Central Juvey. I
simply couldn't create a happy children's story after dealing
with juvenile victims and criminals all day. William
Blake's chimney sweeps were a barrel of laughs after that
kind of work. My publisher was after me to do more and
the networks wanted the rights for a Saturday morning car-
toon. I said that I would consider it.

"Mr. Devon is on sabbatical," I said. "Meanwhile, what
will you be expecting from Mr. Surrey? And why the secrecy?"

She put her hand on my arm. "Detective Surrey. I give
you my word that you will not be asked to do anything
against or above the law. You will not be asked to do anything illegal or immoral. Not one single solecism will you
be asked to commit.

"What you will do will be hard work, great fun, and
richly rewarding. The excitement you will feel just coming
to work every day will add a spring to your step, a smile
to your face. I'll even throw in a free tennis lesson or two."

I looked at her and smiled. "Well, when you put it that
way . . ." I smiled again, but I also took a close look at
those two polished and accomplished women. I searched
inwardly for a gut instinct, which no cop ever goes against.

All of me said "Go! Go!" There was not a single negative vibe in all of my being.

"About those tennis lessons . . . can you teach me your killer serve?"

Corny laughed and squeezed my shoulder. "You can join our club," she said. "Consider it a perk."

I lived in a fashionable high-rise on the corner of Wilshire and Beverly Glen. I had sublet the condo when my new job began working out and I really started rolling in it. Between book royalties, my salary, and the careful investments I was making in my travels through time, I was pretty loaded for an ex-cop. Not that I had much to spend it on; a single guy with simple tastes who hated nightclubs (except in the Seventies) wasn't going to go broke paying his Visa bill. Even my Cessna wasn't much of an expense as it was purchased in cash and was more deductible than a nun's habit. My apartment had a huge sunken living room with two gas fireplaces, a kitchen I almost never used, and two bedrooms, one of which doubled as an office and workout room. It was on the tenth floor, which some folks thought was suicidal in L.A., but I was too much of a Californian to worry about earthquakes.

I flipped the wall screen on to catch the news, although I don't know why I bothered. It was always the same: another innocent kid gunned down in a drive-by, another AIDS cure revealed as a hoax, another Marine killed in Bosnia, the economy bit the hairy banana and would for at least the next eight million years, the Cossacks advancing on Moscow, more foreigners deported from Germany to the delight of jeering crowds. I flipped off the television—both ways.

I decided to hit the rowing machine before going to sleep. I was feeling antsy, disoriented, as though I had a huge bubble in my head. Maybe thirty minutes on the machine would do it.

I gave up after five. Sometimes I was just too bored to exercise. I grabbed a cigarette from my hidden stash and walked out onto my terrace. I had begun dabbling in the habit on my frequent trips back in time, and although you could still buy cigarettes, smoking in public was now punishable by a stiff fine and grounds for dismissal at all workplaces. I had nevertheless found it oddly nostalgic, and indulged from time to time. I could have made a fortune bringing back cartons from the past and selling them on the black market to the smoking clubs, but that wasn't my style. It had amazed me, the first time I visited the past and sat down in a restaurant and lit up—just like that. It was incredible, like taking a stroll down Beverly Boulevard naked, no one saying a word.

I took my battered volume of Shakespeare down from the shelf and flipped it open. My, I was reckless tonight: smoking *and* Shakespeare. To make things really balanced, I should have stopped off on the way home and bought a black-market steak.

I often enjoyed playing a little game with myself: I'd open the book and start reading wherever my finger landed. Usually, I'd come up with a winner, as it was Shakespeare, after all. This time, I hit the jackpot, John of Gaunt's "this happy breed" speech from *Richard II*. What interested me tonight was not the evocative description of England—which never failed to put a lump in my throat—but the opening and closing lines:

> His rash fierce blaze of riot cannot last,
> For violent fires soon burn out themselves;
> Small show'rs last long, but sudden storms are
>   short;
> He tires betimes that spurs too fast betimes;
> With eager feeding food doth choke the feeder;

And then:

> That England, that was wont to conquer others,
> Hath made a shameful conquest of itself.

Violent and politically incorrect as all get-out, which was why it was discouraged in schools and theaters. But read lines like that—which might have applied to Richard's England then and surely my L.A., as well—and you'll see why people on the street punch each other's lights out for no reason at all. Our air is clean, but our factories are rusting. Our cattle roam unmolested, but many of our bellies are empty. Our thoughts do not offend, but neither do they enrich.

Hell! I was becoming a heavy son of a bitch in my dotage of thirty-seven. The world was a shithole—this is news? I had visited every decade for the last hundred years and I knew better than anyone that nostalgia was self-deluding crap. Every era had its anguish, its sacrifices, its injustices. My grandparents always waxed poetic about their youth in 1930s. Hey, I've been there. People were hungry and homeless, just like now. Bigoted clerics spewed racist and anti-Semitic harangues over the airwaves and to huge live audiences, just the way they do today. The economy was a shambles—just like it is now—and Europe was every bit as much of a powder keg as it is today.

But there was an element that was missing from my home era. I had felt it in my bones for many years and had never been able to make any sense of it until now.

Hope.

In every era, there was hope. The Depression of the thirties, the war years of the forties, the Vietnam era of the sixties, and the so-called "malaise" of the seventies; the mindless greed of the eighties; the well-meaning but desperate, ill-conceived, panicky measures to right every wrong of previous eras in the nineties. No one had the slightest doubt that things would eventually pick up.

Not so today. America was a distant fifth in manufacturing, lagging far behind the EEC, Mexico, China, and Japan. A pundit had recently coined the first decade of the new century as the "Laundry Era," and he was right. We took in each other's laundry. The strongest and supposedly richest nation in the world was now entirely based upon a service economy.

There were 1700 murders in Los Angeles last year; 500 car-jackings, 221 residence invasions. There were an esti-

mated 470,000 gang members in Los Angeles. The LAPD
had been pared down to 5,100 officers and the L.A. County
Sheriffs, 3,800.

Consumer confidence was largely considered a thing of ·
the past. The University of California had closed its campuses at Riverside, Irvine, and San Diego; eighty percent
of UCLA's campus was leased out for commercial use.
USC had only one academic building left. Cal State had
closed all of its campuses except Fullerton; the Long Beach
campus, sold years ago to Disney, had been taken over by
the homeless when the project was abandoned. No one
could afford college anymore.

The was plenty of litigation, however. The Pauley Pav-
illion at UCLA was now the Los Angeles County District
Political Court, and it prosecuted an average of five thousand violations of PC statutes each year. It was often observed that you could get more jail time for calling someone
an asshole than you could for slicing them a new one.

In my own way, I tried to help. I gave away as much
money as I could, but charity had always been little more
than a Band-Aid on a slashed artery. We needed something
else; we needed to work again, to build, to create.

I laughed at myself. People had been saying the same
thing for years, and no one had ever listened. It was rather
like the old Aristotle quote about today's youth having no
respect; it had applied to every generation since.

I missed my parents. They had moved to New Zealand
years ago, and would never come back to Los Angeles.

"We're not leaving L.A." Mom had told me. "It left us
sometime back in the nineties."

I still heard from them once a month, long chatty letters
accompanied by photos of rolling green hills that stretched
as far as the horizon. My parents lived in the middle of
nowhere, but since they owned most of it, they were quite
content.

"This place can bore the crap out of you," Dad wrote
me, "but in a good way."

Yet they were homesick. Their letters and phone calls
betrayed an element of wistfulness and I knew that they

wished they were back in L.A. How much can you fish? How much clean air and green countryside could you stand? And who gave a damn about sheep? But the L.A. in which they had been born and raised was long gone, and my parents had never been the sort of people given to whining about things they couldn't change. Even my sister had moved her family there. They'd make the best of New Zealand. Maybe I'd join them someday. It wasn't as if I had anywhere special that I wanted to go.

THREE

IT'S ODD, THE WAY HISTORY OFTEN CHOOSES UNREMARK-able men to perform remarkable tasks. Go back thirty years to a section of the San Fernando Valley called Chatsworth, visit a Little League game in Petit Park on a summer afternoon, and pay close attention to the barely adequate shortstop. Just one of the players on the team sponsored by the local Thrifty's, an average-looking kid whose uniform—like everyone else's—is a little baggy, whose play is without fault but uninspired, whose popularity is no more than acceptance as one of the crowd.

Would you predict, even imagine, that this most ordinary of children would grow up to be the first man to travel through time?

Go forward: an average student skating by in his classes at Cal State–Northridge, intent only on the eleven percent differential in pay a bachelor's degree would command upon joining the LAPD. Is this the Magellan of a new age?

Visit the obstacle course at the police academy. Look at the crewcut rookie, hanging dreamily from the pull-up bar, eyes straining through the trees for a free glimpse of the Dodger game going on at the stadium across Academy Road. Is this the fearless explorer of the undiscovered universe?

I had never believed in fate, destiny, or anything else that indicated a higher power. Even as a child I had been what I would later verbalize as an existentialist, a firm believer in self-determination. But as I took my first trip back through time—a short hop into the previous week—the realization struck me that I was one with Columbus, Byrd, and the Mercury astronauts. In a small way, of course, but facing every bit as much danger.

Cornelia had been sending inanimate objects back through time since completing the module a few years before. Then animals: a monkey, a hamster, a dog. But I was the first human being ever sent back in time, and it all happened rather suddenly. Right after I was hired, Corny simply told me, "Congratulations. You are going to be the first man to travel through time."

"Thank you for the honor," I replied drily. She said nothing more about it, and I had to actually step into the Zoom Room before I figured out she wasn't kidding. The next thing I knew, I was literally knocked into last week.

The apparatus could place you anywhere within a fifty-mile radius in any selected past era, although for medical and sociological reasons, the farthest back we had gone was a hundred years. The future was out of bounds: Corny felt that having knowledge of the past was an advantage, while the future would be far too great a risk. I took that to mean that the future was off-limits to *me*; and that Corny, as usual, had a grand scheme of her own. But I had enough to do. As Security Chief, my job was not only to keep an eye on our tourists, but to act as the lead scout. For example, it was I who had to go back and lease the Haas's vacation cottage, and brief them on the year they would be visiting.

On rare occasions, I had to trace fleeing tourists and bring them back, which was where my experience as a Fugitive Squad detective came into play. I once stayed in 1929 for two weeks as I chased a tourist all the way back to Chicago. He had wanted to visit the Lexington Hotel and "do lunch" with Al Capone. I had to sit on the guy all the way back to L.A. on the 20th Century Limited; people had stared at us like we were a couple of pervs.

I had made a few discoveries about time travel. A time traveler always latched on to the first sympathetic soul met, which led to some serious heartbreak early on. I had almost gotten married (again) in 1940, and came just as close to being fired upon my reluctant return. I almost got killed in the Zoot Suit riots of 1941; there was a sailor with a broken arm he hadn't suffered the first time around.

The high cholesterol content of food in most of the twentieth century made me quite ill; the medical teams had to reconstitute a special universal vaccine before sending me back. I got stoned out of my gourd watching The Doors play the Whiskey in 1966 and took no end of heat from Cornelia for *that* one. I got shot—just a nick, fortunately— in a Van Nuys drive-by in 1993.

By now I was very much the sophisticated world traveler. No one, I was convinced, knew more than I did about our kind of travel. Had it not been the best-kept open secret around, I would have been world famous. But I settled for rich. I made a few investments—real estate here, gold there, stocks and bonds—all very open and aboveboard. Cornelia approved, considering it another one of my "perks." As long as I didn't get greedy, she had no complaints.

As yet, we had done nothing to change the history of the world. Apparently, everything that I, or our tourists, did in our travels was a part of original history. There was not even the slightest change in the world as we knew it.

The job agreed with me. There is something rather lofty about being given free run of an entire century, and Cornelia had been quite right: I did walk to work with a spring in my step.

Our customers came to us strictly by referral. Our clientele was carefully screened, for which a functioning travel agency eventually was opened in the Canon Drive office ("Time travel? Surely you jest, Madam! Now, Princess has some lovely cruises . . .").

Our real office was a large, windowless, one-story concrete structure just off Mulholland, high above the San Diego Freeway. Security was tight, so tight that we could run a license before a car reached the outer perimeter. I carried a firearm while on the property—concealed, out of respect to our customers' sensibilities. The fortress-like mentality would have bothered me if I had been in any other business. But it was our little secret, and we guarded it jealously. There were eighty-seven employees, and each of us owned a piece of the action; even the janitor had privately held shares that made him easily the wealthiest man in the history of broom-pushing.

Of course, we were all sworn to secrecy. Each of us had a signed contract that held us both financially and criminally liable if we leaked anything to anyone from the U.S. Government to the *National Enquirer*. But we were well-compensated for our loyalty. Cornelia gave me the impression that money was the last thing that concerned her, and she constantly found reasons for surprise bonuses and her famous "perks."

The result was a close-knit group with an extremely high morale and profound company loyalty. We all interacted on the cheerful personal level of a happy family working for a generous, favorite aunt and sharing a wonderful secret; which, in fact, we were. Cornelia also insisted employing as many married couples as possible—to keep the secret in the family, I guess—and in some cases, Felice had shamelessly bribed employee spouses away from other careers.

Of course, only a few of us knew for sure what it was we really did. Some, like the medical and currency teams, might have suspected, but only four of us—Corny, Felice, Terry, and myself—knew for sure. The others believed that we were working on highly secretive "government stuff" and were pleased to let it go at that. After all, in the not-so-distant past, Southern California had been the center of the national defense industry, and secret projects had been as commonplace as corner 7-11s. Or hold-ups of corner 7-11s.

The next morning I rose early and went to the club for my weekly game with Cornelia. The company had paid my initiation fee, and Cornelia had kept up her part of the bar-

gain. I still had trouble with her serve, however. She could
ace me more than half the time. Well, what do you expect?
She had once been number one in the world and I was just
a beginner.

She beat me 6–0, 6–0—I was improving, though; I did
manage a few rallies. "You're getting a lot better," she
told me as we sat down to a courtside breakfast. "Or else,
I'm just getting older."

"I will maintain a dutiful silence, ma'am," I said with
put-on humility. "Either in appreciation of your first comment, or denial of the latter."

"You're such a politician," she said. "Now to business."

Of course. The Haases.

"The Haases. I understand there was a slight . . . misunderstanding yesterday."

"Not at all. They were having such a good time, they
just wanted to stay another week."

She waited until coffee and orange juice were served
before continuing. "The Haases are almost broke. They
can't afford to stay another week."

"What if they buy a few shares of IBM or Mc-
Donald's?" I suggested. "Or an empty lot on Wilshire
Boulevard?"

She shot me a Corny-look that shut me up instantly.
"They want to stay, don't they?"

I wasn't going to get a lie past her any easier than a
return of her serve. "Yes, they want to stay."

"Why didn't you bring them back?"

"I wanted to give them some more time."

"You wanted to give them some more time. *You* wanted
to give them more time."

"Yes, ma'am."

"You haven't the right. Or the authority. Are you aware
of that?"

"Yes, ma'am."

"But you're going to do it, anyway. Or am I mistaken?"

"No, ma'am."

She softened and gave me a look that I hoped was one

of affection. "Peck's Bad Boy, that's you. What sold you on them?"

"Their kids."

"John Surrey, why don't you just get married again and have some of your own? You know what a wonderful father you'd make."

"The right girl is always taken," I grinned.

"Well, then she's not the right girl, is she?" Corny said smoothly. "All right, they can stay. But—" she cautioned me sharply, "I want this done within the bounds of good taste. I'd better not open tomorrow's paper and read about former President Haas or Haas Oil or Haas-neyland or the Haas Cable Network or a Haasvision in every home. Understand?"

"Yes, ma'am," I replied brightly.

"And one other thing. From now on, all condition threes go through my office first. Is *that* understood?"

"Oh, indubitably, ma'am."

She rolled her eyes. "Peck's Bad Boy," she sighed.

I scooted off to tell the Haases that they had just won the top prize from Publishers Clearinghouse.

But as I showered and dressed, my delighted whistle slowly became flat and my step lost its bounce. And in response to the system slowdown going on in the rest of my body, my gut began doing a slalom down K2. A sexy little computer voice in my brain warned, "This is a red alert. You are about to be played for a schmuck. Please take appropriate defensive action. Red alert. You are being set up."

I phoned Terry Rappaport. "Say, Ter," I said in a slightly strained voice, one that I hoped sounded almost normal to anyone listening in, but odd enough to attract a former undercover cop's attention. "I'm on my way in, but I thought I'd stop for quick circuit in the Cessna first. How about meeting me at my tie-down on the Woodley side— near the Aero-Squadron?"

"Deal," he said as though the odd invitation was a common occurrence. Although we had a good working relationship, we had not become social friends yet. "Just let me close up the shop."

"Good. Oh, and don't trip on the way out."

"Funny guy." He hung up; I figured that if he was too dumb to understand my blatant double meaning, I wouldn't be able to trust him to begin with.

It was just after the morning rush, so I was able to negotiate the Sepulveda Pass without raising my blood pressure. I hadn't known Terry for long, but if you couldn't trust a guy who had spent much of his life in deep cover without giving in to temptation, then no one was safe.

Terry and I had both been detectives throughout our careers. He had been a detective first grade in New York, and I had been a detective III in L.A., approximately the same senior rank. Neither of us had been seduced by the higher grades; the farthest either of us might have gone was lieutenant if we'd stayed around long enough, but even that lofty position bordered on useless as far as we were concerned. All a lieutenant ever did, in our experience, was stick his head out of his office and whine about overtime. We had each decided that if we had wanted to spend our careers pushing papers around, why be cops at all? We needed action, which was what had attracted us to the job in the first place.

"God, I miss the job," Terry said, causing me to jump and bang my head on the flap I was inspecting. "Right now I'd be sipping an espresso with Big Ralph at Fanucci's on Mulberry Street, talking about last night's Yankee game, while he farted and counted his millions. Ah, the good old days."

Big Ralph was doing thirty-to-life thanks to the case Terry had built during the two-and-a-half years in which he had become the mob boss's most trusted bodyguard. And yet, when Terry revealed his true identity, all Big Ralph had done was throw his big head back and laugh uproariously. Still, the big bust had cost Terry his left shinbone, courtesy of another bodyguard who carried a shotgun but had no sense of humor.

"If you're going to ask me to choose sides, you'd better

have a strong case," Terry said before I could get a word in. "I put a thread in the door and a hair on the control panel in the Zoom Room. So you've got my attention for now. Whether or not you keep it is up to you."

"Fair enough," I said. "Can you get in all right?" I opened the passenger door and motioned him inside.

"To tell the truth, I don't know. I've never been in one of these things before."

"Well, then you're in for a treat."

He stepped into the aircraft with some discomfort, but his face bore no expression. I got in, flipped on the radio, listened to the ATIS, and began my pre-flight check.

"If you're up to it," I told him, "I'll let you take the stick once we're up. And put on those earphones so you can hear what's going on."

"I can't be bribed," he said. "But okay."

I cranked her up. As usual with first-timers, it got Terry's attention. There's a sense of no turning back when the engine kicks in.

"Van Nuys Ground, this is Cessna two-nine-four-three golf at Woodley tie-down, ready to taxi with information Delta."

"Good morning, four-three golf," came the disk-jockey voice of the Mike The Ground Control Guy, whom I had known only by that name and voice for more than ten years. "Four-three golf, you are cleared to taxi. Hold short of runway one-six left and contact tower."

"Four-three golf, thanks, Mikey."

"And a very good morning to you, sir."

I looked sideways at Terry. He was starting to get juiced, his mind already making the trade-off of control over one's life for a chance to experience flight. He tried to remain calm as I began to taxi, but tough guys like Terry especially hate it when their lives are in someone else's hands.

I held at the first turn-off and set the brakes.

"Why are we stopped?" Terry demanded.

"Checking the magnetos."

"What the fuck is a magneto?"

"Relax, Terry. Oh, barfbag's on your right."

"You're all heart."

I revved the engine and everything behaved well, remaining in the green. I set the flaps to take-off position.

"Van Nuys Tower, this is Cessna two-nine-four-three golf holding short of runway one-six left, requesting permission for takeoff."

"Cessna two-nine-four-three golf, stand by."

"That's Van Nuys," I told Terry. "I once waited twenty minutes for clearance. Busiest general aviation airport in the world." I looked over his right shoulder. "But I don't see any landing lights coming in, so maybe we—"

"Cessna two-nine-four-three golf, this is Van Nuys Tower."

"Four-three golf."

"Four-three golf, you are cleared for immediate take-off."

"Four-three golf, thank you." I turned to Terry. "They cleared us quickly but I'll bet they want us out of here now. So I'm going to—"

"Just take off, already!"

I pushed the throttle slightly forward and wheeled the plane onto the runway. Then I set my feet firmly on the rudder pedals and jammed the throttle to the wall. The prop roared and we hurtled down the runway, becoming airborne as what seemed like only an afterthought.

Flying a light aircraft is a completely different experience for those who have only flown in a huge, jet airliner. You can feel every bump and current, and to the uninitiated, a sense of the fragility of the gift of flight. I could see that Terry was both slightly unnerved and pleasantly surprised. A light aircraft offers something else that an airliner doesn't: a decent view. He turned and looked down at the runway dropping away behind us.

I turned out of the pattern over Ventura Boulevard and followed it west toward Encino. "There's Balboa Park and the Sepulveda Dam over on your right," I said. "Feel okay?"

"Fine," he said. "This really is something. But now that

you have me at a total disadvantage, what did you want to
talk about?''

"Terry," I began, "you know what we do at Timeshare,
don't you? I mean all of it.''

"You mean the . . . excursions? Yeah.''

"What made you apply for the job?''

"You asked me this shit when you interviewed me five
months ago," he replied. "And I told you: The salary was
unbeatable; the benefits were good; and I wouldn't have to
walk—or limp—the graveyard shift, rattling doorknobs in
an empty building.''

"What else?''

"Cornelia visited me in the hospital and asked if I would
be interested in working for her when I recovered.''

I became an instant soprano. "She what?''

"Cornelia visited my hospital room two days after they
gave me a metal shinbone," he said matter-of-factly. "She
had somehow found out that the department was going to
either pension me off or stick me behind a desk.''

"How did she know about you?''

"She read about the bust in the papers, I guess. It made
the national headlines, after all. Anyway, she told me that
she needed an honest man to help you out in security. She
figured that I was honest, she said, because I had been
undercover for more than two years and could have easily
been tempted to go south. She offered me double my salary
and helped me to get a carry permit out here.''

A permit to carry a gun in Los Angeles was harder to
get than a decent slice of pizza. Even for ex-cops. But
Terry, who was still in danger of retaliation from the mob,
never went anywhere without one. As we spoke, I knew he
had two on his person, a Sig Sauer .45 in his waistband
and a .40 Glock 27 in an ankle holster. I could only begin
to guess what strings Cornelia had pulled to secure the permit.

"I'm not asking you to choose sides, Terry. I know this
sounds stupid, but I really want to know what's going on.
That's all.''

Terry looked at me noncommittally. I could see why he

had been such an effective undercover operator. His attitude wasn't one of "Oh, gee, I hope they buy me." Instead, he immediately took a subtle offensive, hanging back and making the mark sell *him*.

"Terry, the console has a meter that logs in every excursion, right?"

"Right."

"And since we, as the lead security team, have the only authorized access to the Zoom Room, the meter reading at the beginning of the next day should be the same as it was when we left it the night before, right?"

"Right."

"And? Has it been?"

I throttled back from full to cruising power, and the cockpit became slightly quieter with the lowered pitch of the engine's roar.

"Nope," he said.

I somehow wasn't surprised. "How many?"

"Someone uses it once or twice a night. I can't tell how many per trip or where they go. Somebody really knows the system, though. I can't do any kind of trace, and the computer shows no record of any use at all."

"Okay, then our asses are covered. We launch a simple investigation—just you and me—in which we have discovered that the meter didn't tally. Nothing wrong with that. It's a security matter, after all; and we are the security division."

Terry looked at me for a long moment. "All right. But if something turns up, let me know what's going on before you go off half-cocked. Now show me how to fly this sucker."

FOUR

I DIDN'T LIKE THE LOOKS OF THE CREEP CORNY HAD
brought into the Zoom Room. He was of medium height,
slim, and with the decidedly humorless look that a mus-
tacheless beard had given everyone who ever wore one except Abe Lincoln.

Spook, Terry mouthed as we felt the room become
wrought with tension. Corny, who hadn't been intimidated
by anyone since stepping out onto a tennis court to play
Martina Navratilova almost forty years ago, seemed almost
as white as bleached linen.

"John," Corny began, her voice uncharacteristically
thin, "this is George Obranovich, of the National Security
Agency."

I had spent much of my life dealing with anal retentives
like Obranovich appeared to be. The first thing you had to
do was defang them.

"George!" I said heartily, shaking his limp hand while
slapping him on the back. "How the hell are ya!"

"Nice to meet you," he replied haltingly. Plainly a man
who neither liked to be touched nor even called by his first
name.

"Let me show you our set-up here," I continued enthu-
siastically. "It's beautiful!" Terry shot me an approving

wink; Corny looked at me as though my dog had fouled her geraniums.

"Ms. Hazelhof has really outdone herself here," I continued. "We're just proud to be a part of it. Now what can I do for you?"

I stood over him, remaining disconcertingly close. Things were not going the way he had planned them at all. "I mean after all, you're national security, I'm project security—we're all on the same team, right?" I looked over at Terry, who was trying, not too successfully, to keep a straight face. "Can we get some coffee for George here? You look to me like a decaf man, right, buddy?"

"I-I don't have the time," Obranovich stuttered. "I just . . . here." He flipped a thin, manilla-covered folder at me, which I made no move to catch. It fluttered to the floor by my feet. Then he turned and fled, followed by Corny, who shot me a look that clearly indicated her lack of amusement.

Terry shook his head with a rueful grin. "Nice try, but no cigar," he said, bending down with a lot more discomfort than he allowed himself to betray. He unfolded the paper, and whistled.

"Congratulations, John. It's from the United States Congress. You've been subpoenaed."

It was cold at Malibu. We sat outdoors at a frightfully expensive, minimalist seaside restaurant that was so exclusive, and whose chef was such a tyrant, that no one had the guts to come out and say the food and service both merited the death penalty.

I was slightly hunched over in my seat from the chill. Corny sat across from me, unaffected by the cold, occasionally tilting her face to the sun.

"So, when was it decided that I was to be the fall guy?" I asked her, trying to sound casual.

"Oh, please, John. No one decided for you to be the fall guy. I've never traveled in time; you have. In fact, you're the expert. That's why."

"Bullshit." My unaccustomed rudeness startled her. "Goddammit, Cor—Ms. Hazelhof, I've never been anything but one hundred percent honest with you. Why can't you show me the same courtesy?''

I had hurt her. Never before had she looked vulnerable to me. ''John, there's something I must do.''

''What, Christ's sake?''

''You're right. I haven't been fair to you. But you'll just have to trust me.''

''Why? If you trusted *me*, you'd let me know what was going on.''

''I do trust you! My God, John, you're like one of the family to me!''

A nice thought, but I wasn't buying. ''Tell me something—anything.''

''I can't. Please. Trust me a little longer.''

''All right. But what do I tell the Congressional Committee?''

''Anything they ask you.''

''Fine,'' I said, getting up. ''But when I get back, the two of us are going to have a long, long talk.''

FIVE

SENATE INTELLIGENCE COMMITTEE, 3.31.07
A: "My name is John Surrey.

"I was born on July 19, 1970, in Northridge, California, just north of Los Angeles in the San Fernando Valley. I grew up in nearby Chatsworth and attended its public schools. My parents, who have since retired and moved to the South Island of New Zealand, owned a small chain of successful greeting-card stores.

"After high school, I joined the United States Marine Corps Reserves. I served on active duty in Kuwait and was awarded a Bronze Star. After Kuwait, I returned to my studies at Cal State University–Northridge, where I majored in history with a minor in literature.

"Shortly before graduation, I applied for an appointment to the Los Angeles Police Department. Competition was fierce, but I knew that if I did well, the extra points I would receive as a combat veteran would push me over the top.

"I received my appointment and joined the LAPD in June of 1993. I served as a patrol officer in the Devonshire, Rampart, and Newton Street Areas before my promotion to detective in 1997. I was immediately seconded to the Fugitive Squad, working out of headquarters at Parker Center.

"I enjoyed my service with the Fugitive Squad. It was

our job to track and arrest felons who had escaped from our jurisdiction. It was exciting work. You never knew in the morning where you would be spending the night. We were a close-knit, special group of cops and considered ourselves the elite of the force.

"However, this did not contribute to a sound marital relationship. I had gotten married just before my assignment to the squad; the constant absences soon took their toll. We parted amicably, and I remained on the squad.

"But several years ago, the city, economically straitened for as far back as I can recall, went bankrupt. Our squad, like many of the elite, somewhat esoteric branches of the department, was disbanded and its officers reassigned. I was sent to the Juvenile Squad in Central Division.

"The largest criminal class, as well as a preponderance of its victims, are now juveniles. Sociology aside, by the time someone reaches adolescence, his or her life pattern is set. It is virtually impossible, in my experience, to change that pattern once it has been that deeply ingrained. I state for the record and without apology that every single case I worked brought me heartbreak and despair. I simply could not inure myself to constant exposure to brutal and vicious children who were beyond redemption.

"Even worse were the victims. They suffered brutalities and degradations not to be believed. I sent in request upon request for transfer, but was denied each time. No officer could be spared from Juvenile duty.

"With no other choice left to me, I took the examination for the rank of lieutenant, figuring that if I couldn't get transferred out of Juvenile, maybe I could be promoted away from it. I finished near the top of the list, but then the city announced that because of economic conditions, it was freezing all promotions for five years.

"Therefore, in the interest of my own mental well-being, I was forced to tender my deeply reluctant resignation from a job I had grown to love.

"My financial situation was not desperate, but I still needed a job to maintain my own sense of purpose. I contracted with a headhunter, and almost immediately found a position as chief of security at Timeshare."

Q: "Were you aware of the true function of Timeshares, Unlimited?"

A: "Not at that time, Senator. First of all, I was quite over-whelmed by Ms. Hazelhof, who as you know is a very impressive woman. And I was flattered that they had heard of me at all."

Q: " 'Heard of you?' "

A: "Yes, ma'am. You see, in addition to my police work, I wrote children's books as a sort of a sideline. It became quite lucrative, to tell the truth."

Q: "Your books sold?"

A: "Yes, sir. Surprisingly well."

Q: "Did you write under your own name? I don't recall having ever heard of John Surrey."

A: "No, sir. My pen name was J. S. Devon."

Q: "*You're* J. S. Devon? My children have been reading *Danny Dreamer* for years! You write wonderfully, Mr. Surrey. You must love children."

A: "Yes, ma'am. I do."

Q: "Your last book was three years ago. What happened?"

A: "Juvey, ma'am."

Q: "Understood. Now, Mr. Surrey, when did you first learn the true function of Timeshare?"

A: "About a month after I was hired. Ms. Hazelhof and Ms. Link sat me down and told me exactly what was going on."

Q: "What was your reaction?"

A: "I laughed."

Q: "You laughed? Why?"

A: "It was funny. It was also unbelievable. I used the old Briticism in response. I said, 'Pull the other one.' "

Q: "And what was their reaction?"

A: "Ms. Hazelhof gave me a look."

Q: "A look?"

A: "If you knew Ms. Hazelhof, you'd know what I mean. Then I knew it was for real. When she told me that I would be the first traveler through time, my feet almost left the ground."

Q: "You were excited?"

A: "Senator, I recall the feeling I had exactly. I had the same sensation when I knew I was going to make love for the first time."

Q: "I think we can imagine your feelings at the time, Mr. Surrey. Now, your first trip through time. Was it in the past or future?"

A: "The past, ma'am. Mrs. Hazelhof absolutely prohibits traveling into the future, and I happen to agree. I—"

Q: "Are you quite all right, Mr. Surrey. You're very pale."

A: "Just a weird feeling for a moment. I'm fine now. Must be nerves at appearing before such an august body."

Q: "Your flattery is duly noted, Mr. Surrey. Why do you agree that future travel should not be attempted?"

A: "I have a master's degree in history, ma'am. In addition, I have made it a hobby to further my studies in the subject. When I go into the past, I'm prepared. I know what to expect. I'm familiar with my surroundings. But in the future? I doubt I would have that same sense of security. I could get into trouble, and so could our clients."

Q: "What was your first trip like?"

A: "Brief. I went into the previous week. One of our employees had gone to a Dodger game and kept a meticulous scorecard. I watched the same game and everything happened just as the record stated."

Q: "Did your presence change anything?"

A: "No, sir. It would appear that everything that happened when I was there was a part of history."

Q: "Where was your first extended trip? Or should I say, when?"

A: "One of my first trips took me back to the year nineteen-sixty-six. I went to the Whiskey on Sunset Boulevard with the objective of getting an autograph from Jim Morrison."

Q: "Jim Morrison? Of the The Doors?"

A: "Yes, sir. I caught him on the way into the club. He was pleasant, but extremely inebriated. He seemed to be

torn between laughing in my face and falling ove
wards. He performed quite well, however.

Q: "And you?"

A: "Sir, I must state that I myself had my consciousness
somewhat altered. There was a great deal of marijuana going back and forth, right out in the open. I thought I might
as well try it, for the sake of research."

Q: "What happened when you returned?"

A: "Ms. Hazelhof was very angry. I was extremely, shall
we say, unlike myself. I believe I made a lewd suggestion
that offended her very deeply. However, I had accomplished my mission, and the following day I was appropri-
ately sheepish. We never spoke of it again. However, from
then on I avoided all alcohol and drugs on missions, despite
the temptations."

Q: "What was it like? Being in the past, I mean."

A: "At first, it was the same as visiting a foreign country
where the landmarks are somehow familiar. In general, I
found that people are much the same wherever you go.
Styles may change, and even values from time to time, but
like the popular kid who makes friends wherever he goes,
people react to you in the same way then as they do now.

I've always gotten along well with people; adaptability
has always been a strong point of mine. I always figured
that if I could make it through boot camp in the Marine
Corps, anything else would be a breeze. Also, in police
work, the most successful cops are the ones who know how
to talk to people; I like to think I was that kind of cop. I
always brought a certain enthusiasm to every period I visited and people seemed to respond to it. There was
also . . ."

Q: "Was there anything else?"

A: "Well, yes, ma'am, but I hesitate to bring it up. It
would make me sound . . . well, rather narcissistic."

Q: "It's quite all right, Mr. Surrey. We're quite used to
character flaws here in Washington."

A: "Okay, but understand that I don't mean it the way it's
going to sound.

The simple fact was that when I went back into the

past—and especially the further back I went—I was simply more attractive than most other men. I was healthier, stronger, and in better shape. My teeth had received much better care. People noticed—especially women. I attracted attention wherever I went, and people seemed to like talking to me."

Q: "Okay, so your teeth were a big hit. Tell us about your first big trip. When was it?"

A: "Spring, 1940. My objective was an interesting one."

Q: "And that was?"

A: "To be cast in a major motion picture of that year."

Q: "And were you?"

A: "Yup. But that wasn't the best part."

Q: "Oh? And what was 'the best part?' "

A: "Althea."

Q: "Althea?"

A: "The girl I almost married."

SIX

MY FIRST TRIP BACK IN TIME MAY HAVE BEEN HIGHLY
classified, but that didn't stop me from consulting my Uncle
Jack. Jack was more than twenty-five years older than I,
but he was and is my closest friend and personal adviser.
There was a good reason for this: In addition to my being
his namesake, we had also shared the unusual, but not un-
heard of, distinction of serving in combat together.

When my Marine division pushed into Kuwait, we were
given air support by several elements, one of which in-
cluded a squadron of A-6 Intruder aircraft from the carrier
America. Serving as Air Group Commander was none other
than my old uncle Jack, who told me he made his boys
take special care when they covered a certain group of jar-
heads making the early push against Saddam's Scumbags.

Uncle Jack, or Vice-Admiral John Surrey, USN (ret.)
was every inch the dashing naval officer. Uncle Jack had
been shot down in Vietnam in 1967 and lived in hellish
captivity for almost six years. It was during that time that
I came into the world, and as my uncle was missing and
firmly believed dead, I became his namesake.

When he was released in 1973, it was much to everyone's profound surprise, not least of all my then-aunt Janine—who had already mourned Uncle Jack and found her

solace with a Hughes Aerospace executive. But Uncle Jack, who weighed less than a hundred pounds at the time of his return, believed in starting over with a clean slate. He saw the hesitation in Janine's eyes right away, slapped her on the ass affectionately, and said he hoped her new guy was treating her right. They both laughed, and after an awkward good-bye, he went about his recovery unfettered. "I was a totally self-centered prick that first year back—as I had every right to be," Jack told me much later. "She was far too nice a girl to be stuck with a jerk like I was then. Anyway, fair's fair. She thought I was dead, and it couldn't have been easy for her. She had to mourn me and then let me go. It was almost bad taste for me to be alive again."

Uncle Jack spent the next year building himself back into shape. He had been advanced two grades during his captivity and when he regained his health, he was offered the chance to switch from the reserves to the regular Navy. Much to the outraged disbelief of my parents, he jumped at it. And the new lieutenant commander, in a Jaguar purchased in part with his back pay, drove to Pensacola to become reacquainted with the A-6.

Uncle Jack's naval career became nothing less than stellar, an incredible achievement considering that he was not an Academy man. He commanded an air group, and later served as captain of the carrier *John F. Kennedy*—a plum assignment for a comer like Uncle Jack. He was twice stationed at the Pentagon, served in NATO and in various prestigious assignments around the world.

He was fluent in five languages and was as much at home at the Court of St. James as on a pitching carrier deck. And since returning from his years as a prisoner of war, he was extremely health-conscious. Never forgetting his weak and shriveled form, he became an obsessive bodybuilder. At sixty-two, he had the physique of a man less than half his age. "A woman will forgive you many things," he once told me, "but not skinny arms."

It was Uncle Jack who taught me about the two things he loved most in the world: women and flying. Uncle Jack's pilot's recklessness was betrayed only while in the air. On the ground, he simply let loose with his ambassadorial charm and let nature take its course.

Jack lived in a sumptuous condo in Marina Del Rey— alone at the moment. His forty-foot sailboat, finished with wood and brass fittings, stood ready in the harbor. I spent many invigorating weekends on that boat, which became especially important to me after I was transferred to Juvey and really needed the cleansing of the sea.

Uncle Jack never liked the idea of my becoming a cop. He thought cops were thugs and idiots. "A cop only needs a high-school diploma," he would say, "and for my money, that's pushing it." He wanted me to go to Annapolis so that he could serve as my rabbi throughout my naval career. "I could easily call in enough favors to put you in the CNO's office," he told me. "At the very least, if you don't screw up, I could guarantee you at least two promotions below the zone." When I joined the Marines, he was livid. "You dumb shit, you'll get your ass blown off," he fumed. When I reminded him that flying an A-6 was not exactly beer and skittles, particularly in 1967, he told me to shut up and respect my elders. Nevertheless, he was proud of me and began treating me as an equal from then on.

Uncle Jack had a seemingly endless supply of money. While both his divorces were amicable and his salary was more than comfortable for a single man, it became obvious to me that he lived far beyond the means of even a senior naval officer. Years later, I figured out the truth: It was none other than his loving, favorite nephew who was the source of his riches.

On the day before that trip into 1940, Uncle Jack and I were relaxing in the salon of the *Miss Janine*, drinking cold imported beer. That is, I was relaxing. He was pacing like a caged panther. Jack seemed distracted and, oddly enough, a little nervous.

"So, what's your news?" he asked me.

"Well, Jack, judging from the fact that you haven't sat

down for thirty seconds since I got here, I would hazard a guess that you have some news for me.''

He winced. "No wonder the CIA never recruited me. Yeah, I do have news. But it's top secret."

"Well, hell," I laughed, "so's mine."

"Mine's more secret than yours," he said, attempting humor.

"Is not," I replied.

"Is too."

"Balls," I said. "I bet I can figure out what it is."

"Can not."

"Can too." As you may have guessed, Jack and I are more like brothers than an uncle and nephew. We're also so much alike, it sometimes scares people. Not that I'd mind being like Jack when I'm sixty-two.

"Okay," he challenged. "Take a guess."

"Duh. It's really tough, Uncle dear. You've been recalled to duty and given a fourth star."

Jack looked as though I'd punched him in the stomach.

"How in the fuck did you know that?"

"Hello!" I shouted. "I read the newspapers. How about you? Bosnia's heating up and Germany looks like they're all set to do it again. Oh, and heavens to Betsy, it turns out that North Korea *didn't* shitcan all of its nukes—surprise! So, what're we at now—Defcon 3?"

"Jesus," he whispered, "it's nice to know that top secret really means 'release to national press only.' "

"So, what's your new job? Did they finally wise up and name you Chief of Air Ops?"

"Nope."

"CincPac? CincLant?"

"No, nothing that exciting, I'm afraid. It's rather complicated, but the title is Assistant Chief of Naval Operations."

"For?"

"For?"

"Assistant Chief for what? Training? Personnel? Condom procurement? What?"

"Oh, everything."

"You're gonna be the number two guy in the whole fucking Navy?"

"Not too shabby, huh, kiddo? And wait, it gets better."

"No!" I groaned. "Don't tell me you're gonna be the freakin' CNO! Puh-leeze don't tell me that!"

"I *told* you not to join the goddamned cops, you moron. Yeah, they're grooming me to take over from that doddering old fart in the CNO's office. If it'll make you feel better, I can get you a direct commission as a senior lieutenant commander, maybe in Intelligence or shore patrol. We could bump you up to full commander in a year or so, but at this stage of the game you wouldn't go much higher than that, unfortunately."

"No, thanks. Even so, that's pretty damned wonderful, Unkie. It's what you always wanted. And deserved." I got up and gave him a bear hug. "I'm proud of you," I said.

"It's not going to be any fun," he told me, his mood darkening. "As you said, things are heating up. We're gonna be showing the flag an awful lot in the next few years."

My flesh crawled a bit. "Be careful, Jack."

"I won't be in any danger. I'll be at the Navy Department in D.C."

"Rough life," I said in mock commiseration. Washington was still the best town in America for a single man, especially a guy with the kind of power my uncle was going to wield as one of the nation's top military men. Even if nowadays you did have to wear three condoms and a wet suit.

"So? What about you?"

"You'd never guess this one."

"Oh, yes I would."

"Would not."

"Would too."

"Ladies and gentlemen," I announced to an invisible audience, "It gives me great pleasure to introduce to you the future Chief of Naval Operations. You mature guy. Okay, guess."

"You're about to take a business trip."

"Gee, don't strain your brain, Unkie."

"A business trip back in time."

Now it was my turn to gasp. "No! How in the hell—"

"Hello!" he shouted back at me. "A three-star admiral makes nine grand a month, plus another twenty-five percent in quarters allowance. Not a bad paycheck—but far from Croesian. How the Christ do you think I can afford this place—among other things?"

"Wait a minute, Jack. Are you telling me—"

"Hell, yes, I'm telling you. And I'll tell you something else . . . your Mom and Dad. Oh, sure, the greeting card business was good to them. But how good could it have been? Good enough to buy a thousand acres and a mansion in New Zealand? *I don't think so!*"

Jack went behind the bar and cracked open another beer. He shook his head at me as if he had just visited my school principal and had been subjected to a long litany of complaints about my behavior.

"Don't do this, John," he said softly. "Please, don't do this. I don't need the money, all this."

"What about Mom and Dad? What happens to their place in New Zealand if I change my mind?"

"The hell with it. They're Americans. Fred is my big brother—I think I know him a little better than you. He misses this country, as fucked-up as it is at the moment. They could have afforded a nice place in Rancho Mirage or La Quinta, even without your generosity. They could have been just as happy there."

I sipped my beer and thought hard. Suddenly, I felt guilty. My parents were purebred, second generation Angelenos. They had fallen in love as freshmen at UCLA, and they had never missed a Bruin football or basketball game at home until the programs were discontinued at the turn of the century. They had lived and died with the Dodgers and the Lakers. They had contributed generously to the Music Center, the County Museum, the Thalians, the Hospice of the Canyon, and a dozen other locally prominent and time-honored charities. They had even been named Premiere Parents by the San Fernando Valley Chapter of the

March of Dimes one proud year. It couldn't have been easy for them to leave, yet at my subtle urging, they did.

On the other hand, nothing was the same. The world they had brought me into with such joyous anticipation, the beloved L.A. of their past that they had so looked forward to passing down to me, was gone.

"Jack," I said slowly, "what is *your* problem with this?"

"Hey, kiddo, I'm government, remember? How long do you think this'll stay secret? I give you my word, I won't say a thing. But look at me. I'm the Assistant Chief of Naval Operations. This country's security is my main concern. How long can I wrestle with this phenomenon and then just let it go? If know about this project, how can I, in good conscience, simply ignore it?"

He was completely correct in his thinking, of course, and his strong sense of honor had to be creating a conflict within him. It also opened up a new precedent for the government's responsibility. Did his oath to protect the United States from enemies foreign and domestic also include enemies past and present?

"I know what you're saying, Jack," I said finally. "Eventually, you're going to want to head back to say, 1941, and take the fleet out of Pearl Harbor, head northwest, and meet the Japanese Fleet before they get anywhere near Hawaii, right?"

"Something like that. Can you blame me?"

"Hell, no, I don't blame you. But, Jack, this project is only beginning. I'm the first, the Alan Shepard of this project. I'm going back into 1940, and I'm going to stay for little while. Allow me to at least size up the situation. See how much my being there affects our present, if at all. Let me make a few more trips, if this one works, and see just what we've got. I might not be able to change anything, you know."

Jack gave me a slight sneer. "I doubt that. But okay. For now." He walked over to his rolltop desk and pulled out a small, laminated card.

"Here," he said, handing me the card. "Don't ask me where I got it. This might come in handy."

I looked at the card. It was an identification card from Naval Intelligence, listing me as Lt. Cdr. John Surrey USN, born 19 July 1905.

" 'Lieutenant Commander?' You couldn't even do the decent thing and make me a Marine, for God's sake?"

"If you get into any trouble with the cops, flash that and they'll have to leave you alone," he said, ignoring my comment. Jack had always refused to participate in the long standing interservice rivalry between the Navy and the Marines. He never rose to the bait when I provoked him about it, which was almost every day.

Despite the glaring error that made me a Navy man, it was a nice thing for him to have done. But I also noticed that he couldn't meet my eye.

"Jack? How did you know I was going into 1940, specifically?"

Jack gave me a sickly grin. "I forgot. You used to be a damned cop."

"That's right. When did you meet with Cornelia?"

"Who says I met with . . . whoever you said I met with."

"Jack . . ."

"Oh, all right. Last week. I knew she was your boss, and, of course, I knew of her. But I had no idea what she wanted. She didn't ask me for anything. All she said was, 'You're his family, I thought you should be informed.' Nephew old fellow, I think you're in way over your head here."

"I know."

"I don't think you do. This is one smart lady. I'm no dummy, but she makes me feel like one. There's something going on, and I—"

He paused suddenly and walked slowly to the window. He stared out at the marina for little while before continuing.

"John. Please be careful. I have a bad feeling about this."

"What kind of 'bad feeling?' "

"I'm afraid . . . afraid that you're going to reap the whirl-wind."

I nodded. But his ominous prediction did not have the effect that such momentous words should have had upon me.

"You're wrong, Jack," I said after a long pause. "We've *already* reaped the whirlwind."

"And you think you can put things right?"

"No. I don't know if I can. There are too many things that've been put wrong. But one of these days I just might have to give it a try."

The money, I noticed as I prepared for that first extended trip back into 1940, was real. How Corny got her hands on twenty thousand dollars in legal tender from that era was beyond me. The bills were new, yet they were real. Con-clusion: Corny had friends at Treasury. It was only a pass-ing thought, however, because I had a lot more to think about. The Zoom Room was buzzing with activity and I was at its center. Doc Harvey, a Felice-bribe who had for-merly been the head of pathology at Beth Israel Hospital in New York, pumped my arm with so many vaccines that the slightest touch caused no little pain. I had to swallow a tasteless grainy mixture full of anticholesterol and me-gavitamins. I also had to wear clothing of the era. A heavily starched white shirt and navy blue tie, and a charcoal-gray wool suit. The trousers rode high above my waist and re-quired suspenders and the jacket wasn't vented. I even had to wear that which I despised even more than suspenders: a hat.

"You look smashing," Corny assured me.

"I feel like a jerk," I replied. "I look stupid."

"You'll be the handsomest man in 1940," Corny in-sisted.

"He's not bad for 2006," Felice added, entering the room. She handed me my Decacom and Taser. She and Corny had decided that while there was no way they'd al-low me to carry a gun back into the past, I still might need a defensive weapon, so the powerful Taser—which could drop a man at ten feet—was added to my equipment. If I lost it, they warned me, I'd better not return until I had found it.

The Decacom was no different than the sort of pager that had been the unanimous choice of crack dealers everywhere for the last decade. When I was in range, the Zoom Room could home in on it and get me back safely from any era. I was to keep it on my person at all times, no exceptions. Well, maybe one or two.

Corny stepped behind the console while Doc Harvey took my blood pressure a final time. He also slipped a few packets of Mylanta tablets into my coat pocket. My stomach had never traveled well. Even during my days on the Fugitive Squad I suffered acute constipation as a result of extended manhunts that disrupted normal sleeping and eating habits. It was the only part of the job I didn't like . . . or miss.

"How are his vital signs, Doctor?" Corny asked.

He placed the digital stethoscope next to my chest. "He can play the violin whenever he wants," the Doc replied. Turning to me he said, "Try to eat as much salad and fruit as you can back there. It'll be hard, but try to avoid fried foods and overdoing it on the dairy. You'll probably be eating a lot of red meat, so make sure it's grilled and well-done. And for God's sake, don't drink anything stronger than beer or a light wine."

I nodded sincerely at him, knowing that of course his directions would be impossible to follow in 1940, even if I had any intention of doing so. Apparently, he knew it, too, as does any doctor who is well aware that his warnings and instructions have gone in one ear and out the other. He shrugged and walked away.

I picked up my suitcase and stepped into the Zoom chamber. "Where am I going to land?" I asked Corny.

"In an alley on Gower, just off Sunset. Near Paramount Studios."

"No," I said.

Corny glared at me, but I wasn't backing down this time.

''What the hell do you expect me to do at Sunset and Gower?''

Felice, ever the peacemaker, tried to diffuse the budding argument. ''John,'' she said placatingly, ''your mission is to get into Paramount Studios and try to get cast in a movie. Where would you suggest that you start?''

''What am I supposed to do, Felice? Walk up to the guard at the gate and say, 'I wanna be in pitchiz?' They'll boot my ass right out of there. The guard'll look at his little clipboard and guess what? The name John Surrey won't be on it. Then what do you think will happen?''

''All right, John,'' Corny sighed. ''You've made your point.''

''Okay,'' I replied. ''Here's what I what I want. Get me to Rodeo Drive, just north of Wilshire. I'll take it from there.''

''What's on Rodeo Drive?'' Felice asked.

''I've been doing a little research of my own,'' I said. ''You want me to get into the movies, I have a way to do it.''

''I just hope it works,'' Corny said ominously.

''Just make sure it's off the street. I don't want to get hit by a trolley.''

I heard one of the younger assistants whisper ''What's a trolley? Is that like, you know, like a Beamer?''

It was on that note that I left for the previous century.

has all but vanished from the earth. It was a look brought about by hard but sedentary work, no exercise, constant ingestion of cholesterol-laden, high-fat foods and alcohol. Women were more voluptuously broader in the beam, and their hair and make-up seemed less natural. But they were also better dressed than in our time, the men's suits more formal—handkerchiefs always in the breastpocket and, of course, hats. The women's dresses were more dressy—no pantsuits. And in line with this more polite dress code was a more genteel atmosphere: gentlemen tipped their hats to passing ladies, strangers held doors for one another, and allowed others to pass.

A Mr. Mooney type held the door for me as he exited and I entered Fahey's. We nodded politely to each other and I stepped into a world of men's recreation that no longer exists on this planet. In our time, the first thing you see as you enter a sporting goods store is exercise equipment; weight machines, treadmills, stairclimbers, and other fitness paraphernalia. Then there are running shoes, walking shoes, cross-training shoes, basketball shoes, tennis shoes, and other footwear that in the 1940s would simply be known as sneakers. Then we have logoed sportswear and boogie boards, followed by some baseball, football, tennis, and racquetball equipment. Fishing gear is an afterthought, and hunting equipment is virtually nonexistent.

In Fahey's, the theme was unapologetically male and outdoorsy. The decor was strictly paneled, knotholed walls, fishing nets and creels, and flannel shirts. And by outdoorsy, I mean hunting *first*, followed by fishing, camping, and everything else as an afterthought. And when I say hunting, I mean *guns*. Lots of guns. Guns that ranged from kids' air rifles to powerful safari bolt-actions that could bring down a charging elephant. There was no gun-control here, no fifteen-day waiting period, no background check. But there were also no psychopaths itching to take out schoolyards and McDonald's restaurants. People hunted, people had rifles. They didn't jog or lift weights or do an hour-and-a-half on the Nordic Track, they camped and fished and hunted. Nobody was a sicko or a psycho, and if anyone from a gun-control or anti-hunting-and-fishing organization would have come in and begun spouting off, he or she would be laughed out the door.

"Can I help you, sir?" a young, flower-lapelled clerk asked me politely. He was a slender fellow in his early twenties, with his hair slicked down and parted in the middle. His face showed evidence of a teenaged acne problem.

"Why, yes," I replied. "I'm in the market for a good skeet gun."

"Well, sir, you've certainly come to the right place. We have the finest collection in Southern California."

I looked at the wall to wall racks of rifles and shotguns and didn't doubt him for a minute.

"About your bag, sir, would you like me to place it out of harm's way?"

"Yes, thank you." I handed him my suitcase and I could see that he was surprised by its weight. With effort, he placed it behind the cash register.

"Now, sir," he said, "What sort of gun did you have in mind?"

Notice how tactful the young man was; what he really wanted to know was how much I was willing to spend. He knew it and I knew it, but there was no need to be crass when class would work even better.

"The best for my purposes," I replied, and because he seemed like a nice kid and I was suddenly chilled by the fact that he would probably be in combat within a few years, I decided to make his day.

"Money's no object," I declared. "I need the best match-grade shotgun I can find."

His slightly wider smile betrayed him for only a moment. "Very good, sir. This way, please." He walked me over to a counter, behind which were racked the most beautiful and lovingly manufactured weapons I have ever seen. Deep, rich walnut stocks, gloriously embellished receivers, and delicately filigreed barrels. If there was such a thing as gun heaven, I was smack in the middle of it. The only disappointment for me was that most of the guns had side-by-side barrels. Over-and-unders, which were what I had shot skeet with since Boy Scouts, seemed not to exist in any sort of quantity.

"Will you be competing in the Hollywood Tournament on Saturday?" the clerk asked me.

"Hopefully," I replied. "You see, I've only just arrived in town, and I haven't entered yet."

"No problem," he replied, and I breathed an inward sigh of relief. After all, that was the object of the exercise. "After we get you squared away with a fine gun, we'll get you entered in the contest. Don't worry about being late; we have until tomorrow. Mr. Gable and Mr. Ford just signed up yesterday. Mr. Gable bought a very good L. C. Smith yesterday," he said. "Not my personal choice," he added, "but a good gun."

"What would be your personal choice?" I asked him.

He nodded thoughtfully. "Well, sir, to be honest, I'm not much of a skeet shooter, but I have picked up a thing or two working here."

"I trust your judgement," I said.

"Well, you can't really argue against the mass-market brands. Winchester makes an excellent gun. L. C. Smith, of course, and Parker makes one of the best. Stoegers are a bit more dear, but well worth it, I've been told."

"However," I prompted.

"However, it seems to me that a serious shooter would require a more serious gun."

"And you have just the gun."

"I have," he grinned. He reached behind him and took a double-barreled shotgun from the rack. "There it is," he said as he flipped the breechlock and checked the barrels. "A Zephyr Model 401E, Skeet Grade," he said, as proudly as if he had invented it. "Twelve gauge, fully open choke, five pounds, nice and heavy to absorb recoil. Try it?"

I took the gun from him, checked the breech and swung into a skeet stance, following an imaginary target. The gun was almost perfect.

"Okay," I said. "This'll be our safety. What else can you show me?"

He took the gun back and laid it out on the counter. Then he took another gun from the rack.

"Here you are, sir. A beauty." I took the gun from him and instantly fell in love. It was gorgeous, with a checkered walnut stock and simple, elegant engraving on receiver. The important thing was that the balance was perfect. I busted a few imaginary clays with practiced ease.

"You seem to be comfortable with it, sir."

"What kind of gun is it?"

"A Powell Best Grade, sir. Simply one of the finest guns to come out of Britain in years, and probably the last for some time to come, what with all the unpleasantness going on right now. Powell is often called the Purdey of Birmingham, and deservedly so."

"Have you any Purdeys?"

"I'm afraid not, sir. Most English firms stopped imports last October, and we had a run on our Purdeys almost immediately. We're lucky to still have this Powell."

I broke a few more clays. The double trigger would take a little getting used to, but the Powell was definitely a keeper.

"Okay, what'll it set me back?"

He paused only a moment. "With case and cleaning kit, six-hundred and twenty dollars." He winced only slightly. Little did he know that where I came from, the same gun would bring in roughly ten times that much.

"And how much is the Zephyr?"

He hid his disappointment well. He was obviously working on commission.

"Four-hundred and twenty five."

"That sounds reasonable," I said. Then I made his whole week.

"I'll take them both," I said.

"Yes, sir!" he said, grinning hugely.

The total, after I also bought a pair of khaki field pants, a flannel shirt, a shooting vest with a recoil pad, and a case of shells, came to $1,091.20, or about what I would pay in my own time for a single gun of average quality. But the service alone made it worth the price. When I told the young clerk that I hadn't checked into a hotel yet, he immediately called across the street to the Beverly Wilshire and reserved a room for me. He got a stockboy to take my suitcase there ahead of me. All of my purchases would be sent to the hotel tomorrow after the cases had been engraved with my initials. Fahey's own gunsmith would inspect and oil the guns, so that they would be tournament-ready. Then we got down to the business of my entry into the Hollywood Skeet Tournament.

"Okay, Mr. Surrey, which studio are you representing?"

"The biggest," I said. "The United States Navy."

"Hmmm," he said, envisioning his huge commission going up in smoke. "You see, it's for studio personnel only."

"I know," I lied, "but I've worked with both Mr. Warner and Mr. Goldwyn before. They have had need of Navy cooperation on a few of their films, as you know."

"I see," he said doubtfully. "Tell you what, can I see your Navy ID?"

I flipped open my wallet to reveal the Navy credential Uncle Jack had prepared for me. The clerk gave a low whistle.

"Well . . . Commander . . . I don't see any problem here at all," he said, somewhat awestruck. There was even less of a problem when I peeled a twenty off from the roll of bills in my pocket. Whatever that young man's future held, his present was becoming quite agreeable.

"Son of a gun," I heard a familiar voice call from behind me. "Some lucky fella's got himself a Powell."

I turned around and saw John Wayne smiling at me.

"How's this stranger rate a Powell, Herbie?" he asked the clerk with the same good nature that he would use later to address supporting actors in dozens of films yet to come.

"Mr. Wayne," said the clerk. "Good to see you again."

"Don't let his manners fool ya," Wayne said to me. "Herbie won't sell a Powell to just *anybody*."

The John Wayne standing before me was not the established, middle-aged authority figure the world would soon come to know. He was a mere thirty years old, still lean and unlined, and had just seen the release of his first big hit, *Stagecoach*. It was hard to believe, but this man, who died at age seventy, when I was nine years old, was at this moment younger than I.

"Good to see ya, Herbie," Wayne said. The famous voice was still the same, although it would be a few more years before it became the most-imitated voice in the world.

"Mr. Wayne," Herbie said, "this is Commander Surrey. He'll be competing in the tournament on Saturday."

Wayne looked pleased. "Commander, huh? Up from San Diego? Or the Frisco Naval District?"

"Washington," I said extending my hand. He shook it and I thought, *Holy shit, I'm actually shaking hands with the Duke!* He was about my height, though not as beefy as he would be later on, and his grip was about as strong as my own. The funny thing was that he didn't seem like John Wayne, American supermacho icon, at all. He was simply a nice guy who had just become old enough to no longer be thought of as a kid.

"Washington, huh? Say, do you know Frank Wead? He's one a yours."

Of course I knew of Frank Wead, the former naval aviator and one of the original Langley pilots, who had become a respected Hollywood screenwriter. I also knew that in about ten years, Wayne would *play* Frank Wead in a pretty good bio-pic.

"I know of him. Congratulations, by the way, on your performance in *Stagecoach*."

Wayne smiled modestly. I was surprised to see that he was actually a shy man. "Gee, thanks. But Jack Ford deserves all the credit. That guy could direct a baboon into an Oscar nomination."

He could also direct *you* into one, too, I thought, and he will. "I think you and Mr. Ford are going to make some great pictures together, Mr. Wayne."

"Yeah? Boy, that'd be something. And call me Duke."

"I'm John. What are you shooting on Saturday?"

"I've got a Powell like yours," he said. "I'll give you a run for your money."

"I'm pretty rusty," I lied. I've shot skeet at least once or twice a month since Boy Scouts, and in the Marines I won the championships at Camp Pendleton and Twenty-nine Palms. I even waxed the British Army Champion in an impromptu trap contest during the Gulf War, and you know how serious the upper-crust Limeys are about their shooting. The only guy who had ever beaten me is in his eighties and is one of the best in the world even now. As nice a guy as he seemed, I took great pleasure in the prospect of kicking the Duke's butt on Saturday.

However, I said, "I just hope I don't embarrass myself in front of all those movie stars. Who do you think will be the most trouble?"

Wayne lit a cigarette—in a *store*, he actually lit a cigarette, and no one said anything, Herbie just slid an ashtray across the counter—and thought for a moment. "Gable," he said decisively. "He's the best I've seen. Unless . . . there's this nice young fella who comes along with him sometimes, a rich kid—I think Gable knows his old man—and he's a real ringer. Won the World Championship a few years ago. If he shows up, that's all she wrote."

"Oh, well," I said. "Second place shouldn't be too bad."

"What're you doing in town?" Wayne asked me. "Besides the tournament."

"I grew up around here," I said.

"Yeah? Me, too. I'm from Glendale." No kidding, I thought, only about five billion other people know that, plus the fact that you now have an airport named after you in Orange County. I looked a little sadly at his hand holding the cigarette and thought, and a famous cancer research facility, as well.

"I'm from West L.A.," I told him, since the current site of the hospital where I was born was probably an orange grove. "I'm on an extended leave, and I thought I'd come back and visit the old stomping grounds."

"Leave," Wayne said. "I thought you folks'd be pretty busy right now."

"Oh, we are," I said. "That's why I'm taking time off

now, before things really heat up." Like next month, when
the Germans invade Norway and Denmark, or the following
month, when they attack France and the Low Countries.

"Think they will?" I was about to answer when Wayne
cut me off. "Say, you had lunch yet?"

"Why, no," I answered, pleasantly surprised.

"Aw, hell, then let's go to Lakeside," he said. "The
Commander all done here, Herbie?"

"All set, Mr. Wayne, except . . ." Herbie lowered his
voice to a diplomatic whisper. "Your entrance fee, Commander. Twenty-five dollars. It goes to charity."

"Of course," I said, pulling out a loose fifty and handing
it over. "Keep the change, Herbie," I added. "You've been
a great help." Which was the understatement of the century
so far. I was sure there would be many more to come.

My mission up to this point was a smashing success. I had
been in 1940 for exactly fifty-eight minutes and I was already enrolled in a celebrity skeet-shooting contest, had
bought two guns that would be worth about fifteen or
twenty thousand upon my return, and I was sitting in the
passenger seat of John Wayne's Hudson convertible on my
way to lunch at one of the most exclusive country clubs in
the city. Pretty damned good, so far.

We were behind a slow-moving trolley, the red Pacific
Electric Line that had once been the envy of cities everywhere. Wayne, however, was in no hurry. He drove calmly
and quite well, taking command of the luxurious vehicle in
the same way that he would later take charge in his own
films. He was a man who obviously did physical things
well, with or without the aid of a script. But there was much
more to him than met the eye. In many of the parts he
played, much of the respect he received was due to the role
in which he was cast. He was like that in person, as well,
even as young man. But the one thing that I had never seen
on film was that he was a friendly and solicitous person
who enjoyed being liked as much as the next fellow.

How did this affect me, the disorienting feeling of being

in 2006 at one moment, and in John Wayne's convertible the next? I'll tell you exactly.

One lonely weekend, shortly after my divorce, I stayed home and watched a marathon of Fifties movies. I mean about fifteen straight hours of couch-potato-ism. I fell asleep in the middle of *I Was a Teenage Werewolf* and had a marvelous dream. I dreamed that I was on the set of a Roger Corman movie, and I was co-starring with whole slew of Young Turks from that era: Jack Nicholson, Steve McQueen, Dennis Hopper, James Dean, Don Gordon, Michael Landon, Sal Mineo—you name them. And the best part was, I having a sheer, unadulterated blast imitating the lot of them, and making them laugh while doing it. Except Nicholson. It annoyed him for some reason, even though I did it well. Or, perhaps because I did it well. And it seemed so real that I could hardly believe it when I woke up and found that it hadn't really happened. I recall feeling cheated because it was only a dream.

Well, it felt the same way in Wayne's convertible. Hearing that voice, seeing the familiar side-of-the-mouth grin, it was as though someone was imitating him just for me, and damned well. But this time it was for real, which made it all the more wonderful.

"Ever been to Lakeside?" Wayne asked me.

Actually, I had. A lot of powerful men in the city, both in and out of show business, belonged there. I had attended numerous charity functions held there, and had been invited to lunch a few times, as well. But that was far in the future.

"No," I said. "But I heard it's quite a place."

"It's all right," Wayne said. "I'm not a member, but the studio has a deal that allows us to go there for lunch when we're working. They pick up the tab, too. You'll meet some interesting folks, I'll bet."

Not bad, I thought. Lunch with John Wayne and Jack Warner footing the bill. There's your alley on Sunset and Gower, Cornelia, I thought smugly.

We drove straight down Franklin to Highland, where I could see the Max Factor building to the south. Hollywood, even in my time, has retained many of the older buildings,

so I wasn't too shocked. What I wasn't prepared for was
the 101 Freeway—or, rather, the lack thereof. I almost
never traveled that route because it was always jammed and
supremely irritating, but I was not prepared for the absence
of the ramps and highway roads. I must have looked puzzled, because Wayne turned to me with a quizzical look.

"Been away awhile?" he asked.

"Years," I replied truthfully.

"Yeah, this place keeps changing every day."

We drove up Cahuenga and into the Valley, turning right
and climbing the hill on Barham Boulevard. The sprawling
Oakwood apartment complex seemed to have disappeared.
There was only rolling hillside in its place. As we headed
downhill, I saw that what would become Lakeside Plaza,
the office park, was now a vacant flatland.

But the Warner Studios were there. And they looked exactly the same. *Exactly* the same. If I had closed my eyes
and been whisked back into my own time, I couldn't tell
the difference. Even the main entrance, with the steel Art
Deco lettering *Employees*, was unchanged.

Wayne turned down a side street and drove for about a
quarter of a mile, straight into the entrance of the club on
Toluca Lake. The guard at the gate smiled at Wayne and
passed us through.

We parked near the clubhouse and walked past the first
tee. A chubby man of about fifty, wearing plus fours, was
about to tee off. The men with him laughed as he fiddled
with his club, working his wrists to give the wood a co-
medic rubbery effect. But they stopped laughing abruptly
when he dug in and swung the club in earnest, making
graceful contact with a solid *thwack*, and sending the ball
a good two hundred and fifty yards on the straight.

"Stop kiddin' around and play some golf, Babe!"
Wayne called out.

The chubby man turned around I was stunned to see that
he was a Tweedledummish-looking guy with a little Hitler/
Chaplin mustache under his nose.

"Get your clubs, Duke," Oliver Hardy called back. "I'll
spot you six."

"Not today, Babe," Wayne said. "I'm getting fond of my money. I'd like to keep it for awhile."

Hardy chuckled and with a friendly nod to me, turned back to the game.

"Made the mistake of taking him up on it, once," Wayne said. "Ten bucks, automatic press. He damn near cleaned me out. He's a hell of a golfer, Babe Hardy is. I hope those suckers have their checkbooks ready."

We went through the club entrance, which was virtually unchanged from my time. I recalled the feeling I had the first time I had ever gone to Lakeside, which was one of having stepped into a well-preserved past. Now I was in that past.

We entered the private dining room, which was still decorated in a plaid motif. Many of the photographs covering the walls were still there in the future, but virtually all of the members pictured were currently active in the present with flourishing careers—some with their greatest glories still ahead.

Leon Errol, the famous vaudeville and short-subject comedian, brushed past us with a brief nod. Bing Crosby, looking about thirty years old, sat at the bar, puffing his trademark pipe and talking quietly with a man I didn't recognize. "He's been the club champion four years in a row," the Duke whispered as Crosby gave us a wave and returned to his conversation.

A slender, thin-haired man sat alone at a table with his back to us. As Wayne pulled out a chair nearby, the man turned around. Seeing the Duke, he smiled.

"Ride 'em, cowboy," the man said with a grin. "Pull up a pew and siddown, Duke."

Wayne smiled hugely. As a new star, he still seemed in awe of the great legends with whom he was now on almost-equal ground. It was a forgotten and interesting aspect of his character that I found extremely likeable.

"Thanks," he said. "This is my friend, Commander John Surrey of the U.S. Navy."

Humphrey Bogart stuck out his hand and I shook it. I was surprised at how skinny he was, but his grip was firm.

"Nice to meet you, John," he said. "I'm a Navy man myself. U.S.S. *Leviathan*. Whaddaya drinkin'?"

"I've had a long trip, Mr. Bogart," I said apologetically. "Just coffee for me." He and Wayne glanced at each other. These were drinking times in America. Even the most enlightened people betrayed a slight distrust of those who didn't indulge with regularity.

A waiter appeared magically at Bogart's elbow. "Gimme another Rob Roy," Bogart ordered. "Bourbon for the kid and a cup a coffee for the Navy."

"Will the gentlemen be having lunch?" the waiter asked.

"Try the steak sandwich," Bogart said, pointing to the finished plate in front of him. Wayne and I nodded. "Two," Bogart said, and the waiter scurried off.

"John's in from Washington," the Duke said.

"Yeah?" Bogart replied. "What brings you out here?"

"He's in for the skeet contest on Saturday."

"Well, good luck to you." Skeet was of little interest to Bogart. "How long will you be in town?"

"I haven't decided, Mr. Bogart," I said. "At least a week. Maybe two."

Bogart looked at me frankly. He was not a guy who could be conned easily; his eyes didn't seem to miss much. These were not times when leading men owed their successes to years of method-acting classes that demanded they "become" fire hydrants and gorillas. Much of what you saw on the screen was just as clearly evident off the screen. "You look a little young to be a full commander, John," Bogart stated.

"I'm not," I said. "I'm a very junior lieutenant commander."

"I was gonna say, because it takes you guys years to get another stripe."

"John says things are gonna heat up, Bogie," Wayne said.

"I believe it. Whaddaya think that Austrian twerp is gonna do next?"

"Well, it's just a thought, Mr. Bogart—"

"Bogie."

"Thank you. But I would say that he's going to attack in the west."

"Why?"

"Because he can."

Wayne asked, "What about this 'Phony War' they're talkin' about? Both sides are just sitting on their duffs, from what I can see."

"The Allies are. You'll notice, however, that the Germans are constantly probing the lines, sending reconnaissance flights into France and Belgium. When was the last time a British or French plane flew into Germany to take a look?"

Bogart drummed his fingers on the table, but not out of boredom. He had a lot of questions, and he was preparing them in his head.

The waiter brought our sandwiches and drinks, including a pot of coffee for me. I looked in vain for a package of Equal or Sweet'n Low, but had to content myself with two cubes of sugar. Nevertheless, the coffee was strong and rich, easily as good as what we now pay three bucks a cup for in a designer café.

Bogart rubbed his lower lip with his thumb and thought for a moment. "Mike," he called. The waiter reappeared instantly. "Mike, go into the library and find me a map of Europe. Maybe they got an atlas in there. And get me another pack a coffin nails."

Bogie lit a cigarette and winked. "Lotta questions," he said. "I got a lotta questions."

That was understatement number two. Bogie had a keen mind and he was right on top of current events. To me, all of this was fact, well-documented in history books and films. I had digested and assimilated these facts through years of study until it had become an area of expertise for me. I could discuss the causes or give an in-depth analysis of specific battles as easily as I could give someone directions to Beverly Hills from Burbank. For these people, however, it was current affairs, with most of the plot yet to unfold. Wayne listened intently, asking few questions.

Bogie, on the other hand, wanted to know the whys and wherefores of everything I said.

"I need the map," Bogie said by way of explanation. "Things are a lot clearer to me if I can place them somewhere."

He asked me where I thought Hitler's attack would come, and why.

I pointed to Poland. "He's got his buffer zone in the east," I said, feeling slightly sick as I thought of the brutal policies being enforced against Jews and other Poles right now on that dry corner of the map. "He's protected against Russia—for now."

"Doesn't he have a treaty with Russia?" Wayne asked.

Bogie looked at him archly. "I could throw the little bastard a lot farther than I could trust him."

"Okay, his eastern flank is secure. Now he's got his work cut out for him. On the western flank he has the French, the British, the Dutch, and the Belgians."

"Don't the Frogs have the biggest army in the world?" Bogie noted.

"About the same size as the army the Poles had."

"Which turned out to be useless," Wayne said.

"They were brave, but their equipment was obsolete." Like ours, I didn't add. "And their leadership was pretty second-rate. Plus, their terrain just begged to allow an army of tanks to plow right on through."

Bogart thought for a minute. "Okay," he said to me, "You're Hitler. You got Poland, all that extra room, all those farms. You got a bigger frontier against Russia, and you can feed everybody with all that new fertile land. What's the problem? Why screw around with the Frogs and the Limeys?"

I heard someone murmur "Yeah, why?" and noticed with some alarm that we had attracted a crowd. Crosby stood behind my chair, thoughtfully puffing away on his pipe. Wayne Morris, inexplicably attired in a tuxedo this early in the day, sat at the next table with Howard Hawks, both of their chairs turned toward us. Dennis Morgan pulled up a chair behind Duke Wayne. And those were just the people I recognized. The were five or six others grouped nearby.

"Because I've got bigger plans than that. Okay, I've got Poland. But I've got the Allies to the north and west. The first thing I do, I take out Norway and Denmark. They've got nothing to speak of in the way of an army, I can roll right in."

"What's in Norway and Denmark?" Wayne asked. "If they don't have an army, where's the threat?"

I jabbed the British Isles with my finger. "The biggest Navy in the world. They can roam the North Sea like a Rottweiler in a backyard. They can ferry troops to Norway or Denmark and use it as a staging area. Then you've got a northern flank to worry about."

"I still don't get it," Wayne said. "What's he after?"

"He spelled it all out in *Mein Kampff*," I said.

"Who the hell read that piece of shit," Bogie said.

"Well, I did," I said, not adding, as research for my master's thesis sixty years from now.

"So?" Bogie asked. "What's he after?"

"Russia."

Howard Hawks snorted. "Serve 'em right," he grunted.

"The whole shebang," I continued, ignoring Hawks. "Just like the Schlieffen Plan in the last war. Hit 'em in the west, knock them out, and turn east. With Poland, Russia, and the Ukraine he could feed every German like a Roman orgy."

"Looks like you got it all figured out," Wayne remarked.

"So does Hitler," I said.

Since Bogie was heading in my direction, back to Beverly Hills, he offered me a lift. Wayne had to go to the studio for a wardrobe fitting, but said that he would call for me at eight o'clock on Saturday morning and we would drive to the match together. I felt proud to have John Wayne as a new friend.

"Nice kid, the Duke," Bogie said as Wayne drove off. "He's gonna go real far, if you ask me."

"I don't doubt it," I replied. We got into Bogie's Cadillac convertible. He looked at his watch. "Three o'clock," he mused. "Won't Mayo be pleased." He turned to me and added, "If my wife jumps all over me for being late, you'll have to answer to her."

It was hard to think of Bogie having been married to anyone but Lauren Bacall, but this was 1940 and Bogie was smack in the middle of a boozy, stormy marriage to his troubled third wife, Mayo Methot. As we spoke, Bogie was unaware of the existence of the love of his life, currently a sixteen-year-old theater usher and aspiring model.

"Can you sail?" Bogie asked out of nowhere. Then he gave himself a light tap on the head. "What a dumb question to ask a navy officer. Of course you can. Oh, but I forgot, you're going skeet shooting this weekend."

"You don't shoot?" I asked him.

"Every day. In front of the camera. Otherwise, I keep away from guns. They have a nasty habit of going off."

EIGHT

I WAS UNUSUALLY FATIGUED WHEN I CHECKED INTO THE
Beverly Wilshire. My luggage was already in my room on
the fifth floor, the first hotel room I had ever seen that had
no television. But it was comfortable, even luxurious—
there were fresh flowers and brocade everywhere—and the
bed was a welcoming sight. I stripped quickly and jumped
in, snuggling under the cool covers like a little kid on a
snowy night.

What seemed like four seconds later, but was actually
closer to four hours, I was awakened by the ringing—it
actually rang, instead of chirping—of the bedside telephone. The receiver seemed to weigh a ton compared to
what I was used to.

"Fancy a night on the town, Commander?" I heard Bogart ask.

"Why not," I said. I had all the next day to sleep. "Give
me an hour?"

"Sure," Bogart said. "I'll pick you up in front of your
hotel."

It occurred to me as I showered that if I had received
this phone call under any other circumstances, I would have
dismissed it as a practical joke. But the fact was, except
for Herbie and the stockboy at Fahey's, no one in the world

but Bogart and John Wayne knew where I was. How many people who have ever lived could say that?

I wasn't sure just how formal a night on the town was supposed to be, so I compromised with gray flannel trousers, a blue blazer, and a white shirt with a club tie—in other words, that safest of wardrobe selections both now and sixty-six years in the future. When Bogie showed up I was relieved to see that I wasn't far off the mark; he wore virtually the same thing except for a bow tie—an article of clothing I wouldn't be caught dead in no matter what the decade.

"Where're we going?" I asked.

"Not far." A cigarette dangling from his mouth, he drove straight up Rodeo and across Sunset, turning in at the Beverly Hills Hotel.

A valet with a more complicated uniform than Uncle Jack's dress whites took custody of Bogie's Cadillac.

"Where's Mrs. Bogart this evening?" I asked as we crossed the lobby.

"Mayo? She'll be along. She wants to meet you."

We walked through the hotel proper and made our way toward the "bungalows," which today go for a good twenty-two hundred a night and were probably not much cheaper in 1940s currency.

The door was open at the third bungalow, and I heard piano music from within. Good piano music, playing Gershwin's *How About You* with the flourish of a clearly superior musician.

Two men stood outside the front door in earnest discussion. In the darkness I could see that one was tall and quite slender, and the other was shorter but powerfully built.

"Why the hell do I have to read for it?" the stocky one demanded. "After all these years, I thought I was past that crap." His voice sounded familiar, but I couldn't quite place him. The other was about to answer, but heard us coming and turned around.

"Bogie!" the slender one greeted. "How the hell are ya?" I recognized the gruff, throaty voice in an instant.

"Hiya, John," Bogie said. "Bart, long time, no see."

The three shook hands and Bogie jerked a thumb at me. "This is John Surrey, in town from D. C. John, this is John Huston, who's tryna get me to be in a movie of his even though he's never directed before, and I'm sure you recognize Barton MacLane, who he's probably also tryna con." After we shook hands I thought MacLane had broken at least two of my fingers.

"Nice to meet you, Mr. Surrey," Huston said, sounding exactly as I would have imitated him. "I'm sorry to see that you've fallen in with such low company. Do me a great service and just tell these two louts that I'm doing them a favor by considering them for my film."

Bogie laughed, or cleared his throat, or both. "They made the damn thing twice, John."

"Third time's the charm, Bogie," Huston said. "Cortez and William were both wrong for the part. They just didn't get it. But with my prodigious writing and directorial talents . . ."

"Well." Bogie chuckled. "It's a good story, I'll give you that."

As soon as Huston mentioned Cortez and William, I was able to put two and two together. Unfortunately, it was not up to me to tell Bogie that he was a schmuck if he didn't jump at doing this picture.

"What do you say, John," Bogie asked me. "Ever read this Dashiell Hammett story—"

"*The Maltese Falcon*!" I blurted, like an idiot. The three of them stared at me. "Uh, it was the Cortez and William that gave it away," I mumbled.

"Is this guy from Goldwyn or Fox or somethin'?" demanded MacLane.

"Naw, he's a Navy officer," Bogie said with a grin. "But I guess he likes movies . . . and detective stories." Bogie put his hand on my shoulder. "We need a drink," he said. "All this shop talk is makin' me thirsty."

The first thing I saw as I entered the room was the piano. A smallish man with delicate features sat fiddling with the keys. A gold-tipped cane lay across a low table nearby. The man suddenly swung into a refrain of *You're the Top*, taking one hand off the keys to wave at Bogart. "There he is," Bogie called. "Showin' off again, huh?"

Cole Porter nodded, and began to sing the lyrics—that is, the lyrics he had written for gatherings like this, for these words had never been on any recording of the song *I* had ever heard. But the general conversation stopped as Porter's high thin tenor voice began the song.

> "You're the top, you're the tits on Venus;
> You're the top, you are King Kong's penis.
> I'm your flaccid chum, who has yet to come
> A drop,
> But if, Baby, I'm on bottom, you're on top!"

The song continued to much general laughter, the verses getting raunchier and raunchier, if such a thing was possible. But it was all in fun, and I found myself wondering, *Whatever happened to fun?* I had been to my share of Hollywood parties, even the more intimate gatherings like this one, but I had never seen a group that seemed to be so honestly enjoying themselves like these people. Of course, at the parties I had been to, there had never been any cigarette smoke, nor was there ever any alcohol stronger than wine. Here, people seemed to drink and smoke with careless abandon. But they also laughed a great deal, and with Cole Porter at the piano, and another impeccable-looking fellow waiting for his turn at the keys, you can believe that the music was a hell of lot better than anything on a CD player.

Porter took his cane and rose from the piano with enormous difficulty. I recalled reading that he had been seriously injured in a horseback riding accident from which he would never recover. He tried to affect a swagger, but the tight set of his face gave him away. He reached into his pocket and withdrew a vial of pills, washing a few down with champagne.

Meanwhile, the impeccable fellow who replaced him at the piano was tinkling out the Porky Pig theme with two fingers. That didn't fool me, though—his dynamics gave him away as a great talent.

> "Turks do it, Greeks do it,
>   Even young men who sell antiques do it . . ."

I almost kicked myself when I heard that. How could I not have recognized Noel Coward? I began laughing uproariously along with everyone else. It wasn't just that Coward's lyrics were hilarious; it was out of the sheer joy of being where I was.

> "Sods do it, twits do it,
>   Even pompous little shits do it.
>   Let's do it, let's fall in love.
>
>   The Nazi swine on the Spree do it,
>   Tho' they lack in panache,
>   Frogs in Paree do it,
>   For the right sum of cash.

Bogie, seeing that I was beginning to have a good time, did something I had never seen him do in the movies, and that was more out of character for him than anything I could ever imagine. He walked over to the piano and sat on Coward's lap. Coward, not missing a beat, reached his arms around Bogart and continued playing. What Bogie did next could have landed him PC Court on a major harassment charge and ruined his career in my time. He bent his wrists, pursed his lips, and began singing along with Coward in a high falsetto with absurdly sibilant esses. But he and Coward were obviously good friends, and it was taken with good humor.

I hadn't laughed that hard in months. There were tears rolling down my cheeks and my stomach was beginning to cramp. But here I was, in a bungalow at the Beverly Hills Hotel, surrounded by the likes of Leslie Howard, Raymond Massey, Joan Fontaine, Tyrone Power, Ward Bond, Brian Donlevy, Maureen O'Sullavan and a whole bunch of other people whose names I was sure I would recognize once introduced, and Humphrey friggin' Bogart was going for a big yuck for *my* benefit by sitting on the lap of Noel friggin' Coward. If a better time could be had anywhere, I wasn't aware of it.

I stepped back and almost tripped over an ashtray on the floor, which caused me to spill part of my drink, narrowly missing a dark-haired, petite young woman.

"I'm terribly sorry," I apologized, reaching for a napkin.

"That's all right," the girl said. "No harm done."

She smiled, a winning and engaging smile, the effect of which went straight down to my toes. I had received such an introductory smile from just three other women in my life: The girl I went steady with all through high school; the woman who eventually became my wife; and a lady I sat next to on an airplane to Chicago and never saw again— she made a connection to Rome and passed out of my life forever.

"John Surrey," I said.

"Well, John Surrey to you, too."

"No, that's my name," I said, extending my hand.

She shook my hand firmly. "Oh. I thought that's what people say where you come from."

I grinned. "What're you, a wise guy?"

"Not I. It's a pleasure to meet you, John Surrey. I'm Althea Rowland. Are you an inmate?"

"Excuse me?"

"An inmate. Hollywood."

"No," I laughed. "I *am* from around here, but I live in Washington now."

"And you're not in The Industry?"

"No."

"Thank God! Let's have a conversation . . . *please*. What do you do in Washington, Mr. Surrey—no, let me guess. I can usually tell by looking at someone what they do."

She narrowed one beautiful brown eye at me and regarded me critically. "Well, I'll be damned," she said finally. "You're a cop."

It took virtually all the self-control I had not to spit out my drink, but I recovered nicely. "How could I afford our children's school fees on a cop's salary?"

"Oh? Are you rich, Mr. Surrey?"

"I have a private income."

"Remittance man, eh?"

"Not quite. I also have a job."

"Really? A steady job?"

"I'm a naval officer."

The bantering mood vanished. "I want to talk to you," she said sternly.

She took my hand and led me over to a small couch. She was about to speak when Bogie appeared. "Leave it to a sailor to find the prettiest girl in the room." He leaned over and kissed the top of Althea's head. She reached up and rubbed his shoulder affectionately.

"John," said Bogie, "see if you can talk her out of going to England. We can't afford to lose a great actress like her."

I suddenly recalled that Althea Rowland was an up-and-coming young actress in the late Thirties who had been nominated for Best Supporting Actress in 1937 and 1939. She was about to graduate to stardom when her career was mysteriously halted. I was determined to find out why, although I already had a bad feeling about the reason.

"You're sweet, Bogie, but there's no shortage of good actresses out here."

Bogie gave me a man-to-man wink and said "Talk to her." Then he went back over to his friends.

"Why are you going to England?" I asked. "You're a wonderful actress—you're going to be a big star." I remembered seeing her in *Dead End* with Bogart and *Stage Door* with Katharine Hepburn. She almost blew Hepburn off the screen in that one—not an easy thing to do.

"I have to go home," she said simply. "My country needs me."

"Your country?" She sounded American to me. Her accent struck me as pure Californian seasoned with heavy dialogue coaching.

"I'm half-American, half-English. My father. He's been

called up, you know." Her father was even more famous than she was. You may recall Angus Rowland won more Oscars than any other set designer of the era. "They actually made him a colonel, although for what, I have not the slightest idea."

"When are you leaving?" I asked.

"Next month. My commission in the WAAFs should come through any time now. What are you, a captain or something?"

"Lieutenant Commander. Look—can we get out of here? I think we should talk."

"Why, yes. I often leave parties alone with men I've known for three minutes."

"Just outside, where there's less noise. Don't worry, your virtue is safe with me. I am, after all, an officer and a gentleman."

"Oh, well. *That*'s a comfort."

I stopped at the bar for a couple of drinks on our way outside. As we left the room, I noticed that we were under the aegis of Bogart's watchful eye.

"Who's putting you up to this?" she said as we settled into lounge chairs by the pool. "Bogart or John Huston?"

"Excuse me?"

"Huston wants me for his new movie—which by the way, I'd commit murder and mayhem to do at any other time in history. But I have a previous engagement, thanks to Mssrs. Hitler and Mussolini."

I immediately tried to imagine her in the role that Mary Astor had immortalized. No problem.

"What do you hope to accomplish?"

"Accomplish? I hope to accomplish an end to this stupid war, that's what I hope to accomplish. I hope to do my share and put Hitler behind bars where he belongs."

"It's going to take a long time to accomplish that. This war is just beginning."

"I know," she said. "But as long as we keep Hitler from going any further—"

"Won't happen," I interrupted, a little more gruffly than I had intended.

"Well, then," she said, sounding a little annoyed, "what *will* happen?"

"He's going to attack and win, attack and win, and attack and win. Then we'll stop him. But by then, it'll almost be too late."

"Too late for what?"

"Althea! Althea," I heard an English-accented voice call. "Oh, there you are." A superbly tailored young Brit, strolling with the easy grace of an athlete, came into view. "I just wanted to say good-bye before—oh, hello."

"I just can't avoid sailors, can I," Althea said to the air.

"That's why you should listen to me and join the Navy instead of the Air Force, darling," the man said, kissing her on the lips. He seemed like a decent fellow, but I didn't like his kissing her, just the same.

"What, me with those Cheltenham snobs? I'm used to working for a living. The RAF for me, thank you. Here's a fellow Navy man for you. Lieutenant Commander John Surrey, U.S. Navy, meet Lieutenant Ian Fleming, Royal Navy Volunteer Reserves."

I stood and shook Fleming's hand. The creator of James Bond seemed overjoyed to meet me. I, on the other hand, was not too thrilled to meet him at the moment.

"I'm honored, Commander."

"A pleasure, Lieutenant. What brings you to Hollywood?" *And takes you away from Althea very soon, I hope?*

"Just showing the flag for our film community friends, sir. I had to speak at a Defend America by Aiding Britain reception. Doug Fairbanks and friends. In fact, I'm due back in Washington next week. I came to say good-bye to Althea."

"Well," I said, suddenly heartened. "Do join us, won't you?"

"Thank you," he said, pulling up a deck chair and sitting on the edge.

"The Commander here was just telling me that Adolf is going to attack and win, attack and win, and attack and win," Althea said.

Fleming looked at me appraisingly. "He's probably right. But I've got to say, Commander—"

"John, please," I said.

"John," he nodded. "Having just come from—and soon to be returning to—Washington, that doesn't seem to be the prevailing view among your colleagues at the Navy Department. In fact, most of them seem to think we should accept his 'outstretched hand' and leave well enough alone." He gave me look that asked for a comment.

"They're misinformed," I said. "But the Navy isn't interested in Europe. They're concerned with Japan."

Fleming nodded his approval. "As they should be. But if the balloon goes up, will America get into the war?"

"We'll get into it, all right. Just not right away. The President has public opinion against it at the moment. What you guys should be worried about is when he attacks in the west."

"We'll stop him in his tracks," Fleming said confidently. "After all, why hasn't he attacked up to now?"

Well, Ian, I thought, *he was going to attack on November 12, but his generals wisely talked him out of it because they weren't ready. They'll talk him out of it another eighteen times, too, but the twentieth will be the charm, and all hell will break loose.*

"I'm sure he has his reasons," I answered. "If you folks were smart, you'd attack him while he still has his pants down."

"To what end? He's not going anywhere. Not with our Army, the French, and the Maginot Line."

"You don't seriously believe that the Line can't be flanked," I asked him.

The very idea seemed to amaze him. "Where?"

"Through Belgium."

"But Belgium is neutral."

"Oh, Hitler will respect *that*," I said sarcastically. "If it were up to me, I'd take that huge white elephant the French call an Army, your BEF, and both Air Forces and invade Germany, and I mean *right now*. Catch 'em flatfooted; take back the Rhineland. They'd have to sue for peace and hang that Austrian loony-tune by his thumbs with the rest of his gang of cutthroats.''

"Do unto others *before* they do unto you. Right, John?" Althea said.

I hadn't realized how heated I had become. But for some reason I was exhausted, and the futility of all my knowledge of things to come sat on my shoulders like a giant anvil. There were thirty million people alive right now who would be dead in five years, and there was nothing I could do about it. There were thirty million people, many of them asleep in Europe at this very moment, who were destined to die. And it could have all been avoided at any time in the last six months by one massive Allied attack. "I'm sorry," I said tiredly. "I'm sure you're doing all you can."

"No, John, continue," Fleming urged, "I insist. *Please.*"

There was something about his tone that made me decide to shoot my mouth off. Here was a good man whose country was about to come within a hairbreadth of being destroyed in the coming months, and he deserved any possible advantage he could lay his hands on. I also didn't give a damn anymore. The year 1940 was fast losing its charm for me. I felt as if I were dining at the captain's table on board the *Titanic*. The world was just about to explode. I'd met a woman who, so far, seemed like she could be the next Mrs. Surrey if I wasn't careful, and I was going to lose her almost immediately. I was on top of a deep canyon, irresistibly drawn to the edge.

"All right, Ian." I looked at Althea, whose eyes were shining. She put her hand over mine and gave me a reassuring squeeze. "The Germans will attack Norway next month. You folks will give them a go at sea—pretty much end the war for their surface Navy. But the damage will have already been done, because their northern flank will be secure. The following month, on May tenth, they'll launch a massive attack against Belgium and Holland. Belgium will fall soon after paratroopers take Fort Ebn-Emael. They've been rehearsing all winter with a cardboard mock-up, so they'll do it in twenty-four hours—eighty men led by a sergeant.

"Holland will stage a brave defense, but it won't be enough. They're good but just too small. Down they go. Of course, you fine folks—that is to say, the French and British—will rush your armies up to Belgium to try and plug the hole. Your Brits will fight pretty well, but the French will have to pull whole armies from the Maginot Line. Not that it matters: Who'd be fool enough to attack a fortified defensive network like that? Anyway, it won't make a difference, because you're doing just what the Krauts hope you'll do. Bring everybody and his goddamned brother up across the Meuse; protect that border. Be Adolf's guest, if you're stupid enough to think that his invasion only has one prong."

"Where's the other prong?" Fleming asked hoarsely, his mouth completely dry.

"Well," I said expansively, "it's funny that you should ask. About, oh, five or ten years ago, there were some army colonels. One was American, a dashing cavalryman named George S. Patton; one was a Frenchman, a rather tall, saturnine boyo named Charles de Gaulle; and two were German—one, a dapper aristocrat named Heinz Guderian; and the other, his most trusted subordinate, a gent from a working class background named Erwin Rommel. All four of these splendid fellows had one thing in common: They were all staunch proponents of the power of the armored attack. That, for our Spanish listeners, means tanks. Now, our American cousin, Colonel Patton, is unfortunate enough to be in an Army so small that there *aren't* any tanks to speak of. Oh, well. The Gallic Colonel, Monsieur de Gaulle, has the misfortune to be in an Army that spends more time planning parades than tactics. Who'd the Frogs ever beat in the last hundred years, after all?

"But our Teutons—ah, they know military genius when they see it. And they knew that one day, they'd need a couple of bright boys like that to lead their armored corps into battle. So, when these fellows wrote books about armored tactics, instead of saying, 'Great, but where's the money going to come from?' like the Americans; or 'Really, Charles, who the hell cares and polish that button, you're a disgrace' like the French; the Germans said, 'Okay, sport, you're up. Draw us a battle plan and let's kick some ass.' Pardon my French,'' I added, to Althea.

I swallowed the rest of my champagne. ''Now, then, boys and girls, the sixty-four thousand dollar question for tonight is: What are these two extremely brilliant Krauts going to do when Germany opens hostilities in Western Europe—which, again for our Spanish listeners, is what the German High Command calls *Fall Gelb*, or Case Yellow. Where is this armored attack going to be? Althea, for that beautiful lounge suite? No? Lieutenant Fleming, for a new Buick? No?

''Well, kids! There's a forest in Northeastern France, and it's called . . . the Ardennes! Yes, ladies and gentlemen, those Nazi armored divisions are going to just pour through that supposedly impenetrable forest, and nothing is going to stop them. The French and the British, scared silly, are going to rush headlong for the nearest port, because they won't want to be completely encircled. Fortunately for them, there is one last port that Germans won't have captured just yet, a nice little seaside burg called Dunkirk, a good place for a miracle because, by God, are you going to need one.''

I stopped abruptly, my angry words still hanging in the air. There were tears pouring down Althea's cheeks, and Fleming's face was completely frozen.

''How could you not know?'' I whispered bitingly to Fleming. ''What the hell do you think they've been *doing* all winter while you jerks were sampling French cuisine?''

Althea had turned her head away from me and was weeping softly. Fleming looked as though Joe Louis had punched him in the solo plexus.

''Ian,'' I said slowly. ''I know there's nothing we can do. But can't you at least get them to fly over Western Germany and take a look? See the troop buildups? The huge movements that have to be going on right now?''

Fleming drew himself up. I'd spilled something in his

lap that he didn't want. It was too big and he needed to think. "I can't ..." he began weakly, "I ... Commander, where can you be reached?"

"I'm at the Beverly Wilshire," I said. "But do not contact my government, or the Navy Department and ask about me. Is that understood?"

"Of course," he said.

"Don't even give anyone my name, Lieutenant. I'm not kidding. If you do, I'll deny ever saying anything. If I hear that you've been checking me out—and I will hear about it—that's the end. Is that understood? If you talk about me to anyone, use a cover name. That's a direct order, Lieutenant Fleming."

"Yes, sir. Who should I ... uh ... what 'cover' name?"

I couldn't possibly resist; who could?

"The name," I said, using the intonation I had heard in two dozen movies, "is Bond. *James* Bond."

After Fleming stumbled away into the darkness, Althea, once again dry-eyed, turned to me. "Well," she said, "you sure know how to get rid of the competition, don't you?"

I shrugged and leaned all the way back in the deck chair. "I'm a lot bigger than he is, and just about as good-looking."

"How much of that was true?" she asked.

I shrugged again. "If it isn't true, then no one's lost anything. Where I come from, it's called a win-win situation."

" 'A win-win situation.' I like that. Does such a thing exist in the real world?"

"It can. Under ideal conditions."

"These are hardly ideal conditions."

"It's a dilemma."

"Poor Ian." She turned to me suddenly. "Are you really an American?"

"Am I what?"

"There's something strange about you. I can't quite put my finger on it. Are you a Nazi spy or something?"

"Ve haf vays uf makink you talk," I replied tiredly.

"I'm serious."

"Like I'd tell you if I was. Come on, Althea, what the hell would I spy on in Beverly Hills?"

"Then how do you know all that about the German attack?"

"I can't tell you that. And why would I give away invasion plans to a British naval officer?"

"Maybe they're the wrong plans."

"Nope. I can guarantee that."

"How?"

"Oh, history will bear me out," I said airily. "C'mon, I want gossip. I heard Gable has false teeth. Is that true?"

"No shop talk. I'm a semi-famous actress; everybody knows about me. I want to know about you."

"There's nothing to know about me. I was born here in Los Angeles, joined the Navy, and here I am."

"Exciting life."

"It has its moments. I'm here with you, aren't I? Look, I'm pretty rich. I could make you happy."

"Is that a proposal?"

"I'll tell you when I know you better."

She sighed. "You'd better get to know me fast. I won't be here much longer."

I sat up suddenly. "Althea. If you go to England, you'll die." I had said it so plainly, and so simply, that she was taken completely aback. She gave a brief shiver.

"God, you just gave me the chills. What do you mean, I'll 'die'?"

"Do you have any idea where you'll be assigned?"

"No, but there's a good chance it'll be Manston or Biggin Hill." Both of those RAF bases were clobbered six months later during the Battle of Britain.

"Great." I stood up. "It would have been a pleasure to get to know you. You seem like a bright, possibly wonderful woman. I would have liked to have courted you, see if a relationship could have developed, but I guess that's just not in the cards."

She shook her head at me. "You're nuts."

"I sure am. I hope—"

I suddenly heard glass shatter. As I turned towards its source, Bogie came skittering out of the bungalow. There was a small but very bloody gash on his forehead.

"Christ," I said, taking a handkerchief from my pocket and pressing it to his wound. "What happened to you?"

"Oh, no," Althea groaned, rolling her eyes. "Mayo's on the loose."

A slight blurry figure in a beige evening dress and wrap came charging out of the bungalow, grasping an empty champagne bottle like a club. Bogie wrenched away from me and ran around the deck chair. Giggling with fear, he dodged away each time she tried to bludgeon him.

"Son of a bitch!" Mayo hissed. She chased him around the deck chair, rudely shoving me each time. I couldn't help noticing, however, that as loaded as she was, she instinctively avoided contact with Althea.

"What happened, Bogie?" I asked as he took refuge behind my back. Mayo slashed away with the bottle, coming a hell of a lot closer to me than to him.

"Oh, I was a fiend," Bogie said. "I think I said something like"—he turned me suddenly to avoid a flanking movement by Mayo—"something like, 'hello, dear.' Am I a no-good prick, or what?"

"Sweetheart," Bogie said in rapid-fire to Mayo, "this is John Surrey, who I told you about, and of course you know Althea."

"Nice to meet you, Mr. Surrey," she slurred, swinging away at Bogie and narrowly missing my head. I began thinking seriously of disarming her and getting her into a wristlock, but I had declared myself free of that crap forever when I made detective. Like a true friend, Bogie solved the problem for me. He whispered, "I'll call you tomorrow," and took off into the night. Mayo went in hot pursuit, bottle held high.

"Well, that was an evening's excitement," Althea said, drawing a gold cigarette case from her purse. She took out a cigarette and put it to her lips, looking at me expectantly. I held out my empty palms. I had never known a woman who smoked after my mom quit when I was a kid, and I don't think I had ever lit anyone's cigarette before. Althea took out her lighter and lit up for herself.

"This has happened before, I take it?"

"Every night," she said, exhaling. "I wish he'd dump her and find someone nice. He insists that she was once a great actress, before the booze. I have my doubts."

"I couldn't help but notice," I said, "that as drunk and maniacal as she was, she didn't go near you."

"She came after me once. It was during the filming of *Dead End*. It was just like this. She saw me and took a swing at me, just for the hell of it. She's got a mean right hook, as Bogie can tell you."

"What did you do?"

"Not much. I told her I was aware that she had a few problems to work out and that I understood."

"Is that all?"

"For the most part. Oh, then I threw her against the wall and said that I didn't care how drunk she was, if she ever touched me again, I'd beat the living shit out of her."

"I guess she believed you," I nodded.

"Come on," she said, rising suddenly. "I'll buy you a cup of coffee."

I was not surprised to discover that Althea drove like a maniac. A skilled maniac to be sure, but I was still in agony over the fact that this was an era long before seat belts and shoulder harnesses. I gripped the windwing post and planted my feet firmly on the floor. The car was a brand-new Packard convertible, and as she took the turn from Rexford Drive onto Lexington, I had frightening visions of being tossed out into the night and being left with a fractured skull.

She slowed down considerably as we wended our way up into the hills. " 'Either you ought to be more careful,' " I quoted, " 'or you oughtn't to drive at all.' "

"*The Great Gatsby*," she said. "Jordan Baker was a vapid bitch. I'm not. Who are you, Nick or Gatsby?"

"I used to be Gatsby," I said, adding predictably, " 'in my younger and more vulnerable years.' Now I'm definitely Nick. When you're young he's sort of boring, but I find him and what he has to say more interesting the older I become. And poor Gatsby becomes more pathetic.''

"Pathetic? How cruel." She jinked the car to avoid some overgrown brush on the side of the road.

"Not at all. You can't help but like the poor guy, but he lives, and then dies, for a woman who couldn't give a damn about him."

"And you'd never do that?"

"Not now. Maybe twenty years ago. Or as Nick so aptly put it, 'I'm too old to lie to myself and call it honor.' "

"Then you're not a romantic?"

"God, no." Six months in Juvenile Division had effectively purged me of any last vestiges of romanticism I had left.

"No blinking green light at the end of a dock for you."

"Nope. Because there'd be a blinking green light in my *head*, and it would say, 'Suck-errr.' "

"That's good to know," she said, sounding unconvinced. She pulled into a driveway of a pretty, one-story house built into the hillside. We got out of the car and walked across a dimly lit, meticulously kept garden. At a pair of huge double doors, she stopped and fished in her purse for her keys.

The first thing I saw as I entered the dark house was a panoramic view of the sleeping city. "It's beautiful," I said. "I could stare at it for hours."

"I sometimes do. I'll miss it when I leave." She turned on the lights, revealing a green and peach decor that successfully brought to life a turn-of-the-last-century English living room. Like many houses in Beverly Hills, it had looked deceptively smaller from the outside. The interior was gigantic, with everything on a grand scale.

She put her finger to her lips and turned on a hall light. Then she led me to a darkened bedroom. A sleeping blond head poked halfway out of the covers.

She leaned down, lightly ruffled the tousled hair, and kissed the sleeping boy's forehead. There was a purr as the boy moved slightly beneath the covers. Althea put her finger to her lips again and we tiptoed out of the room.

"I didn't know you had any kids," I whispered.

"Neither did I," she replied. "That's my little brother, Tony. Well, half brother, but it doesn't mean I only love him half as much. Dad sent him here when the war broke out. There were all kinds of bomb scares and gas masks and kids being sent to the country for safekeeping. I told Dad I'd take care of him."

"Does he like Los Angeles?"

"God, he's crazy about it. He was homesick for about ten minutes."

"What'll happen when you leave?"

"Why, I'll take him with me, of course. The danger's over with, isn't it?"

I shook my head. "It hasn't even begun. If you're too damned stubborn to not go to England, at least save *his* life."

She was about to speak, probably to tell me I was beginning to be a bore on the subject, when a rotund little woman with a bright, ruddy face entered the room. She was wearing a bathrobe over a heavy nightgown, but didn't look sleepy at all. She gave me a disapproving glance.

"The hours you keep," she scolded Althea in a heavy Irish brogue.

"It's eleven o'clock, Mairead," Althea said. "I'm off tomorrow."

"Bringin' a strange man home at this hour . . ."

"Mairead, this is Commander John Surrey, U.S. Navy. I assure you I'm quite safe. He's a gentleman."

Mairead sized me up with a doubtful look. "He's too damn good-lookin' to be a gentleman. Sailor, huh? Probably been on a ship and ain't seen a woman in months."

"Pleased to meet you, ma'am," I said with a bow. "And no, I haven't been at sea. I've been behind a desk in Washington."

"Hmmmpph. You'll be wantin' coffee, then?"

"I'll make it," Althea said. "You go to sleep."

"I'll go to sleep when I'm damn good and ready. Now

you go and entertain the Commander. I'll have your coffee in two shakes.''

"Come on, John," Althea said. "I give up. We'll be in the living room, Mairead.''

Mairead dismissed us with a wave of her hand and began bustling about the kitchen. We went into the living room, sat down on a sofa, and stared out at the winking city lights below.

"She likes you," Althea said.

"Oh, it was obvious," I replied.

"I've never brought home a man this late before, and she trusts my instincts," she said. "She's seen men pick me up for dates, but I never brought any of them in afterwards. She loved Errol Flynn but told me to get rid of him. She turned out to be right. He's a sweetie, but . . .''

"A . . . masher," I experimented with a word of the era. "A wolf?"

"To be blunt. But enough about my love life. You're not married, are you?"

"I wouldn't be here if I were."

"I'm glad to hear it. Have you ever been married?"

"Yes. Long ago. She was a nice girl. We just didn't belong together."

"Couldn't adjust to being a Navy wife?"

"Something like that," I replied ambiguously. "I was away a lot." Tracking down felonious scumbags in faraway cities, I didn't add.

"There's something odd about you," she said accusingly. "What I asked you before, about being an American—"

"Brooklyn Dodgers," I interrupted. "Nathan's hot dogs. The Santa Monica Pier. Mom and apple pie." I debated with myself whether to add that I was circumcised, but decided against it. This *was* 1940, after all.

"I'm serious. There's something about you that doesn't quite fit. It's like you're a foreigner, but you're *not* a foreigner. You seem to be a little out of step with everyone else—in a cute way, of course."

"Really. Okay, then how do I know who's going to get your part in *The Maltese Falcon*?"

She practically jumped off the sofa. "Ooh, tell me! Who?"

"Mary Astor."

She thought for a moment. "I guess I could see her in it. I'm a lot better looking, of course. And younger."

"You're a lot better looking than *most* women."

"Thank you. So, John. Where do you *really* come from?"

"Excuse me?"

"Oh, come on. I'm supposed to be an intelligent woman. If you're a naval officer, then I'm Eleanor Roosevelt."

"Hey, you could do a lot worse."

There was a glass container of non-filtered cigarettes and a tear drop shaped lighter on the coffee table. I took one and lit it. After a cough that made my eyes tear, I handed it to her.

"Well, you don't smoke," she said, grinding the cigarette out in a swan-shaped ashtray. "I thought we established that before. I take it that people don't smoke where you come from?"

"Not anyone I know."

"An abstemious bunch. I also noticed that you don't drink. You nursed one glass of champagne through that entire party. Is it a religious thing?"

"No, I'm just healthy."

"Well, you sure look healthy. Are you a physical-culture nut, or something?"

"No, I just like to keep in shape, stay young."

"How old are you, anyway? You don't look a day over thirty."

"Long past it. I'm thirty-six, almost thirty-seven."

She looked shocked. Really shocked. In those days, when you reached the age of thirty-seven, apparently you were supposed to start looking like a St. Bernard. Or Mr. Mooney. Nowadays, a thirty-seven-year-old who works out regularly looks like a twenty-one-year-old who stayed up a little late studying for finals. I could understand how she felt, though; Bogie, for example, was only three or four years older than I and he looked like he could have been my father.

"All right," I said, "I'll level with you."

"The truth at last!" she declared triumphantly.

"I'm from the future."

"I knew it was something like that!" she squealed. "What year?"

"The year two thousand six."

"Oh, how wonderful! Do people drive around in little spaceships?"

Mairead, who had entered with a silver coffee service, had obviously heard the last part of our conversation. She stopped suddenly, and then quickly put the tray down in front of us.

"I didn't hear nothin'," she said, crossing her heart. "And I don't wanna hear nothin' else, neither. I'm goin' to bed." She backed out of the room before either of us could say anything.

"Tell me more," Althea said, pouring my coffee. "Cream, sugar?"

"Both."

"Are there still movies?"

"That's debatable, from a qualitative standpoint, but, yes, there are. There are also videocassettes and laser discs."

She handed me my coffee. "And they are?"

"It's like a tape from a . . . like a dictaphone. A laser disc looks like a small record. You put it in a machine connected to the television and—"

"Television? I've seen those! You're very good, John. This is really entertaining."

"Okay," I said. "Forget it."

"Sorry," she said. "I just wanted to see how far you could go."

We sipped our coffee in silence for a little while. I was beginning to get addicted to 1940 coffee.

"Neville Chamberlain has cancer," I said.

She almost choked on her coffee. "The prime minister?"

"He's got about six months to live."

"How do you know that?"

I shrugged. "It's history. He's only got another two months as PM before they throw him out, though."

"I never liked the man," she said solemnly. "But I wouldn't wish that on anyone. Who's going to replace him?"

"Winston Churchill."

She laughed. "Oh, that's a hot one. *Winston?* The next prime minister?"

"They didn't make him First Lord of the Admiralty last September for nothing," I said.

"Winston? What's he ever done right?" I had to admit, that within the context of her era, Althea's reaction was a normal one. Historical hindsight has obscured the major catastrophes Winston Churchill presided over up till then. We seem to remember only his dynamic wartime leadership—with good reason, perhaps. But to Althea's generation, he was at that moment nothing more than a witty screwup. Like Henry Clay, James G. Blaine, Mark Hanna, Hubert Humphrey, or Richard Nixon before 1968, he would come tantalizingly close but never quite make it. And, when taken with some of his gigantic mistakes, it made him seem just a little foolish.

"He'll go down in history as the greatest prime minister Britain has ever had," I said. "His leadership will keep the nation going during the dark times ahead. Of course, they'll kick him out when the crisis is over, but then they'll bring him back again a few years later."

"Winston," she mused. "I can't get over it." She turned to me accusingly. "What 'dark times?' You don't mean we're going to lose?" She put a hand to her cheek.

"No, but it'll be close. *Damned* close."

"Worse than the last war?"

"Much worse." I was sorry as soon as I said it. Her face seemed to crumple, and although she did not weep this time, she seemed to be frozen in deep pain. World War I has never captured the public imagination in the same way that its successor has. There have been fewer books written about it, fewer documentaries, far fewer movies. Its characters move jerkily through shadowy, grainy pictures. It has become something akin to a historical embarrassment on both sides, like two close friends who inexplicably get into a drunken, brutal fistfight and then are embarrassed about it the next day. But in Althea's time, the horrors of that war were still fresh in everyone's memory. The idea that any war ever again could cause such destruction was unthinkable.

"I wish I could help," I said, somewhat idiotically.

"But can't you . . . warn someone. Maybe Ian can help. Or tell me everything. I'll be in the WAAFs. Maybe I can reach out to someone—"

"They'll never believe you," I said. "They won't believe Ian, and they certainly won't believe me. My father's parents met . . . will meet . . . during this war. What if I did stop it? They'd never meet, and he and my uncle would never be born—much less yours truly. Not that I wouldn't give up my life to prevent it—I've risked my life for a hell of lot less, believe me—but no one would listen."

"It's worth a try," she said.

"Yes it is," I agreed. "But even if I went to the President himself, I'd wind up in the loony bin and nothing would have stopped it. The only history I'd change would be my own."

"Then what do I do? Just stand by helplessly while the world goes to hell?"

"You do your part," I said. "But you try not to get killed in the process."

"And you think *I'm* going to be killed?"

I paused. "I'm sure of it."

If this were a movie scene from my day, she would have run out of the room and threw up, or had some such violent, dramatic reaction. But all she did was say "Oh," in a very small voice.

I wanted to do something, maybe take her in my arms and apologize or give her some comfort, but all I did was sit there.

She straightened up. "Oh, well," she said in a flawless

English accent. "*Dulce et decorum est pro patria mori* and
all that."

"Maybe not," I said.

"What do you mean?"

"I mean . . ."

When I awoke the sun was shining brightly through the
panoramic windows. I was still fully dressed but someone
had taken off my shoes, loosened my tie, and thrown a
blanket over me. A towheaded kid of about nine was staring
at me with his eyes wide.

"Hi," I croaked. "You must be Tony. I'm John." I sat
up stiffly. I felt like I had just come in from a stakeout.

"Are you a battleship captain?" the boy asked me.

"Nope," I said. "I'm a desk commander. Are you a
battleship captain?"

"I will be when I grow up," the boy said. "A big battleship. My daddy's in the army."

"No battleships there," I said. "My Uncle Jack's an
admiral," I added.

"No!" the boy's eyes grew wider still. "An admiral!
Does he command a battleship?"

"He did, before he got promoted. Not a battleship, an
aircraft carrier."

"Sol-id, man," he exclaimed, the slang sounding a little
odd in his plummy accent. The kid was obviously getting
used to L.A.

Mairead came in and began shooing the boy out. "Come
along, Tony, your school bus'll be here any minute." She
avoided any contact at all with me—even eye contact.

"It was a pleasure meeting you, John," Tony said with
public school formality.

"When I see you again, we'll talk some more, Tony. I'm
looking forward to it." Mairead gave me a look that said
over my dead body and left the room lightly prodding the
boy ahead of her.

I must have drifted off again, because the next thing I
knew, someone was holding a cup of coffee under my nose.
I opened my eyes and saw Althea standing over me with a

smirk on her face. I tried to say something, but yawned hugely instead.

"Morning," I said. "What the hell happened?"

"You fell asleep in mid-sentence," she replied. "That's a new one on me, I must admit."

"Hell," I said, sitting up suddenly and instantly regretting it. "I'm sorry. I don't know what could have happened. What time is it?"

"It's after eight. Come on, I'll drive you to your hotel."

"Oh, I couldn't put you out—"

"Why not? You did last night."

My face flushed. "I'm sorry."

"I know," she said kindly. "Are you quite all right?"

"I've been better." But my strength was beginning to return; I could feel energy beginning to pump back into my system.

"Come on."

I was unwashed and I looked, well, like I'd just been kicked out of bed, which I had. But Althea drove me straight to the Beverly Wilshire—and not like a maniac this time. Still, the trip took only a few minutes and, at the hotel, she surprised me by getting out of the car with me and handing her keys to the valet.

I must have looked pretty rumpled, because the manager glanced up at me and called, "Can I help you, sir?"

I had a wiseass retort all set but Althea cut me off. "The Commander is a guest here," she said sternly. "He was in an automobile accident last night and has just been released from the hospital."

The manager might have suspected she was lying, but he also recognized who she was and wisely decided not to press it. Instead, he allowed a convincing look of concern to crease his forehead.

"Nothing serious, I hope, Commander? Is there anything we can do? The Beverly Wilshire is at your disposal."

"Just send up a nice breakfast to Commander Surrey's room. And have a valet pick up the Commander's suit for pressing."

"Absolutely, Miss Rowland."

"Thank you."

I almost collapsed in the elevator, falling heavily against the wall. The elevator boy, a goofy-looking kid with long slicked-back hair, gave me an amused glance, but turned quickly back to his job after a daggerlike glare from Althea.

In my room, Althea had me hand her my suit through the bathroom door. I took a long hot shower and shaved, emerging from the bathroom in a terry-cloth robe with the hotel's crest emblazoned on the left breast pocket. The valet had picked up my suit and a sumptuous breakfast was set out on a room service cart. There were scrambled eggs, toast, fruit, orange juice and coffee. Not a 2006 breakfast, I couldn't help noticing; there wasn't a lot of fiber on that table. I didn't care, though. My own time was becoming abstract and 1940 was becoming real to me. I still had my roots in my own time, but with Uncle Jack in Washington and the rest of my family in New Zealand, I was alone in California no matter what the year.

We ate in silence, and it occurred to me that Althea might be a bit uncomfortable in the presence of a man who was completely naked under a bathrobe. Thinking about it began to turn me on, so I concentrated on other things. Baseball, airplanes, skeet-shooting. It didn't help. Anything can have sexual connotations if you think about it enough. Or try not to.

"I wanted to ask you something," Althea said, breaking the silence.

"Fire away," I said.

"What you said before, when you pretty much said I was doomed."

"I apologized for that."

"Never mind that. You said that you would have liked to get to know me better, 'to see if a relationship could develop.' "

"You're a quick study."

"I'm an actress. I'm paid well to be a quick study. Did you mean that?"

"Yes. I did mean that."

She looked out the window, and then back at me. "When I go to England, and I'm sent wherever I'm ordered to go, how much time will I have left?"

"Althea . . ."

"Merely a technical question. No judgment, no criticism. How much time will I have left?"

"Althea, I can't—"

"You're the expert," she said. "I just want to know: How long do I have. Don't *speak* unless you give me the answer."

I did some quick, morbid figuring. It was now March; the Battle of Britain, in which many WAAFs would die in attacks on British airfields, would climax in early September. Then the London Blitz would begin, and it would last for months, killing service personnel and civilians indiscriminately.

"Five months," I answered softly. "A year at the outside."

"And you wanted to know me better."

"Yes."

Her eyes drilled through mine. "Then we'd better get started," she whispered.

I was relieved that she wasn't a virgin. It was, after all, 1940, and sexual liberation was far in the future. I later found out that I was only her second lover, however, the first being her fiancé at the Royal Academy of Dramatic Art. The engagement broke up, and since then, although she dated a lot and with some of filmdom's most famous and horniest stars, she had not gone to bed with anyone.

We had known each other for a grand total of twelve hours, and for five of those hours I had been asleep. That fact alone should have given both of us pause—especially her—but it didn't. It had taken a year of going steady before my high-school girlfriend and I became intimate, but my wife and I had also made love on our first date—and we had moved in together three days later. It's like that for some people, and I guess in that respect I've always been one of the lucky ones.

I had drawn the curtains and she undressed herself while

I slipped off my robe and slid under the covers. Women wore complicated underwear in those days: garters with strange-looking straps and hooks, and brassieres that looked like they needed a safecracker to open. It was too tender a moment to deal with the low comedy my undressing her would have provoked—it could have broken the mood. Instead, I stared diplomatically at the ceiling until I felt her slip into bed beside me.

The foreplay of my era was shockingly different than hers, if the concept existed at all. In fact, she seemed downright appalled at some of the things I did—at least, at first. Her fiancé in London, I was to learn, was obviously as new to sex as she was, because he knew nothing about pleasuring her. I'm no Casanova, but I did learn early on how to make a woman feel good—and, just as importantly, to know when she was ready.

But it was all new for Althea. "What are you *doing*?" she would moan breathlessly at least a half a dozen times that first day. It was a little surprising to me that a woman as accomplished and sophisticated as Althea could be so inexperienced in sexual matters, but in 1940, perhaps women were supposed to be ignorant about making love. I wondered if this was true of all the people I had met over the last twenty-four hours; if Bogie or Wayne or any of the others knew any more about such things than Althea's fiancé. At this time there was no wealth of literature on the subject, no talk shows and film plots. Sex was a private matter, for better or for worse.

I'm not a piston engine, but is true that the first flush of romance shoots the adrenaline through your body and gives you stamina and recuperative powers far beyond the norm. After number of liaisons, Althea, begged me for a break.

"John," she said, lighting a cigarette. "Let's keep this to ourselves, or else pretty soon *everyone*'ll be doing it."

"They already do," I said. I took the cigarette from her and puffed on it, careful not to inhale.

"Not the way you do it," she said.

"They do in my day," I said.

"Really? Well, how do they . . . learn about it?"

"Experience. Books. Movies. TV talk shows."

"They do it in the movies?" She was scandalized.

"Sometimes it's done tastefully."

"I like your time," she said. "What year was it again?"

"Two thousand six."

"The twenty-first century!" she exclaimed. "It seems like a million years away."

"It's okay," I said, not adding, *It sucks. That's why I'm here in the first place.* "Anyway," I said, "people are pretty much the same wherever you go. Or *when*ever. The inventions, the technologies, well, they don't mean very much compared to the way people are."

"What are—" she was interrupted by a knock at the door. Her face froze in terror, and I almost laughed. I half-expected her to hiss "My parents!" But then I realized that in 1940, there were still hotel establishments that frowned upon unmarried couples sharing connubial bliss under their roofs, and some even had hotel detectives to enforce such morals. Not only that, as a public figure, Althea could endanger her career and her reputation if she were caught in such a compromising position.

"Go into the bathroom," I whispered calmly. "I'll soon sort this out, whoever it is." I didn't have to tell her twice. She grabbed my shirt off the floor, held it to her breasts, and scampered out of the room.

The knock came again. "I heard you," I called out. "Give me a second, will you?" As I searched the darkened room for my robe, I considered my options. A house detective, as security men were called in those days, could possibly be bribed. It would be even money that a house dick would be an ex-cop, so threats wouldn't work. Maybe the one-cop-to-another routine would play—if I didn't have to produce a badge. I'd just have to play it cool. In a pinch, I supposed I could Tase the guy and check out while he was unconscious.

The knock came again. I hitched up my robe, took a deep breath, and strode toward the door.

It was a bellhop. There were four large packages on a luggage cart beside him.

"Commander Surrey?" he asked.

"That's me."

"Your delivery from Fahey's, sir."

Fahey's. My guns! I'd completely forgotten about them. "Why, bring them on in," I said heartily. "Just here by the door is fine."

"Right away, sir." The bellhop tactfully kept his eyes down, avoiding the rumpled bed, the room service setup for two, and probably the electrifying sexual current in the room. In doing so, he earned himself an exorbitant tip.

"Thank you, sir," he said with an amazed look at the twenty I gave him. "Anything you need, anything at all, you just ask for Murph." He gave me a smart salute, which he held until I realized I was supposed to return it. Since I hadn't saluted anyone since receiving my Medal of Valor from the Chief of Police years ago, mine was sloppy. Murph nodded to me and did a crisp about-face, stepping out of the room and shutting the door behind him. I waited until I heard his footsteps recede down the hall.

"It's allll-right!" I called in a falsetto approximation of Billie Burke. "You may all come out!"

She had a towel wrapped around her body. I have always thought that there is nothing more sexy than that, and nothing has ever changed my mind. "Jesus, who was that? Almost gave me a heart attack."

"That is yet to come," I said, taking her in my arms and kissing her neck.

"What's all this?"

"Oh, I was at Fahey's yesterday, bought out the store."

"Oooh, Fahey's. What'd you buy?"

"A couple of skeet guns for the tournament tomorrow, some sporting duds, and a case of shells."

"Really? Come on, let's have a look." She hitched up her towel, and picked up the nearest package. She tore away at the brown paper wrapping, which revealed a burnished leather case. She opened the two snap-catches and gasped at what was inside as if it were a diamond necklace.

"A Powell Best Grade!" she exclaimed. "Oh, you lucky devil!" She pointed to the gun, which gleamed with fresh oil. "Oh, why didn't you tell me you were a skeet-shooter?"

"The subject never came up." The gun was broken down into two parts, but Althea assembled it expertly. She took a shooting stance and followed the flight of an imaginary clay. Wrapped only in a towel, she made a comical sight. Then she laid the gun back down in the case.

"I keep finding out new things about you," she said, coming into my arms. "And most of them, I like."

I tugged at the towel, which fell away from her.

"What don't you like?"

"I don't like—" The phone rang. "I don't like being interrupted." I picked her up and carried her to the bed. Then I got in beside her and picked up the phone.

"Hello?"

"Mr. Bond?" A voice of strength, low and tough.

"Yes." I straightened up immediately. Althea gave me a questioning glance and I nodded my head.

"I wonder if we could meet."

"Who is this?"

"I wonder if we could meet *now*."

Something in his voice told me not to be cute. "All right. Where?"

"The bar wold be fine."

"Of course it would," I said. "You're English."

"Canadian, actually."

"Okay. Twenty minutes."

"As long as you like," the voice said amiably, but I wasn't fooled.

"How will I know you?"

"Don't mind about that. I'll know *you*." He hung up.

I leaned over and gave Althea a good long kiss. "I've got to go. I think a friend of Ian's wants to meet me."

She looked at me without expression. "All right," she said. "You go get ready. Then I'll clean up and let myself out."

"Are you sure?" I said.

"This is important, John. Maybe you can do some good."

"Maybe I'll get conked on the head and tossed off a cliff."

"*Dulce et decorum est*," she said. "But be careful. Be at my house at eight for dinner, if you can."

"I love you," I said.

"After today, you'd damn well better."

I made sure I had my Decacom and Taser within easy reach as I made my way into the hotel bar. Seated at a low table were Ian Fleming and a short, tough-looking man with a thick neck and arctic blue eyes. There was something about this fireplug of a man that instinctively put me on my guard.

Neither man stood, although they each shook my hand. The stranger's grip was surprisingly soft, but something told me that he shook that way on purpose.

"Commander . . . er, Bond, this is Mr. Stephenson from our . . . consulate in New York."

Oh, shit, I thought immediately. "Not *William* Stephenson?" I blurted before I could stop myself. I was so shocked that I actually said what I was thinking. I felt like standing up and giving myself a swift kick in the ass. But I didn't, tempted as I was.

Stephenson calmly raised a pale blond eyebrow. He clear wasn't used to being recognized by anyone; that was his job.

"Forgive me, Mr. Bond," he said. "I had no idea that I was so . . . celebrated."

And I didn't realize that my jaw was hanging open. "Holy shit," I thought, "The man they called *Intrepid*!" And I also didn't realize, that once again, like a *schmuck*, I had said aloud what I was thinking.

Stephenson and Fleming's heads swiveled toward each other so quickly that I thought I heard their necks pop. I don't mind telling you, that for the first time since arriving in 1940—in fact for the first time in years—I was scared out of my wits. I was bigger than the both of them, well-schooled in hand-to-hand combat, and armed with a powerful Taser, but I had no wish to tangle with Intrepid. Not the most-gifted and cold-blooded covert operative in the history of Allied Intelligence. I had read his biography twice, and thinking of what I had read made me strongly consider pulling my Taser, zapping him unconscious and getting the hell back to 2006. But then again, I could always punch the red button on my Decacom and be zoomed back instantly. With this precarious ace in the hole—and the thought of Althea showering upstairs—I decided to stay. And to keep my lip buttoned from here on.

"Let's all have a drink," Fleming said. He shouldn't have, because once again, I couldn't resist.

"Vodka martini," I said. "Shaken, not stirred."

"How odd," Fleming said, wrinkling his brow at me. "That's *my* drink."

"Is that a fact," I said innocently. "Well, I was just kidding. A beer will be fine."

"Whiskey and soda," Stephenson said. "No ice."

Fleming got up and walked over to the bar. Stephenson leaned toward me. "Well, Mr. Bond," he said softly. "It seems that you've some explaining to do."

"I do?"

"Please, Mr. Bond." He paused, pretending to be thinking. "I wonder if you might be so kind as to clear up a little confusion."

"Anything I can do," I said.

"Could you explain to me why it's so difficult to find a Lieutenant Commander John Surrey on any of our U.S. Navy personnel listings? I'm baffled."

"You haven't contacted the Navy Department?" I demanded.

"Of course not," he replied jovially. "Unlike your country, which has no agency for gathering intelligence abroad, we have bumf by the ton."

I pulled out the Naval Intelligence ID card that Uncle Jack had given me. Stephenson gave it a cursory skim.

"Identification can be forged," he said matter-of-factly.

"That's true," I said.

"But fortunately for you, yours isn't."

It *isn't*? I thought—to myself for a change. "Of course it isn't."

"Just so," he nodded. "I apologize," he continued, "for violating your agreement with young Fleming, but it wasn't an agreement made with *me*." He reached into his pocket and took out a small envelope. "Lucky for us, we have friends in the Navy Department. We have enemies, but we like to think our friends outnumber them." He pushed the envelope across the table at me.

I picked it up and extracted a flimsy sheet of Teletype paper. Keeping my face expressionless as I read it was a supreme test of willpower on my part, especially as I could feel Stephenson's eyes studying me intently.

RE: JOHN NMI SURREY, LCDR USN

B. 19 JY 1905, LOS ANGELES CA. ED.

HOLLYWOOD HIGH SCHOOL, GRAD 1923; US NAVAL ACAD, GRAD 1927. ENS, USS WARD, 1927–29; NAVAL INTEL, 1929–30, LTJG, USS CLAY, 1930–32; DETACHED TDY, STANFORD UNIV. 1933; LTSG, USS NEVADA, 1934–36; DETACHED TDY, WAR DEPT 1937; LCDR, USS CALIFORNIA, 1938–1940. CURRENTLY ON LEAVE OF ABSENCE. DUE FOR NAVAL STAFF COLLEGE, 1941.

"Well," I harrumphed, "I'd say that about sums me up." Oh, Ja-ack! Uncle Jack! You've got a little explaining to do . . . including admitting that I wasn't the first member of the Surrey family to go back to 1940. But thank you, you crazy old bastard. As for Cornelia, she was going to get quite a talking-to.

"His Majesty's government," Stephenson continued, "is pleased to have such good friends abroad." He stopped to gesture toward me, "Such as yourself. But we—"

He stopped again as Fleming arrived with the drinks. We gave each other a silent toast and sipped.

"But . . ." I prompted.

"But," Intrepid continued, "how in the *hell* did you come by this information?"

I was glad to see him lose his composure, however slightly. It made him seem more human . . . and less dangerous. It gave me the opportunity to take the upper hand.

"I can't tell you that," I said shortly. "No more than you could tell me how you came by yours. My government is isolationist right now, and I could land in the brig if I were caught meeting with you. Telling you all this amounts to treason."

"Then why are you doing it?" asked Fleming.

"Because we'll be fighting them anyway, and I want to save American lives."

Stephenson nodded and leaned back in chair. "You know I can't do anything with your information right now. I wish I could, but the evidence of one sincere American Navy commander won't be enough."

"I know," I said. "You'll have to wait till after Norway."

"Christ," said Fleming dejectedly.

Stephenson raised his glass. "Well, Commander 'Bond.' To a long and happy association."

"Allies," I said.

NINE

SENATE INTELLIGENCE COMMITTEE 3.31.07
Q: " 'James Bond, shaken not stirred.' If you don't mind my saying so, Mr. Surrey, that is a hoot."

A: "Yeah, I thought so, too."

Q: "Well, Mr. Surrey. You'll have to excuse me, but I always believed in the butterfly theory."

A: "I know what you're talking about, Senator. The story about the people who went back in time—I believe to the prehistoric era—and their guide told them not to deviate from the path that had been marked out for them. One person took a slight misstep and flattened a butterfly. And then, when they returned, absolutely nothing was the same. Is that the one?"

Q: "That's right. You've done quite a bit more than mush a butterfly."

A: "I think it's a lot of crap, as theories go, Senator. As far as I know, I only changed one thing. I found that being back in time doesn't necessarily change everything. It just might change one thing. Whoa. Sorry."

Q: "You're getting pale again, Mr. Surrey. Is that related to your time-travel experiences?"

A: "Directly."

Q: "How? You're not traveling back in time now. Unless

you're visiting us in the future—your future." (GENERAL LAUGHTER)

A: "No, ma'am. I'm in the present. Mine and yours." (LAUGHTER)

"But I have found that because the mind never stays still, we have a tendency to weigh options even when we are at rest, or are thinking about other things. So, at various junctures, I may be making a decision that could contribute to my own destruction—without even knowing about it."

Q: "You mean to say that some changes can effect your existence and others don't?"

A: "Exactly. One of my earlier guided tours was for a gentleman of Mexican ancestry. He told us that he wanted to visit 1941, and see—from a distance—the arrival of his family in Los Angeles. That was fine—we have found a lot of people want to see their parents as young people, to view first hand the origins of family legends. But this guy wasn't honest with us. That wasn't why he wanted to go back at all."

Q: "Why did he want to go back?"

A: "Because his grandfather had been severely beaten by sailors in the Zoot Suit Riots of 1941. He wanted to interfere, prevent it if he could, and if not, take revenge."

Q: "What happened?"

A: "I had briefed him to avoid the area. We often do that if we can't keep a Tourist out of a high-risk era altogether. But I could tell that he was fobbing me off. I don't know, maybe it was the instinct of a former cop—something didn't quite jibe for me. So I followed him back into 1941 and kept a close surveillance."

Q: "Did you do anything? Did you stop him?"

A: "Yes, sir. I saw him pulling a young man from a fight and trying to get him into his car. I ran up, helped him with the kid, and told him to beat it out of there. As they drove away, I saw that I was facing five very angry young tars."

Q: "Did they attack you?"

A: "Well, they tried. I Tased two of them right off. Two others saw that and ran. The last guy came at me with a broken beer bottle. Excuse my alliteration."

Q: "You're forgiven, Mr. Surrey. Were you injured?"
A: "No. The sailor was pretty drunk. He lunged at me with the bottle, and I caught his arm and . . . well, I broke it."
Q: "You broke his arm?"
A: "Well, he was going for my jugular, ma'am. I had to do something. Then I took off. When I got back to the rendezvous point and met our Tourist, he and his young grandfather were loaded on tequila, celebrating the boy's deliverance. I had a few stern words for our Tourist, but he was so damned happy he wanted to make me godfather to his next child. But the point I want to make is, that particular episode didn't change anything. A young man was not beaten into insensibility, and a bigoted sailor got out of fatigue duty for a few weeks while he recuperated. No major changes to speak of."
Q: "All right, Mr. Surrey. Let's return to your on-again, off-again weakened condition. You're saying that it is controlled by your subconscious?"
A: "That is correct."
Q: "Could you give us an example?"
A: "Okay. I'm strongly considering going back to the year 1934. It is April. My grandfather has been picking up part-time work as a stuntman for Warner Bros. After a hard day's work, he likes to unwind with a few beers at a bar called Henry's. It's a rough place. I'll go in there and watch him for a few minutes. Then I'm going to take out my old undercover piece, a Taurus 85CH. That's a small .38-caliber snubbie with a concealed hammer. I will walk up behind him and put one shot behind his ear. That's it. No problem; I'll do it first thing tomorrow."
Q: Mr. Surrey? Mr. Surrey! Can we get the paramedics in here? Now!"
A: "I . . . It's all right. Just kidding. I'd never do anything like that. Sorry, Gramps."
Q: "Are you sure you want to continue, Mr. Surrey?"
A: "Yeah, let's get this over with."
Q: "All right. So, you've just illustrated for us the old 'grandfather theory.' You go back, kill your grandfather, and you're never born."

A: "Right. Now, that would change my future. However, it might not have anything to do with *your* future. Or if I were to kill your grandfather, back in . . . uh, Wyoming is it, Senator?"

Q: "Well, technically, my grandfather would have been in Vermont at the time. But I see your point."

A: "That's right. Nothing at all might happen to me. But it'll certainly effect you."

Q: "So you're telling us, then, that these random options that go through your subconscious may or may not effect you?"

A: "Exactly."

Q: "Now, what you've told us about your trip to 1940: You've crossed a great many paths, touched many lives. You even gave the plans for the German Spring Offensive—Case Yellow—to a senior British Intelligence Official."

A: "You can't prosecute me for that. It'd be a waste of government funds. Besides, I saved lives."

Q: "Oh, did you?"

A: "That was not secret information of the American government, it was history long within the public domain. And all I did was inform a friendly government of the intentions of a criminal government—you remember the Nuremberg Trials? We did find the Nazi government to be criminal, so where's the harm?"

Q: "Well, I mean . . . Mr. Surrey, did you in fact change history?"

A: Oh, yes. Not as much as I would have liked. But enough to make me feel a little better about things."

Q: "What did you change?"

A: "Don't you know?"

Q: "No."

A: "No, I guess you wouldn't. Before I left for 1940, a total of 335,000 British and French troops were rescued at Dunkirk. Twenty-five RAF fighter squadrons were held back by Air Chief Marshal Dowding in anticipation of what would become the Battle of Britain. I suggest that you send one of your pages out to the library or nearest bookstore for a history of World War II."

Q: "Very well, Mr. Surrey. Ten minutes."

(RECESS)

Q: "This is very odd, Mr. Surrey. According to this respected history of the Second World War, the number of British and French service personnel evacuated from Dunkirk is close to 480,000. I have also noted that Air Chief Marshal Dowding held back not twenty-five, but thirty-eight squadrons for home defense."

A: "I always felt really good about that."

Q: "Where did you get this other number—this 335,000?"

A: "History. Fleming and Stephenson couldn't go through regular channels. All they could do was to hit up the military commanders who they or their fellow operatives knew well. A few regiments broke off from the fight and headed for Dunkirk a little earlier, that's all. To this day I don't know how Stephenson got to Dowding."

Q: "You're talking about thirteen extra squadrons. As it was, RAF Fighter Command lost eighteen percent of its pilots."

A: "That's a hell of a lot better than twenty-five percent."

Q: "Mr. Surrey, that's 150,000 lives. You saved an awful lot of people. That must have changed the world somehow."

A: "Perhaps. There were plenty of other battles still left to go. I did do a little research, and about 35,000 of those men were killed in later battles. Mostly at El Alamein and Arnhem."

Q: "How do we know any of this is true?"

A: "I'm under oath. I'm a former Marine and a former police detective."

Q: "This is quite a bind you've put us in, Mr. Surrey."

A: "Not all, Senator. I saved Allied lives, ultimately, American lives. What're you going to do? Prosecute me for not allowing the enemy to kill as many men as the original plan called for? Where's the legal precedent? And what about public opinion? And what about all of those veterans with families instead of graves?"

Q: "What do *you* suggest we do, Mr. Surrey?"

A: "I . . . You know what? Never mind. This'll give all of us a headache."

Q: "All right, Mr. Surrey. We'll return to it later. I'm curious about something else. What about your involvement with Althea Rowland? The actress?"

A: "I wasn't as lucky there."

Q: "Would you care to elaborate?"

A: "Not really. But okay."

TEN

A MAKESHIFT GRANDSTAND HAD BEEN CONSTRUCTED NEAR the lot in what would later come to be known as Woodland Hills. Currently it was used by the studios to film location shots for Westerns.

There were three skeet ranges set up in front of the grandstand. Althea and Tony were seated somewhere in the middle, flanked by Ian Fleming on one side and Katharine Hepburn on the other. Little Tony was clearly taken with Hepburn, she—looking young and vibrant and without the shakes—sent him into frequent gales of laughter. Ian was talking somewhat urgently to Althea. I couldn't help but think that when Ian saw the three of us arrive with John Wayne it couldn't have improved his day.

With my Powell at the ready, and wearing my stylish shooting duds, I reported to the center circle when my name was called. I was glad that Wayne was going to be shooting with me.

"Wuh-huhl, you're a fast worker, John," he said, nodding toward the grandstand. From anyone else, it would have seemed an insult. From Wayne it was a statement of sincere congratulations. "She's quite a gal," he said. "I always liked her."

"I never met anyone like her," I said.

"Ya won't, either. Not in this town."

The next circle was called. I hadn't been paying attention when my own group was called, so I didn't know with whom Wayne and I would be shooting. I noticed, however, a slight breath of relief from Wayne when John Ford was called for another group. He smiled a little guiltily.

"I love the guy, but I'm afraid I might kill him," Wayne said ruefully. I understood: Althea had told me that Ford had made Wayne's life miserable during the shooting of *Stagecoach*, jumping on him at any time for the slightest real or imagined misstep. It had been a hard filming for Wayne, despite its obvious rewards.

"Don't do that," I said. "You two are going to have a long and prosperous alliance."

"I hope you're right." He saw two men and a woman striding toward us in the distance. "Uh-oh," he called. "Here comes trouble!"

"Go on, ya big galoot!" I heard a female voice call, followed by a waterfall of laughter. Wayne's smile thinned slightly. "Looks like we're sunk, John. Here's the ringer."

Coming into view with shotguns pointed downward were Carole Lombard, Clark Gable, and the fellow I mentioned earlier, the gentleman in his eighties who is the only person, including Uncle Jack, who has never beaten me in a skeet match. But he wasn't in his eighties here. He wasn't even in his forties, which is when he captured the Emmy as a famous crimefighter. He was just twenty, young, lithe, and recently, a world champion.

"Carole Lombard, Clark Gable, I'd like you two to meet my friend, Commander John Surrey."

"Ooh, I just love a man in uniform," Lombard cooed, batting her eyelashes.

"Maw," Gable cautioned her with good humor. "How do you do, Commander?"

He stuck out a tractor-seat for a hand and we shook. I was glad for Lombard's presence. Even fifty years dead, women still moon over him, and deservedly so. Alive and in his prime, no one's girlfriend was safe. Even Duke Wayne seemed somehow diminished standing next to Gable. I snuck a look at the grandstand for a look at Althea, but she was talking across Tony to Hepburn. I was relieved that her attention was elsewhere. In the dictionary under the word *man*, a picture of Gable would get the point across quite succinctly. He could even give Uncle Jack a run for his money.

"C'mon over here, per-fessor," Lombard called to the young man hitching an ammo pouch to his belt. He looked up and smiled. "Hello, Duke," came the far younger but still familiar voice.

"Go get 'em, kid," Wayne said. "John, say hello to Bob Stack."

"Nice to meet you, Bob," I said. "I'm looking forward to shooting with you."

He smiled a little shyly. "It looks like it'll be a lot of fun."

"He'll beat our fannies into the dust," Lombard said. "Right, per-fessor?"

"I don't know, Carole," he said. "You're getting awfully handy with that Stoeger."

"Oh, sure. I'm a regular Annie Oakley." She turned to me. "Bobby's taught me everything I know," she said. "Sometimes I even hit something."

The first round ended in a four-way tie. Lombard had managed a seven, showing good form but not enough concentration. Stack, using the same Parker with which he had won the World Title, coolly ran up a perfect score. Gable— using the Stradivarius of skeet guns, a Holland and Holland—missed the first double but used his option and tagged it. Wayne and I were each flawless, but it was only a matter of time. Busting a clay is not a difficult thing to do, but hitting it two-hundred and seventy-five times without missing is damn near impossible. We knew that Stack's youth and championship experience would eventually give him the edge.

Gable loosened up a bit toward me when he saw that I wasn't a dilettante, and even offered to swap guns with me for the next round. He seemed like a tough guy to get to know, and I was glad that he was giving me the chance.

The Holland felt perfect in my hands, even better than the Powell, which had turned out to be a dream to shoot. With Gable's Holland, shooting was completely effortless, as though gun and clay were connected by some invisible, electric current. I didn't miss a single clay during the next round, and I almost offered to buy the gun from him right then and there. But shooting a round of skeet with Clark Gable, and using his own treasured shotgun, was enough for me.

Stack was pretty quiet, fully concentrating on the task at hand. He asked me a few questions about the Navy, which he said he would join if we got into the war. Since I knew for a fact that he later became an aerial gunnery training officer, I kept my answers short and to the point. Looking at him as a blond and athletic twenty-year-old, I was amazed at how little he would change over the years. He was certainly the youngest octogenarian I had ever met, and the by far the best shot. In his twenties, there was no doubt that there was a great career ahead of him.

Lombard was eliminated after the first round, and Gable and I found ourselves in a group with John Ford, Spencer Tracy, and a tall blond guy named Lawrence. Ford and Tracy were both little guys, Tracy much smaller than he appeared on the screen. Ford was a balding guy with two brown front teeth, a result no doubt, of the cigar constantly clamped in them. Gable kept calling Tracy "Shorty," which I took to be in bad taste until I realized that they had just finished shooting *Boom Town* together and that that had been the nickname of Tracy's character.

Tracy was a quiet sort of guy, but like Bogie, I had a feeling that he didn't miss much. He looked up at the grandstand and waved at Hepburn, who waved back. Then I saw his eyes widen as Althea blew me a kiss.

"Nice kid, Althea," he said to me.

"I couldn't agree more," I replied.

"You're a lucky fella."

He had said it noncommittally, but I could see a slightly veiled threat behind his words. *You'd better not be just playing with her* was the obvious implication.

"I am a lucky fella," I said, and Tracy nodded.

It made me care for her all the more, the idea that so many people in a town like Hollywood would so instinctively want to protect her. I vowed not to let any of them down.

Lawrence, the big blond guy, was an experienced shot, probably an upper-class guy who had grown up around quality shotguns, but he was outclassed by Gable and me. Clark—he insisted I call him that—had found his rhythm and was really starting to shoot well. Ford and Tracy were way out of their league and just having fun.

My own shooting was lousy. My score was perfect, but I was on autopilot. For one thing, I was exhausted, and it made me fire under or behind the target. Althea and I had spent half the night talking, and the other half trying to make love as silently as possible without waking Mairead who, from the filthy look she gave me this morning, knew exactly what had been going on.

But that wasn't the only thing that made me tired. Just being in 1940 was beginning to wear me out—much the same as being on a planet with a stronger gravitational pull. A few more rounds and I didn't think I'd be able to lift my shotgun.

"I understand that you are a naval officer, Mr. Surrey," Lawrence said.

"That's right," I said, thinking, why you sonofabitch, you're a German! He spoke with no trace of an accent, but his grammar and careful pronunciation gave him away. They were far too good. *"Wilkommen in Amerika, Herr Lorenz,"* I added.

He laughed softly. "You speak German well, Mr. Surrey."

"Actually, that's all I know. Excuse me." I took my turn and easily popped two from the number three spot. This Lorenz guy was starting to piss me off, and the adrenaline helped my shooting. I was right on the money, leading the two clays with perfect deflection.

"You shoot like a gentleman," he said.

I turned to him abruptly. "Let's knock off the sales pitch,

mein herr. What's your rank, SS *Sturmbannfuhrer*?"

He kept his smile but a shade dropped over his eyes. In the social circles he ran around in, there was very little of the frankness I had just expressed. "Well, I suppose, technically, that would be my rank."

"And I'm a lieutenant commander, so we're equal in seniority. What can I do for you, Major?"

"Please, call me Karl."

"I'm John."

"I'm pleased to know you, John. It's good to meet a military man in this . . . *milieu*."

"Oh? Why's that?"

"Well, this is a rather . . . frivolous industry. The influences are not always . . ."

"What influences?" I was going to make the Nazi bastard work for it.

"Oh, certain . . . types of people. Not like the sort of Americans you have in the Navy."

"Oh," I said, pretending to finally get it. "You mean Jews."

"Exactly."

"I wouldn't be so sure. I mean, you never know. Gable over there?" I motioned toward Clark, who missed and growled "Shit" under his breath. "His mother," I whispered, "is a nice old lady in Chicago named Minnie Goldfarb, but he likes to keep it under his hat."

"He does?" Lorenz exclaimed in a whisper.

"Oh, yeah. John Ford? The great director over there, who just missed by a mile and said 'Aw, fuck' a little too loud?"

"Yes?"

"Isadore Bronstein. The real kicker is—you know Jack Warner? The head of Warner Bros.? His real name is Horace Wickersham III. He just changed it so he could get work out here."

Lorenz nodded. "You're having a little sport with me," he smiled. "I don't blame you. We do have a reputation that is largely undeserved."

"Oh, I'm sure," I said. "Like those ghettoes you're

making the Jews build in Warsaw and Lodz.''

"For their own protection," he said insistently. "You know how the Poles are. Virulent anti-Semites, they always have been.''

"Well," I said. "Lucky for them, they have friends like us.''

"Quite right. I wonder, Commander, if we could meet later and perhaps discuss a few things.''

"All right," I said. "After the match.''

"Good," he said. "I look forward to it.''

You won't when I'm done with you, I thought.

Stack missed. He actually missed one, and then another. I couldn't believe it. "What happened?" I asked him.

He smiled. "I'm good," he replied. "I'm just not perfect.''

Well, if Robert Stack could have even one bad day on the skeet range, then anything was possible. It came down to a dream team play-off. John Wayne, Clark Gable, and me. The fatigue had completely disappeared, and was replaced by an energy I hadn't felt in years. Perhaps it was where I was and who I was with. Maybe it was being in love for the first time in years. Or, it could have been the prospect of setting up a real, live, arrogant Nazi asshole. Whatever it was, I felt marvelous and ready to take on the world—beginning with the King and the Duke.

"Clark," I needled him as we began, "Can I use your Holland this round?''

Gable gave me his trademark grin. "Not on your life, Navy. Me and my Holland are gonna whip your ass for bragging rights.''

"Loser buys the drinks," Wayne said. "And no coffee this time, John.''

"Just don't sneeze on my shots, Duke," I replied.

It was great, standing there kidding around with two icons as we prepared to face-off in a supremely macho contest. You could cut the testosterone with a knife and spread it on a ten-foot sesame roll.

The last shot in a skeet round is the easiest. You stand

in the center of the half circle and the disc comes out from the high house and flies directly over your head. All you have to do is stick the gun straight up as soon as you yell *pull*, and blast it to bits. It has never given me a problem. It also gave the Duke no difficulty. Gable, on the other hand, missed it completely. For some reason, he brought the Holland up a second too late and twisted his body around trying to chase it.

"Goddamn it," he rasped. "I *never* miss that fucking shot."

Because the special rules of the contest called for a sudden death play-off with no options, Gable was out of it. He smiled, almost graciously, and patted my shoulder. "Nice going, John," he said. "Good luck to you."

"Hey, what about me?" Wayne said.

"Aah, I hope ya choke," Gable retorted. Then he threw an arm around Wayne's shoulder. "Here's luck, kid."

The grandstand gave a loud cheer for Gable as he left the field. I saw Althea looking at me with something close to adoration—and I don't say that out of conceit. It's a typical situation: a girl brings her new boyfriend to a gathering of her friends and colleagues, and wants him to make a good impression. Well, I was making a hell of an impression. I saw Ginger Rogers, who was sitting behind her, whisper to Althea and point to me. Althea laughed and nodded vigorously. It was a heady moment, I assure you.

Wayne nudged me. "Looks like we got us a beer frame, old buddy," he said.

"The battle of the Powells," I replied.

"Care for a little side bet," he winked.

"Sure," I said. "Five thousand?"

He roared with laughter. "Five thousand *what*? Pennies?"

"Scared?"

"Yeah. Of my wife if I lose. Let's just make it a gentlemen's bet. Loser buys the drinks."

"You're lucky I'm not much of drinker."

"Well, I am, so get out your wallet."

It only took four shots. The first two were singles, first

from the high house and the second from the low house; followed by a double. Wayne did all right on the singles, but missed the second shot on the double. The grandstand gasped.

"Sorry, Duke."

"You ain't won nothin' yet, John."

But I did, almost immediately. I felt as though I were sleepwalking through the last four, easy shots. The double looks harder than it is, and I blasted both clays dead center.

The grandstand erupted. People came pouring onto the field, and I almost expected music to swell and the scene to fade to a slow-motion sepia like a cornball made-for-TV movie. Wayne pumped my hand and called me a sonofabitch, and Gable gripped my shoulder and gave me a man-to-man nod. They gave me a surprisingly small trophy, just a simple winner's cup, but it remains a valued possession that I keep over my fireplace. FIRST PLACE, SHOOTOUT OF THE HOLLYWOOD STARS, *1940, Lt. Cdr. John Surrey, USN*, it reads. It makes for a hell of a conversation piece, believe me.

Althea jumped into my arms and Tony kept yanking at my sleeve. I felt like I had just quarterbacked in the Super Bowl and I held every second of it close to me. "I'm goin' to Disneyland," I muttered under my breath.

"What?" Althea shouted into my ear above the din.

"Private joke," I shouted back. "It's a future thing."

"You're a hell of a shot, Commander," Bob Stack said to me. "I hope we can do it again sometime."

"You can count on it," I replied. "But I'm sure I won't be so lucky."

"Luck had nothing to do with it, Commander," he said. "You're good."

It was the best compliment I received all day.

The party to follow that night would be, in the words of my dear old pal, the Duke, "a pisscutter to end them all." Everybody who was anybody in Hollywood would be there, and everybody who was nobody would be parking cars or serving hors d'oeuvres. It would be hosted by some studio head—I never did find out who—in a mansion that was outrageously luxurious even by Bel Air standards. The Duke dropped me off at my hotel and promised to meet Althea and me at the party. Althea and Tony had hitched a ride with Hepburn and Tracy.

Feeling diminished as I entered my lonely hotel room, I was nevertheless relieved to have a little time to myself to unwind. Despite the kindness of my new friends and the wonder of new love with Althea, I realized that I hadn't spent any time alone since arriving in 1940, save for about four hours of rest between lunching with Bogart and Wayne at Lakeside and the party in Cole Porter's bungalow. I had only been in 1940 for two days, but so many things were happening so quickly, it felt as though a month had passed. I looked forward to a few hours sack time followed by a long curative session under the showerhead.

Silly me.

I awoke with a dull throbbing in the back of my head. There was a sensation of motion and I realized that I was in the trunk of an automobile. My hands were tied behind me, and the trunk, as roomy as it was, smelled of exhaust and made me queasy. I would have laughed at the cliché-ness of the situation—like something out of a Raymond Chandler novel—but I had other things to think about. The first was freeing myself of the knot binding my hands before we got to wherever I was being taken. I did a sort of a body-crunch so that I could feel my trouser pocket. Fortunately, the Decacom and Taser were still there, and I sighed in audible relief.

Next, I worked for a good five minutes on the rope. It was a pretty half-assed knot, considering the situation, but being unconscious in a car trunk, where could I go? When I had loosened the rope enough to maneuver, I removed the Taser from my pocket and wrapped my fist around it.

The car left the paved road and, judging from the knocking-about I was receiving, was now on a rocky dirt path. After a few minutes, the car came to a stop, its spongy suspension causing me to bang my head on the trunk.

I strained in concentration and made out three people alighting from the car. As the footsteps came closer to the trunk, I slipped the rope loosely around my hands and stuck them behind my back. Then I closed my eyes and feigned unconsciousness.

Two pairs of powerful hands pulled me from the trunk. They didn't handle me roughly, they just picked me up by either end and carried me into what sounded like a wooden shack from the creak of the steps and the whine of the doorspring.

I was plopped into a chair and shaken until I opened my eyes and did my best to look dazed.

"Thank you for coming, Commander Surrey," Major Lorenz greeted me.

"Lorenz," I said, squinting at him. "Nice place you've got here."

It seemed like an abandoned camping shack, lit by Coleman lanterns and the fire from a stone hearth. The room smelled like the standing water in an abandoned fishtank.

"I'm glad it meets with your approval. Personally, I think it's a dump, but there's no accounting for taste."

"You're not doing much for German-American relations here, Karl," I said. "You've kidnapped a serving officer of the United States Navy—in the United States. You're in deep shit, Major. This amounts to an act of war."

"Yes, well, your government will have to prove it. And to prove it, they'll have to catch me."

"You'll look fetching in a sombrero, Karl."

He laughed, and I have to admit, it was a good laugh, nothing phony about it. "Oh, I will miss America," he said with a genuine touch of wistfulness. "What a wonderful place. Everyone has such a good sense of humor. They even laugh at themselves—could you imagine that in Germany?"

"If that were possible, right now there'd be eighty million Krauts rolling around on the floor holding their sides."

He nodded sadly. "We are far too serious as a people, but that's why we are going to win."

"Keep dreaming, pal."

"I don't understand you, John. We have so many friends in Washington, especially in your Navy."

"Not as many as you think," I said.

"I can't imagine why. We even have a few friends out here in Hollywood. A lot *more* than you'd think. Even though this is hostile territory."

"Karl," I said impatiently, "what's all this about? I'd've just met you for a drink later on. What's with the cloak-and-dagger crap?"

"You've made some friends," he said. "Some of whom are enemies of the Reich. Lieutenant Fleming, for one. He seems like a fine fellow, but we are at war with his country. And he has been quite busy. He and an RAF officer, a Flight Lieutenant Dahl, have been cutting a swath through certain circles in New York and Washington, and out here in Los Angeles, gathering support for Britain."

"Roald Dahl," I said, more to myself. "That's right, the writer."

"Dieter!" he called. "Heinrich! *Kommst du hier!*"

His fellow Surrey-snatchers appeared. One was a small, weasely guy, and the other was a walking beer truck without the bottles. Quite stereotypical, I realize, but the Nazis were never very big on originality. Guys like these would become stock characters later on; right now they were the real thing.

"As you might say, John, you've got a big mouth. One of our friends was shopping at Fahey's this past Thursday, and his attention was piqued by the presence of an American naval officer in town. We're always looking for friends in the American military establishment, so we had you followed to see what you were made of. You were never out of our sight from the time you and Mr. Bogart drove off to the Beverly Hills Hotel. Your poolside conversation with Miss Rowland and Mr. Fleming was quite illuminating, to say the least. And troubling.

"And, of course, your meeting with Mr. Stephenson. My heavens, John, have you no sense of decorum at all?"

"Of course I do," I said. "I am universally acknowledged as a classy guy."

"John. I will ask you nicely the first time." he clasped his hands together. "Please answer me. Who gave you the information about Case Yellow?"

"Case Yellow? Sounds like a dog peed on a valise."

"Please, John. Don't make me—"

"Oooh, say it! Come on, I'd love to hear it for real, and not in a movie!"

"What?" He looked confused.

" 'Ve haf vays uf makink you talk.' Come on, Karl, don't let me down."

"John," he warned me, "you're not making this easier for either of us. Please. How did you find out about Case Yellow? Who is your source?"

"Heinrich Himmler. We're old golfing buddies."

"John . . ."

"All right," I said. "I'll tell you all you're entitled to know. 'Surrey, John NMI. Lieutenant Commander, U.S. Navy, USN8185551138.' " The last was my phone number in Studio City, but he wasn't going to know that.

"Is that your last word on the subject?" he asked me with almost-convincing regret.

"I'm afraid so."

"I'm sorry," he said softly. "Heinrich! Dieter!"

The two flunkies came out from behind Karl and began walking toward me. Their manner was nonchalant but their intention was anything but.

Enough was enough. I brought my right hand out from behind me and Tased them all, one-two-three. When Heinrich hit the floor, the cabin shook for long moments afterward.

I tied Heinrich and Dieter back-to-back, but I ran out of rope and had to settle for pulling Karl's jacket down over his elbows. Each of them were armed with Walther P38s, two of which I pocketed, and kept the third for immediate use. I propped Karl up in the chair that I had just vacated and leaned on the table opposite, waiting for him to come around.

Karl opened his eyes and blinked at me. He tried to move his arms.

"Don't bother," I said, gesturing with the gun.

"What in God's name was that?"

"It's called a Taser. Don't worry about it, they're impossible to find right now. Now let this be a lesson, Karl. Never hunt a bear in his own cave."

"I have a diplomatic passport," he began.

"And I have a gun." I finished for him. "You've got a big problem, Karl. I know what you're all about. I know what your lousy country is planning to do. I can't stop it, but I can sure stop you."

"Jew-lover," he sneered.

I smacked him across the face with the butt of the Walther. A bloody gash appeared on his cheek almost immediately. He stared at me with what could only be described as a surprised and hurt expression.

"Let's clear up one thing right now," I hissed in his face. "That shit may go over big in Krautland, but you're in *my* country now. You make one more crack like that and I'll rip your fucking lungs out."

A lot of subtext went into that warning. I was thinking of all of the Jewish people I had ever known and loved; friends, parents, school chums, fellow Marines, cops, and tried to imagine them in the hands of bastards like Karl. It was an ugly thought, and it enraged me that in 1940, much of that depraved brutality was yet to come.

"What are you going to do?" Karl demanded, his voice quivering.

"I don't know," I said frankly. "I always dreamed of kicking the crap out of a Nazi scumbag like you, but you seem like such a wuss that it'd probably be over in less than a minute."

"Wuss?" he wondered aloud.

"Shut up. I can't turn you over to the cops. You'd probably just be deported, and that would cause some kind of international incident. I suppose I ought to just shoot you."

"You can't kill me in cold blood."

I grabbed my chest. "Oh! Oh! You're killing me, Karl! You're right—how could I *live* with myself after doing that?'' I shrugged. "I know what I'll do. But first—Hey, Karl, do me a favor.''

"A . . . favor?''

"Yeah. Repeat after me: '*Hava*,' '' I sang. "C'mon, Karl. '*Hava nagila, hava nagila . . .* ' '' I backhanded his head. "You're not singing, Karl."

"I won't sing that!'' I kicked him roughly in the left shin. "All right," he shouted. " '*Hava . . . nagila, hava . . .* ' ''

It wasn't the best revenge, as revenges go, but it served.

Once I got outside it was easy to get my bearings. I had grown up—or would grow up—just a few miles from the cabin where I had been held. All I had to do was look up to the north, where I saw the dark outline in the night sky of the Santa Susana Mountains. I knew every peak and crag of those hills. I was able to estimate my location at what would someday be Tampa Avenue at about Lassen Street in Northridge. From there it was a question of wending my way south over back roads until I reached Coldwater Canyon.

Karl's Cadillac was a pleasure to drive once I got out onto the paved road. From there it was only another twenty minutes before I reached the Beverly Wilshire.

"I'll only be a minute," I said to the attendant as I pulled up in front of the hotel. I handed him the first bill I could pull from my pocket, a ten. "Just watch it for me."

"Hell, I'll *wash* it for you," he said, staring at the bill.

I walked quickly to the front desk. "John Surrey," I said to the clerk. "Any messages for me?"

He turned to check my box. "Yes, Commander." He handed me a folded sheet of hotel stationery." As I had expected, it was from Althea, demanding to know where the hell I was and giving me the address of the party in Bel Air.

I jumped back into the car and took off. By the time I got to the street where the party was taking place, all I had to do to find it was follow the long line of parked cars.

"Just *watch* the car," I said to the valet in front of the scaled down replica of Fontainbleu. "Don't touch it."

Without waiting for an answer, I ran to the front door.
A butler tried to stop me, but I pushed past him. As I
entered a ballroom only half the size of the Sports Arena,
a ripple of a applause began that grew until the whole
roomful of about two hundred people were clapping and
cheering.

Althea appeared almost immediately. She had probably
been watching the door since she first arrived.

"Glad you made it," she said, kissing me. "You know,
this was supposed to be black tie."

I looked down at my clothes. I was still wearing my
shooting outfit, which made me decidedly out of place.
"Uh-oh," I said. "I'll explain later. Is Ian here?"

"What?" she asked. "Why?"

"Is Fleming here?"

"Why, yes. I think I saw him . . ."

"Get him for me, will you?"

"What—Oh, all right. But then you'd better tell me
everything."

"I will, I promise." She swept off into the milling
crowd, and I felt a hard slap on my back.

"I understand yer wantin' to have your moment, John,"
Duke Wayne said, "But ya might've changed your clothes
by now."

"It's a long story, Duke."

"It would have to be," he nodded. "I owe ya a drink.
And remember: No coffee."

"No, a real drink would go great right now," I agreed.

"Bourbon?"

"Irish," I said. "Bushmills, if they've got it."

"If they don't, I'll kick John Ford's shanty butt back to
Ireland and have him bring you a case," he promised. The
Duke had already caught a slight buzz, I noticed. He cor-
ralled a waiter. "Hey, Ignatz," he said, "a double Bushmills—"

"Rocks," I added.

"On the rocks for my pal here, and make it snappy."

"Right away, Mr. Wayne," the waiter nodded.

"Stick with me," the Duke said, "I got pull around here.

Now the next thing we gotta do is, we gotta get you a tux.''

"I didn't bring one with me this trip," I said. "I didn't know I was going to be in such lofty circles."

"Aw, who cares anyway," he replied. "You're the guest of honor, you can wear whatever the hell you want."

The waiter reappeared with my drink. "It's Black Bush, sir," the waiter whispered to me. "The bartender keeps it for . . . special guests."

"Give him my thanks," I said. "I mean it." Black Bush was twenty-year-old Bushmills—and bartenders only poured it for people who really cared.

"Very good, sir."

"Well," said Wayne, "here's how."

"Cheers," I said. Although I wasn't a drinker, I was known to enjoy an occasional tumbler of the Irish, and I sure needed one now. It was smooth and heavenly.

"John!" Fleming called. I excused myself from Wayne and pulled Ian aside.

"Ian," I said. "Is Stephenson still in town?"

"Why, yes. We'll be leaving together on Monday."

"Good. There's a dark blue Cadillac parked right out front. Take it to wherever Stephenson is. I've got a few presents in the trunk. Be careful when you open it."

His eyes widened. "You don't mean . . ."

"I'm sure you'll have a lot to talk about."

"Let's go then, John."

"You're kidding, of course," I said. "I'm whipped, Ian. Give me a break."

Fleming made an exaggerated moue. "Come along, old chap," he said, in an overdone, upper-class British accent. "Stiff upper lip and all that. For the Navy."

"Oh, for Christ's sake," I complained, reluctantly following him out the door to where the car was waiting. I drained my glass and handed it to the attendant. Another drink magically appeared in front of me.

I was startled by a poke in my back.

"Just where in the hell do you think you're going?" Wayne demanded. "It's the shank of the night."

"I'll be right back, Duke," I said.

"The hell you will."

"Navy stuff, old pal. Take me ten minutes." Still holding on to my second drink, I opened the passenger side door of the Cadillac and got in. I blinked as my vision was flooded by a pair of headlights from a car pulling up behind us.

As Ian started the engine, I heard Wayne get into the car behind us. "Follow that car!" I heard Wayne shout.

"Without a drink?" Bogart's unmistakable voice replied.

Ian was a damned good driver. He drove fast and with great skill, and I could see that the little prize in the trunk had him good and wired. From the shrieking tires behind us, I could tell that Bogie was having trouble keeping up with us, and I worried about him and Wayne getting into an accident.

Fleming pulled up to the first phone booth—an actual booth, with a handheld receiver—and made a brief, urgent call.

Behind us, Wayne demanded another drink as Bogie opened the lid of a cocktail shaker. Those guys were apparently enjoying a normal evening out. In my time, such behavior would create a week's worth of headlines and land them at Betty Ford for months.

Fleming returned to the car and we headed back toward the Valley. I told Ian to slow down as we climbed Laurel Canyon, afraid for the two celebrants behind us, but he kept a firm foot on the accelerator.

I asked Ian where we were going, and I wasn't surprised when he replied, "Burbank Airport." Bogie would be shooting one of his most famous scenes there in just two years, I figured, so he might as well become familiar with the place.

It was more of an airfield than an airport in 1940. There were just a few official buildings, and Lockheed had another year or two before its presence dominated the landscape. Fleming drove directly onto the field and came to a stop at a DC-3 with British markings parked well away from any structures in a deserted part of the airport grounds. The plane's outboard engine was already turning as we pulled up. Stephenson was waiting for us with six very tough-looking young men carrying Thompson submachine guns. They were wearing civilian clothes, but as this was decades before cops and secret agents yielded Scotch and cigarettes to health clubs and fiber, I pegged them for soldiers in mufti.

"Good to see you again, Commander 'Bond,'" Stephenson greeted me, his handshake firm this time. "Ian tells me you've given His Majesty's government a little gift."

"Three actually," I replied. We turned our heads as the Bogart charabanc careened to a stop near us. Bogie and Duke spilled out of the car. They managed to right themselves and affected a highly casual walk toward the plane. Bogie looked at the assembled company and then at Wayne.

"Limeys," he nodded.

"'S okay, Bogie," Wayne said. "They're on our side. No autographs," he called to the soldiers who stood frozen at parade rest.

Stephenson looked slightly nonplussed at the intrusion, but I could also tell that he was a little impressed to see what famous escorts I rated.

Bogie and Wayne weaved toward me. "Guys," I whispered, "thanks for helping me out. But just let us get on with this, okay?"

"Mum's the fuckin' word," Bogie said, pantomiming a zipper across his lips.

"You Limeys go ahead," Wayne said to Fleming. "We're just along for the ride."

I tossed the Cadillac keys to Stephenson, who motioned with his head to the soldiers. Three of them quickly deployed around him, their guns trained on the trunk.

"These guys are serious," Wayne commented.

Stephenson turned the lock and the trunk sprung open. My three erstwhile kidnappers were awake and sprawled at various angles. The other three soldiers shouldered their arms and moved to help the kidnappers out of the trunk. Stephenson's face lit up as he saw Lorenz pulled upright.

"Oh, Commander," he said happily, "what a wonderful present you've brought me! This fine fellow will have so much to tell us."

"I will tell you nothing," Karl said stiffly. "I am member of the diplomatic corps, and you have no right—"

"Yes, I am awfully sorry," Stephenson interrupted him.

"I demand to be returned to the German Consulate at once. This outrage is in direct violation of the Geneva Convention."

"A convention?" Bogie remarked. "Where're the Shriners?"

"Your government will hear of this, Commander Surrey. Your naval career is finished! The Reich will—"

"The Reich?" Wayne said. "Hey, these guys are Nazis!"

"Nice to meetcha, squarehead," Bogie said. "Goldenberg's the name, Emmanuel Goldenberg," he added, giving the real name of his friend, Edward G. Robinson.

"How the hell are ya, sausage-meat?" Wayne said. "I'm Irving Weinstein. Howdja like some matzo balls shoved up your ass?"

For some reason, that angered Karl, probably the humiliating prospect of two famous Hollywood movie stars ridiculing him. He broke loose from the guards and charged. It all happened so quickly that it was over before anyone had a chance to move.

Bogie stuck out his foot and tripped him. Karl fell heavily against Wayne, who grabbed his collar and held him out at arm's length. He gave Karl an appraising look and then with a shrug, he belted the German powerfully in the jaw. Karl sagged and Wayne tossed his limp body to two soldiers.

"I hope he doesn't rate a parachute," Wayne sneered.

Stephenson shook his head, trying to conceal a grin. He gestured toward the aircraft. The soldiers drew their weapons and prodded Heinrich and Dieter up the steps into the plane. Two of them heaved the unconscious Karl into the plane like a duffel bag.

"Where are you taking them?" I asked him.

"We'll be in Canada in the morning," Stephenson replied. "Then it's back to Blighty. This cargo has top priority."

"Have a good flight," I said.

"Thank you, John," he said, using my name for the first time. "I hope we'll meet again—as true allies."

"Don't worry," I said. "It's just a matter of time."

He shook my hand warmly. "I hope it won't be too much time. Good luck to you." With that he turned and quickly made his way up into the aircraft.

"I have to go along for the debriefing," Fleming said. "I may be back, I'm not sure."

"It's been great knowing you, Ian. About Althea—"

He gave me a rueful smile. "The best man won," he said.

"I wouldn't say that," I replied.

"I would. Take care, John." He turned to go, and then faced me again. "That cover name you gave me," he began.

" 'James Bond?' "

"Yes. I rather like it."

"It's yours," I said. "Believe me."

He gave me an uncomprehending grin and climbed up into the aircraft. A soldier shut the hatch behind him, and the pilot started the inboard motor. In another moment, the plane began a slow taxi away from us.

"That was just beautiful," Bogart said, wiping an imaginary tear from his eye. "A beautiful friendship."

"That's the corniest goddamned thing I ever heard," Duke Wayne snorted.

"That's the trouble with you cowboys," Bogie retorted. "You think being sentimental is the same thing as being buggered."

"I'm sentimental," Wayne argued. "I wouldn't flatten just anybody."

I rolled my eyes. "Come on, you two. We've still got a party to go to."

"That's right," Bogie said, pulling his keys from his pocket. I snatched them from his hand.

"I'll take those. I want to get back to Bel Air in one piece."

"Oh, all right." He held out an arm to Duke Wayne. "Come along, Irving."

Wayne took his arm. "Right with you, Emmanuel." They strolled arm-in-arm back to the car.

"By the way, John," Bogie called back to me, "that whole thing was very well done. You ever consider bein' in the movies?"

"Listen, Althea," John Huston was saying urgently, "I'll move the shooting schedule around. It'll only be an extra month, maybe two."

"I can't do it, John," she declared. "I'd love to, but there's a war on. Haven't you heard?"

We were sitting in the panelled study of the Bel Air mansion. After returning to the party, Wayne and Bogie circulated. After a while, virtually every major star in Hollywood was staring curiously at me. I had a feeling that my two fellow-adventurers had been shooting off their mouths, because from the way I was being observed, I no longer felt out of place in my skeet-shooting attire. I mean, when you're waiting behind Gary Cooper at the bar, and he sees you and says, "I'll get it for you, Commander," even though you've never been introduced, you have to know that you've made a sizable splash in Tinsel Town.

"John," Huston said, "talk some sense into her."

I put my hands in front of me in a gesture of helplessness. "Hey don't put this on me," I said. "I've tried, believe me."

"Goddamnit!" he shouted. "I want this movie!"

"Charm won't work," Althea said.

"Well, just tell me what will work, Althea." There was an edge to his voice and I could tell that it rubbed Althea the wrong way.

"Go to Berlin and shoot Hitler, John. That's what'll work."

"All right, this is getting us nowhere," I said, shades of uniform patrol and domestic disputes. "John, excuse us for a moment, will you?'' *Could you go and talk with my partner for a moment, sir?*

Huston gave a bark of laughter. ''Of course. I'm sorry, Althea, I just—''

''It's all right, John. I know how much this picture means to you,'' she said forgivingly. Huston smiled like a kid on his birthday and left the room.

I sat next to her on a the small sofa and put my arm around her.

''I can't do the picture, John,'' she said. ''I'm getting antsy just being here instead of in Britain. I have to leave soon. And if what you said is true, about the Germans getting ready to move . . .''

''It is,'' I said. ''Never mind about the picture. I wonder if there's something you can do for me.''

She turned and kissed me softly on the cheek. God, it was great to be in love again. ''Anything,'' she said.

''Do you believe me?'' I asked. ''All that stuff I told you, about being from the future.''

''I didn't,'' she said, ''at first. But those things you once showed me in your pocket. That little box that knocked out those Nazis. That's a convincing argument. I've never seen anything like them—not even the materials they're made of.''

''I can save your life,'' I said. ''You don't have to die in this war.''

She sat up stiffly, exuding dignity like a strong perfume. ''There's something you don't understand, John.''

''What?''

''I would rather die fighting this war, than avoid it and live.''

Her words chilled me.

''Whoever said that war is only a man's game?'' she demanded. ''If you told me that you had received your sailing orders—if you really *were* in the Navy—would I have the slightest chance of stopping you? Then who are you to stop *me*? Don't women die in air raids? Aren't children casualties of the Nazis already? Then why can't I fight back? They won't let me carry a rifle, or fly a bomber, but I can serve, and I will.'' She turned to me, her beautiful face set in anger. "And no one, not even you, shall stop me."

"Okay," I said. "I won't. But what about us?"

She clasped my shoulders. "Stay here, John. Stay with us. The things you know, the things you could do—even in a small way—"

"I can't stay in 1940," I said. "That's impossible. I don't belong here."

"Yes, you do! You know you do. I like to think that I'm a perceptive woman, John. Do you think I haven't watched you, seen the way you are with people you meet? You love it here! Who the hell do you think you're kidding?"

That's the problem with brilliant women; you can't fool them, even when you're fooling yourself. Still, being a man, you try. "What do you mean, the way I act? I'm with movie stars, for Christ's sake. Duke Wayne and Humphrey Bogart are my best bosom buds! Of course I'm happy to be here."

"That's not what I mean," she said, "and you know it. You must *hate* two thousand six, John."

"That's not true!" I shook it off. "Of course it's true. You don't think I'd love to be able to stay here, and marry you, and go off and fight the only 'good' war we've ever had? You don't think I haven't seen films and documentaries and read books about what the Nazis have done? I have a master's degree in history, for God's sake. Professionally, it's useless, but I can tell you everything you want to know about the first fifty years of this century. I can tell you everything that happened and why. Do you think, after all that, that I wouldn't dearly love to do my best to grind the Nazis into the dust?"

"You want to marry me?" she asked after a long pause.

"Well, not tomorrow, but . . . it could happen."

She snuggled up against me. "John," she said, "we're not the first lovers to be torn apart by this war, and I don't think we'll be the last. We each must do what we must."

"When will you leave?" I asked, my mouth dry.

"When my commission comes through. I'll have to report to the British Consulate right away. I've called several times, but they tell me it could be two weeks or two months. Longer, perhaps. They don't have a dire need for WAAF officers at the moment, John. There's even been talk of a partial demobilization, the way the war has been— hasn't been—going."

"Yeah, well," I said, "they're in for a nasty shock."

"No one knows what you know, John. What was your favor?"

"What?"

"Before we got into this, you said you needed my help. What can I do for you—that I haven't done already?" she added with a sly grin.

"You can help me complete my mission."

"Your mission?"

"Step into my parlor," I said. "I'll tell you all about it."

ELEVEN

BEING BACK IN A POLICE UNIFORM SHOULD HAVE FELT LIKE old home week for me, but it didn't. For starters, the uniform was made of wool instead of the comfortable blend I had once worn with such pride. I also wore an eight-pointed cap. Although LAPD officers are issued caps, they seldom, if ever, wear them after their police-academy graduation ceremony. The biggest difference was the badge. Instead of the bronze and tin oval shield with the clear blue lettering—arguably the most beautiful police badge in the world—I wore one of the seven-pointed variety, with the legend *S.F. Police* engraved in the style of the Old West.

I walked through the milling crowd and stepped around an ambulance.

"What do you want here?" I demanded, flicking my left hand on the chest of a man in a trenchcoat walking toward me.

"I'm Sam Spade," Bogart replied, a barely perceptible smile playing around the off-camera side of his mouth. "Tom Polhaus phoned."

"Oh, I didn't know you at first," I answered, mollified. "Back there." Bogie walked past me and I lightly shoved a bystander away from the ambulance.

"And . . . cut!" shouted John Huston. A bell rang, and grips began scurrying all over the set.

"You're a natural, John," Bogie said. "You ought to do this for a living."

"Yeah," I said. "Me and about a half a million other guys. I'll take the Navy, Bogie. I like steady employment."

"You could do all right," he insisted. "Lookit Bond over here," he said, gesturing at Ward Bond as he joined us. "He's ugly and he can't act for shit, but he works alla time."

Bond reached over and flicked Bogie's ear. "In your ear, wiseass," Bond said. "I don't see you playing Hamlet. It'd be funny, though," Bond added. " 'To be,' " he began in a pretty fair Bogart imitation, " 'or not to fuckin' . . . uh . . . be, yeah, that's right.' "

We all laughed heartily. Although I found movie work dull and repetitive, I enjoyed the camaraderie on the set. I especially liked watching real pros like Bogie, Ward Bond, and Barton MacLane showing me how it was done. There was also the fact that I was there when one of the great film classics of all time was being made. You could tell from the first cold reading that something great was going to happen. Bogie and his co-stars brought instant life to Huston's masterful script and everybody seemed to know it. It was like being on a baseball team that had just clinched the pennant by fifteen games and was a lock to win the Series.

Bogie had been kind enough to visit me at Althea's the night before, and we had spent hours rehearsing our short scene together.

"Just hit your marks," Bogie told me over and over again. "You do that, everything else falls into place." Althea's living-room couch had pulled double duty as the ambulance, and we rehearsed the scene at least fifty times. I surprised everyone by getting it right on the first take.

"What're you tryna do," Bogie hissed at me, "make me look bad? Nobody gets it on the first take."

"Hey, you taught me," I replied. "It's your fault."

I don't remember how many times we shot the scene,

but it was a lot. There were so many different angles and distances, for one thing; and then there was the lighting to get exactly right. Once an extra moved at just the wrong time, and Huston cut the action immediately. Still, it was an experience I wouldn't trade for anything.

I have to admit that I did feel bad about one thing: The actor who originally played my part. Huston had cast him with great care, a man much older than I. But even he landed on his feet; he was immediately picked up for a bigger part in a Howard Hawks film elsewhere on the Warner lot.

Althea came over and took my arm, walking me away from Bogie and Bond. "I knew I was right," she whispered.

"Right about what?"

"The way you wear that uniform. The first night we met, remember? It wasn't so long ago. When I said I'd guess what it was you did?"

"What about it?"

"I said you were a cop. I was right. You wear that uniform far too well."

"It's only a costume," I shrugged.

"You know I'm right."

I sighed. "LAPD, twelve years," I said.

"LAPD!" she exclaimed. "Why, they're all louts!"

"Not in my time," I said stiffly. But I understood her feelings. In 1940, at least half of the LAPD were so corrupt that they'd have taken MasterCard, had it existed.

She looked at me in wonder. "What was your rank?"

"Detective Three—Detective Sergeant," I amended for her benefit. "I was on the Lieutenants list, though."

"I knew I was right! Did you solve murders?"

"No. I was on the Fugitive Squad."

"The Fugitive Squad. My, that sounds thrilling!"

"It was, actually."

"Did you ever . . . shoot anybody?"

I paused. "Yes."

"How dreadful."

"Well, they were shooting at me."

"Lunch, everybody!" the assistant director called. "One hour!"

"Let's take a walk," Althea said. "We need to talk."

Uh-oh, I thought, knowing what was coming. At any other time—that is, in my time—my thought would be, *Oh, Christ, here it comes, the* relationship *talk*. But this I knew would be worse, much worse.

"John!" Huston called, walking over to us. "Hello, Althea," he said coolly. He still hadn't really forgiven her for turning down the part, even though Mary Astor had read wonderfully and was raring to go. "I need your opinion on something, possibly your help."

"Whatever I can do," I said.

"I couldn't help but notice that Duke Wayne is a good friend of yours."

"He is my friend, yes."

"And I also couldn't help but notice that he has been out on the town a lot with you and Bogie; and that he and Bogie seem to get on well together."

It was true. Although Bogie and the Duke were never known to run in the same circles, and they would never do a picture together, the two were a lot alike if you looked closely enough. Both were honest men of outstanding character, with little use for those who weren't.

"I've had an idea for a long time," he said. "There's a story I've always wanted to bring to the screen. With Bogie, of course, and Spencer Tracy. But Tracy's agent a is real pain in the ass. I'll probably never get him. But the more I see of the Duke, and his positive chemistry with Bogie, the more I'm inclined to believe that it would work."

"What would work?"

"A story I've loved since I was a kid," he said. "You ever read any Kipling?"

I gave in to the urge to show off again. "Way ahead of you, John. *The Man Who Would Be King*. The Duke would definitely work as Peachy Carnehan. I think it's a brilliant idea."

Huston shook his head in wonder. "Where does he get it?" he asked Althea.

"You'd be surprised," she answered.

"Anyway," Huston continued, "I've got a script pretty much written. I know Bogie is slated to do a potboiler called *All Through The Night* after he's done with this, but I think he'd jump at it under the right circumstances."

"You're probably right," I said. I remembered Bogie in *All Through The Night*. He played a Damon Runyonesque, golden-hearted gangster who loved his Ma—Jane Darwell, *of course*—supported by a cast of other lovable mugs played by the likes of Phil Silvers, Jackie Gleason, and William Demarest. In it they chased Nazi spies played by Conrad Veidt and one of Bogie's best pals, Peter Lorre. It was a fun movie, but I didn't think the world would change for the worse if Bogie skipped it for the Kipling story.

"Could you talk to the Duke? Just sort of bring it up casually?"

"Of course," I said. "I'd be delighted."

"Wonderful!" He rubbed his hands together. "Of course," he added, "there'd be something in it for you."

"That won't be necessary," I replied. "I'm still in the Navy, John. I'm returning to duty soon."

"Oh, I'm sorry to hear that. Still, if you change your mind, you were good out there today."

"I'll keep that in mind," I replied.

Althea and I never did get to have that lunch and the discussion still loomed. Bogie dragged us over to Lakeside, and there wasn't enough privacy. We did, however, run into the Duke, and I told him flat out, and in front of Bogie, of Huston's proposal. He did the famous John Wayne double take.

"*The Man Who Would Be King*, huh? Lemme at it! Whattaya think, Bogie?"

"I'm in if you're in, cowboy. I can't wait to see what Huston's come up with for a script."

"I think you'll be delighted," I said.

"Did he ever make the movie?" Althea whispered to me.

"In 1976," I whispered back. "It was fantastic. But who knows? That might turn out to be a remake."

Tony was in bed but having trouble falling asleep when Althea and I walked in. I sat down next to him as Althea stood in the doorway.

"I can't sleep," Tony said gravely.

"Why not?" I asked him.

"I just . . . can't."

"You're homesick."

"I . . . I don't know. I love California, but . . . England . . ."

"I know exactly how you feel," I said. "You love it where you are, and you don't really want to leave, but you know you must. It's an odd feeling, because you're not really sure how you feel."

"Yes." He looked up at me. "Is the war going to end?"

"Someday," I said.

"I want to fight the Germans. Do you think they'd let me fight . . . smaller Germans?"

"You remind me of someone I know," I said. "A little boy just about your age."

"Does he want to fight the Germans?"

"Oh, yes. But he can't because he has to go to school. His name is Danny Dreamer."

"Danny Dreamer," Tony repeated.

"That's right. Danny never liked going to school, because there were so many more important things to do. But he loved his teacher, Mrs. Welch. So he tried hard to listen, to pay attention. But then he'd somehow start thinking about the war, and how much he desperately wanted to fly a Spitfire . . . lead a squadron of brave men into battle . . ."

Tony was sleeping peacefully, no doubt secure in the knowledge that when Danny punched the throttle through the gate, the engine gave him a burst of speed that enabled him to turn the tables on the Messerschmitts behind him. And, as Danny explained to Mrs. Welch, it was pointless to try for a deflection shot when you were attacked: Bullets don't travel as quickly as a 109 at top speed, after all, and the only thing to do was to close in right on its tail and blast away while you were too close to miss. Boy, Mrs. Welch, if we only had a 20mm cannon like the Luftwaffe instead of .303-caliber rifle ammo, then we'd show the Hun a thing or two.

"That was wonderful," Althea said. "You really should write children's books."

"Maybe I will, one day," I replied.

She sat me down on the living-room sofa and took my hands.

"My commission came through," she said, looking me squarely in the eye.

I had thought that because it had been hanging over our heads for weeks, when it came it would be something of a relief. It wasn't. I felt my stomach turn over. "When?"

"Monday."

"Oh, God. What about Tony?"

"I need your advice. Dad misses him."

"Where is 'Dad' stationed?"

"London."

"No way!" I exclaimed. "Do *not* take Tony to London."

"All right," she said, placing a calming hand on mine. "My aunt can come down from Palo Alto. She can stay here for the duration. I've enough to cover all the bills, and a little more. Mairead will stay on. Tony won't like it, but I suppose there's nothing else to do."

"Then I guess this is good-bye." I said weakly.

"I guess so."

We melted into each other's arms. "Oh, John," she cried, beginning to weep, "please don't go. Come with me. Please."

"I can't."

"Why not? What could possibly be more important?"

She had me there.

"Your Uncle Jack. I know you'd miss him, and your parents, but John . . ."

"It's impossible."

She stared at me. "Who cares? John . . . to fight the Nazis. An important struggle, the biggest of this century!"

"I've had my war," I replied.

"Yes, your . . . Gulf War. You told me. And you also told me that you let the tyrant stay in power. What kind of victory was that?"

"I also fought a war on the streets."

She waved her hand dismissively. "Yes, you told me about that, too. A war against children. Brutal and vicious children. A war that can't be won. Is that what you're going back to?"

"I don't do that anymore."

"So what are you going back to, John? Is there a woman?"

"Don't be ridiculous."

"Then what! What could hold you there, that future you despise so much?"

"I have responsibilities, work, a life—"

"What life?"

I drew myself up. "I'm the first man to travel through time. It's a great responsibility. I can't just shrug it off."

"Yes you can!"

"This war will be long, bloody, and destructive, but it will continue and it will end with or without me."

"But with you, it could end sooner."

"No it wouldn't. Who would listen? Who would believe me?"

"Stephenson might. You could work for him."

That caught me off guard, and it had its merits. "Hmmm."

"Yes, 'hmmmm.' I've got you thinking, haven't I?"

"Okay."

"One other thing. Your wife left you eight years ago. Have you been in love since then?"

"Only now."

"Why?"

"I don't know why."

"Do you see yourself falling in love again?"

I thought of 2006, and boy, did she have me there. After

Althea, I doubted there was a single woman in the span of centuries who would do it for me. And that's coming from a guy whose philosophy has always been: "Once you get over it, there's always someone else—always."

"You know," I said, "like Danny Dreamer, I've always wondered what it'd be like to fly a Spitfire against the Luftwaffe."

I reached into my pocket and took out the Decacom. I stood up and placed it on the floor. "Say you'll marry me when we get to London."

"John . . . of course I will."

"Stephenson'll have to rustle me up some new identification."

"I'm sure he'll be delighted."

"Darling," I said, raising an imaginary glass, "to the war. *Vive la mort, vive la guerre, vive la sacre, mercennaire!*"

"That's a mercenary toast. You're not a mercenary."

"I know, but it *sounds* so good."

I brought my foot down like a groom stomping the wedding glass. The Decacom shattered into small pieces. The only way I could leave 1940 now or ever, was the same way as everyone else—on New Year's Eve.

Mairead raised a huge stink about it, but I would move out of the Beverly Wilshire and stay with Althea until we left the country on Monday. I had no passport, but we would be going through Canada, and from there embassy connections in Ottawa would speed me across the Atlantic. We would be married as soon as we hit London. I still had over fifteen thousand dollars of my original bankroll left, and between her father's wealth and her own successful career, Althea was loaded.

"The Cincinnati Reds will take the Series this year," I said. "Let's make sure we bet the ranch on it."

"Ah, you're just after my money," she sneered playfully. "Well, from here on out, it's eleven shillings a day."

"I want at least half," I told her.

"I don't know. Does my agent get ten percent of that?"

It would be a wonderful life, I thought, as I drove down Benedict Canyon in the Dodge I had rented a few weeks before. I had been staying at Althea's every night, but prudently returned to my room at the Beverly Wilshire before Tony or Mairead woke up. But the housekeeper knew damn well what was going on, and she didn't like it one bit. All she ever said to me was "hmmph."

Having made the decision to stay, I felt a great sense of relief, much as I had upon my discharge from active duty after the Gulf War or following college graduation. Even though I was going to war, I couldn't stem the exhilaration that coursed through my blood. I would miss California, and I would miss Bogie and Duke and everyone else, but I would be with Althea. And who knew? Maybe I *could* save her life. Maybe we could both return to L.A. in 1945, flush with victory and ready to resume our careers. Money would never be a problem for me, I thought. I knew the outcome of every World Series, every Kentucky Derby, every heavyweight championship fight. Hell, I could buy Xerox, IBM, and McDonald's when they were still penny stocks.

And now, with the woman I loved, I would fight the war that every serviceman in following generations had kicked himself for missing. I'd do my part in helping to turn Nazi Germany into a junkyard.

The question was, what exactly would I do? Join the Army, the Navy? Work for Stephenson undercover, maybe parachute into France and kidnap a few generals? I knew I was in good shape—better than most men of the era. Could I pass for twenty-six, the cutoff age for RAF fighter pilots? It was a dilemma, but one I enjoyed thinking about.

I pulled up in front of the Beverly Wilshire and told the attendant to leave my car alone—I was checking out. I felt so good that I ignored the open door to the elevator and ran up all five flights of stairs to my room. Nice hotel, I thought crazily, I'll have to spend a night here sometime.

I searched my pockets for my room key, wiggling my hand around the Taser—I'd wisely decided to hold on to *that*—fished the key out, and slid it into the lock. As I opened the door, I reached around to the wall and flipped the light switch on. As light flooded the room, I saw that I wasn't alone.

"Just what in the hell did you think were doing?" Cornelia demanded. She took several angry steps toward me and gripped my wrist with her powerful fingers. She held up her Decacom and glared at me.

"No!" I shouted.

But I was too late. Her thumb hit the red button and the room began to swim.

The year 1940 had returned to the past.

TWELVE

CORNELIA DRAGGED ME OUT OF THE ZOOM ROOM, WHERE
I had been standing like a zombie. Doc Harvey ran up to
me and pushed me down into a chair, rolled up my sleeve
and wrapped a blood pressure gauge around my arm. He
placed his stethoscope against my chest.

"He's in shock," he said to Cornelia in a rebuking tone.
"I told you not to bring him back this way."

"Tough," Cornelia spat. I had never seen her so angry.
Felice came from around the console and motioned for all
of the support personnel to leave the room—which they
did in a hurry. "Are you all right, John?" she asked solic-
itously.

"Oh, are you in trouble!" Cornelia said menacingly to
me.

"That's enough," Doc Harvey snapped. He swabbed my
arm with an alcohol-soaked cottonball and jabbed me with
a needle. I began to feel better almost immediately, up-
grading my condition to rotten. "He's suffered a severe
emotional trauma," he pronounced. "John needs a lot of
bed rest, and no stress. Okay, Cornelia? No debrief until
he feels better, and no breaking his balls until he completely
recovers."

"Thank you for that highly professional diagnosis, Doctor,'' Cornelia said sarcastically. "That'll be all."

The Doc closed his medical bag and patted my shoulder. "Bed rest, John. And I would suggest, no television or anything like that."

"Not even . . . old movies?" I asked dully.

"Go slowly. Don't immerse yourself in this time culture too quickly. From what I can see, it won't be an easy re-adjustment."

I stood and walked over to the armoire and took out my clothes. As I slowly changed behind the screen, I couldn't help but feel a slight irritation. My 2006 clothes—jeans and a sweatshirt—actually felt good.

Felice had been talking urgently to Cornelia, who nodded and walked over to me. "Come on," she said, attempting a reasonable tone, "I'll drive you home."

As we pulled out of the complex in Corny's '06 Mercedes coupe, I stared down at the San Fernando Valley. I tried to pick out the spot where Karl and Company had held me prisoner, but all I could see was a built-up city with freeways, houses, and malls. It was as though my life in 1940 had never existed.

But as we sped east on the 101, I knew that I would be haunted for a long time, and I was honestly frightened when I began to imagine the emotional fallout I would undoubt-edly suffer. Bogie was dead. Duke was dead. Huston, Flem-ing, Stephenson, and worst of all, my Althea—all of them, gone forever. I would have wept, but I had never been the sort who gave in to tears.

Somebody was changing a flat tire on the shoulder just west of Woodman, so naturally all five lanes of traffic hit their brakes to better view the thrilling sight. Wonderful. That gave Cornelia just the stimulus she needed to blow up.

"You are in such deep shit," she began. "You cannot imagine the depth or the breadth of the hole you are in. If I decide that you may continue to work for me, you will do exactly as I say. You will follow the book, you will not deviate from your stated mission, you will not *breathe* unless I say so . . . the cost of the Decacom is coming out of your paycheck . . .''

It suddenly struck me, in a wry way, that I had been here before. I recalled my mother bringing me home from school after I had gotten in trouble for some idiotic prank or other. ''You're going to clean up your room, mow the lawn, take out the garbage and do your homework. And you're grounded, young man, until I decide you've earned your privilege to play again!''

''What's so funny,'' Cornelia demanded.

''Nothing,'' I said, ''Mom.'' We got off at Coldwater Canyon, and as we pulled to a stop at a red light I jumped out of the car. ''Back in a jiff.'' Before she could protest I dashed into a Seven-Eleven and asked for a couple of packs of cigarettes and matches. Then I paid the man and ran out, catching Cornelia just as the light changed.

''Where did you go?'' she asked.

I ignored her and opened the cigarette pack, slid one out, and stuck it in my mouth. I couldn't understand why I had a sudden urge to smoke. I never had, and even in 1940, where I was virtually the only non-smoker around, I had had no desire. I guess it had to do with being in shock, like Doc Harvey had said.

''You're not smoking that in my car.'' Cornelia was horrified.

''I guess I am,'' I said. I lit it, took a puff, and flicked it out the window.

''Yech.'' Cornelia waved the air. ''Disgusting.''

''It doesn't make me a bad person,'' I said.

Cornelia pulled into a parking space in front of my condo. ''Are you coming in?'' I asked.

She didn't answer. She just got out of the car and followed me into the building. We said nothing in the elevator. I was beginning to return to 2006; this was my home, my own territory. I had forgotten about it, but it felt right to me.

The place had that nobody's-been-home-for-awhile smell to me, but it must have been an olfactory illusion because I had only left that morning.

"Are you tucking me in?" I asked her.

"Damned right, I am," she replied. She followed me into my bedroom and turned down the bedcover. She pushed me gently onto the bed and I laid my head on my pillow. Cornelia unlaced my shoes and dropped them on the floor.

"Well," she said, sitting on the bed next to me, "did you have a good time?"

I noticed that she was finally smiling. "Oh, you just couldn't imagine . . ." I said.

"Did you make a lot of friends?"

"I made . . . there were . . ." I couldn't get the words out. "You couldn't imagine . . . what a time . . . I—I . . . it . . ."

She lifted me slightly and put her arms around me. "It's all right, John," she said softly, patting my back. "Shhh, it's okay. Go ahead, I'll never tell a soul, I promise."

And so far, she has been as good as her word. To my knowledge no one, not even Felice, has the slightest clue that I spent the next half hour in her arms, blubbering like a baby.

THIRTEEN

I SLEPT A DREAMLESS SLEEP FOR ALMOST FOURTEEN hours. I would have slept for even longer, but I was awakened by the insistent ringing of my doorbell. I padded to the door and opened it.

"Your boss called me," Uncle Jack said. His arms were full of groceries. "Are you okay, kiddo?"

"I've been a lot better."

"Well, you look like hell." He went into the kitchen and began unloading his bags. "Jesus!" he exclaimed, opening the refrigerator. "Don't you ever eat? There's nothing in here." He gingerly held up a package of ancient bologna and sniffed at it distastefully. "Christ! Spanish sailors in the Armada ate better than you." He tossed the bologna into the garbage can.

"Go easy on me, Jack. I've had a rough . . . three weeks." He tossed me a Heineken Dark and I cracked it. "By the way, Jack-o, what did *you* think of 1940?"

He banged his head on the top door of the fridge. "Now, look, John—"

"Don't give me that. Someone covered my ass back there."

"Well, we had to, John. You walk around telling people

you're a Navy officer, sooner or later, *someone* is going to check you out."

"So, how did you do it?"

"It was nothing. I didn't even have to go to Washington. All I did was put on my blues, walk into some office in Long Beach, and tell a frightened yeoman to see that this package—your file—got shipped to DC pronto. Then I got the hell back to the present. I didn't even have time to look around."

"You didn't even look around?"

"That's the Navy, boy: Define your mission and stick to it. Otherwise, all kinds of shit can happen. So it helped?"

"Oh, man, did it ever!"

"You have a lot to tell me."

"There's an understatement for you."

"Okay. I'll make us a few sandwiches and—"

"I'll make lunch, unkie. I need you to run a quick errand for me."

He cocked an eyebrow. "All right."

"Go down to the video store and get me *The Maltese Falcon*. Also, *The Man Who Would Be King*."

"Which one?" Jack asked. "The one with Caine and Connery, or the one with Bogart and Wayne?"

"YES!" I shouted.

Jack drove me to work the next day and attended my debriefing with Corny and Felice. I was still being treated like an invalid—Jack refused to let me drive anywhere by myself, and Corny had Doc Harvey keep a watchful eye on my blood pressure and other vital functions. I had few objections, though I was tired and irritable much of the time, and the debriefing took much longer than it should have.

Jack made me rerun my scene in *The Maltese Falcon* at least a dozen times. "I always thought that guy looked familiar," he mused. "I mean, I haven't seen it in years, but come to think of it . . ."

"Come on, Jack," I said, "It's not as though my role is entirely memorable."

"Yeah, but you were good. You had screen presence."

"It was the script," I said, rolling my eyes.

The 1941 version of *The Man Who Would Be King* was admittedly not as good as the later version, but only because constraints of the era, the budget and location restrictions did not allow the movie to open up as it had in 1976. But the script was virtually the same, and Bogie and Wayne were marvelous. So good, in fact, that the movie received Oscar nominations for Best Picture, Director, Screenplay, Photography, and—I noticed with a great deal of pride— Best Actor, John Wayne. It didn't win anything, but it did wonderfully at the box office and was now considered a classic.

Even better, after further research I discovered that the Duke and Bogie had collaborated on three other pictures: *We're No Angels, Sahara*, and *Destination Tokyo*. Of the three, the strangest was seeing Bogart in the Cary Grant role in *Tokyo*, but as usual, his performance was flawless. *Sahara* was a standard wartime action film, but Wayne in the Aldo Ray part in *Angels* was something to behold. It was as though acting with Bogie set his crazier side free, and his notices for *True Grit* in 1969—when he finally won the Oscar—called it his best performance since *We're No Angels*.

"I did that," I said flatly to Cornelia.

"You did what?"

"Before I left, Bogie and Wayne had never done a movie together. I don't know if they even liked each other. I do know that they hung out with different types. A lot of Bogie's friends leaned to the left and Wayne was slightly to the right of J. Edgar Hoover, minus the tutu."

"John," Felice asked, "are you sure?"

"I'm positive. What else do you want to know?"

"Who originally played your part in *The Maltese Falcon*?"

"I don't know his name—he was an older guy. When Althea and Bogie asked Huston to give me the part, Huston said I looked too young. They put a lot of makeup on me, wanted me to look like an old beat cop. But Huston was pretty happy when he saw the dailies. He said I looked just like a real cop.''

"If he only knew," Felice said with grin. "Are you okay, John?''

"I was just wondering," I replied, feeling depressed. "What did she think when I just disappeared like that?''

"Althea," Corny murmured.

"Yes. What a terrible thing to have done." I wondered when it was that she knew I wasn't coming back. I wondered how Duke and Bogie took it. Maybe they understood, especially since the next day was April 9, the day the Germans invaded Norway and occupied Denmark.

There was a long silence. Felice finally broke it by telling me that she had gone quickly back and recovered my luggage and my toys from Fahey's.

"Thank you," I said. "They'll be worth a fortune today. I hope you'll let me keep them.''

"What the hell would we do with them?" Cornelia said. "Consider them a perk.''

I laughed. "Holy Hell!" I exclaimed.

"What?''

"My hotel bill! The Beverly Wilshire must think I'm a deadbeat!''

"You're covered," Felice calmed me. "I left them some cash in an envelope, explaining that you'd been urgently recalled to duty.''

"Whoa, thanks." For some reason, that made me feel a lot better. Briefly. Because then I started thinking about Althea again.

"What happened to her?" I asked suddenly.

Cornelia and Felice looked at each other. Uncle Jack folded his arms and stared down at his shoes.

"I have a right to know," I said tonelessly.

Cornelia nodded to Felice. "John," Felice said, "she was killed on August 14 at the RAF base at Manston in Kent.''

"How?''

"I don't know.''

"How!''

Felice cleared her throat. "She was running for cover just as Messerschmitt 110s began a strafing run on the airfield. I'm sorry, John, she didn't make it."

"Okay," I said. "All right." There was a lump in my throat, but I really didn't feel anything, just a sort of numbness. The sense of loss, I imagined, would come later. But she had met her death sixty-six years before. It was practically ancient history.

"There's something else, John," Felice said softly. "A letter came for you. It was delivered yesterday to Police Headquarters at Parker Center. They forwarded it here."

She handed me an envelope. I took it absently and put it on the table. Cornelia, Felice, and Uncle Jack rose slowly and filed out of the room, closing the door behind them and leaving me alone.

I waited for a few minutes before opening it. It was postmarked London, and it bore the letterhead of a law firm whose legend proclaimed that they had been in business since 1807.

Detective John Surrey
Los Angeles Police Department
Parker Center
150 North Los Angeles Street
Los Angeles, California 90013

Dear Mr. Surrey:

In accordance with terms specified in the will dated by Ms. Althea Joan Rowland 30 July 1940, the enclosed has been held for delivery until 18 March 2006. With the delivery of the enclosed, we have discharged our final duty to Ms. Rowland's estate.

Yours truly,

Edward Ashton-Hyde Esq., Solicitor

Holding a letter for sixty-six years for delivery to a man
not yet born must have raised a few eyebrows, but leave it
to a good old English firm of solicitors to mind their own
business and get the job done. I reached into the manila
envelope and pulled out a letter. It was made of strong
paper, and although it was yellowed it did not seem to be
falling apart. No doubt it had been kept in a safe for many
years, secure from the ravages of time.

I opened the envelope carefully and extracted a neatly
typed letter. I had never known that Althea could type, but
then again, there were a lot of things about her I would
never get to know.

30 July 1940

My Darling John,

I have to believe that this letter will reach you. I think
its chances are quite good. My family has used this
firm for generations, and they have always delivered
the goods, pardon the pun. Even my precious Tony—
oh, God, he'll be seventy-four!—now probably the
head of the Rowland family, is assuredly a valued client. Anyway, I've convinced myself you'll get it on
schedule.

As the hours went by and you didn't return, I began
to fear the worst. Then I made the most difficult telephone call of my life—I phoned the Beverly Wilshire.
They told me that you had left a note—and more than
enough money to cover your bill—and that you had
been urgently recalled to active duty. It was then that
I knew that you had gone back—or is it forward?—
and that I would never see you again.

Well, of course I cried for hours. But then I realized
that you had probably been forced to go back, or that
you had decided that you simply couldn't stay. Either

way, I knew that whatever had happened, you had done what you felt was right. And I understood.

The next day, the Germans rolled into Denmark, and Bogie told me that he figured you were recalled without a minute to lose. I let him think that I agreed with him, because after all, I couldn't tell him the truth. Both Bogie and the Duke told me that they would miss you. Wayne said you were "a hell of a guy."

Well, I got that out. You're back in 2006, and I'm still here in the "old days." Everything has happened exactly as you said it would. France fell last month, and now everyone here is positive that the Germans will invade at any moment. I feel better knowing that they won't, thanks to you, but everyone tells me I'm crazy. Time will tell.

I've been assigned to the air base at Manston, where I sit next to the station commander and plot enemy formations. Where on earth did the Germans get all those planes? Right now they're attacking our convoys, and we're taking horrible losses. They haven't hit our bases yet, but that'll happen quite soon, I'm sure. Hollywood seems very far away indeed.

If I live through this war, and make it to the ripe old age of ninety-two, I hope you'll take the time to visit a doddering old lady somewhere in Beverly Hills. Who knows? Maybe I'll have a granddaughter who'll be just your type.

I miss you so awfully, John. I know how unhappy you were (are?) in your own time. Don't be. I still have this awful war ahead of me. My country just suffered a humiliating defeat and stands on the brink of total disaster. But I still had the chance to be in love with you, and that makes everything somehow bearable.

Before you agreed to stay, you told me of your profound responsibility as the first man to travel through
time. I now agree with you. It is a great responsibility,
and you should be proud of your achievement. But
more importantly, John, I want you to be happy. It's
hard being without you, but I know that I can't change
it and I must go on. So must you. Maybe I'll fall in
love with someone else someday; I hope I will. And
I pray that you do, as well. It won't be the same, and
perhaps not as marvelous, but because we can love
each other, we can love again. We'll always hold a
corner of our hearts for each other, but we must go
on.

Enjoy your life, John. Live it fully, love completely.
Anything less would be a waste of of time, and who
knows more about time than you?

Always,

Althea

I don't know how long I sat there after reading her letter,
but when I finally stood up and went out to face my em-
ployers and my uncle, I was feeling a whole lot better.
What a woman Althea had been! Thinking of me to the
last, not giving me even a day to worry about how she
badly she must have been hurt. And she had been hurt, but
she had been strong and on her way to recovery. I put the
letter in my breast pocket, next to my heart. In those pages,
she was alive again. I would buy every video of every film
she had ever made, but she would never exist for me as
much as in that letter.

But *I* wasn't as strong as either of us thought. Because,
no matter how much time went by, no matter who I met,
or even married—though I doubted I ever would—I would
never get over Althea. I would live my life, do my job, get
my share of laughs, take what pleasures I could, but the
emptiness of life without her would never change. I could

hope that it would, I could try as I might, but that beautiful, brave, and generous woman could never be replaced in my heart.

I could only hope that, in the few weeks left to her, Althea had filled the void in her heart that my leaving had caused. It was the only consolation I had.

But I couldn't deny that I would spend the rest of my life searching for her in vain. I would forever be troubled by the possibilities forever left unfulfilled.

I guess I did believe in blinking green lights, after all.

FOURTEEN

HAVING FINALLY ACCEPTED THE FACT THAT ALTHEA WAS gone, my own recovery proceeded quickly, and in a few weeks I was ready to get back to work. I assured Cornelia that my emotional health had returned and that I was champing at the bit to resume my singular career.

"Are you sure?" she asked pointedly.

"Look," I said, "I got emotionally involved. Okay, I goofed. Now I know better. It's a normal hazard of the discovery process, and now I'll be more careful."

She gave me a dubious look. "I don't know."

"Oh, come on. I know I'm ready." It was true; for some reason, I was really jazzed. I couldn't wait to get back to work. "Come on, what's my next job?"

"All right," she sighed. "But remember. Quick in, quick out, no attachments."

"I won't let you down," I promised.

"All right. Your next mission is going to be much more simple. You won't need more than an hour. All you need to do is get me an autograph."

"No prob," I replied breezily. "Whose?"

"My favorite rock star when I was a kid," Corny said. "Jim Morrison."

" 'Light My Fire'? That Jim Morrison?"

"God, he was a doll," she reflected with uncharacteristic dreaminess. "Okay, I admit it—we are combining business with pleasure. Why not? *You* got to do it."

I put up my hands. "Hey, no argument here. Glad to be of service. But how am I supposed to get his autograph? I'll never get within a hundred yards of him at a rock concert."

"You won't be going to a rock concert," she said. "You're going to catch him just before he got famous."

"How?"

"You'll be going back to 1966. That's before they got big. They were a popular local act in L.A. at the time, but still relatively small potatoes. We'll zoom you over to Sunset Boulevard, you'll go to the Whiskey A Go-Go, catch him as he comes in, and home for tea."

I liked it. Clean and quick. I had to admit, I wasn't ready for another extended visit to back in time. I had to return on light duty first. I couldn't see myself caring too much about Morrison. To me, he was just another scumbag rocker who OD'd on depraved self-indulgence, just like a lot of other rockers and movie stars who killed themselves at the height of their careers. I felt little more than contempt for people like that. Not because of what they had done to themselves, but because their willful mismanagement of success was an insult to the millions who still struggled in vain and would have made better use of such triumphs.

The Zoom Room was a little quieter this time around. Doc Harvey pronounced me physically fit but added, "I'm not too sure about his mind yet."

As usual, he was ignored, and I turned to Felice, who handed me my costume for the visit.

"No way!" I said. "I am not wearing that! I'll look like a raging queen.!"

Felice laughed. "Come on, John, I can't wait to see you. Go change."

Grumbling, I went into the small changing area and took off my work clothes, changing quickly into the 1966 loon-boy costume.

The Zoom Room erupted with laughter as I re-entered.

Even Corny's lips twitched, and she was unsuccessful in affecting a stern expression as she tried to shut everyone up.

"You look simply divine!" Felice shrieked with laughter. "Oh, John, I've got to get a picture of this!"

"No you don't, Felice," I barked, feeling my complexion redden even more than it had when I first saw myself in the mirror. I wore striped bell-bottoms; a flowing, baggy-sleeved polka-dot shirt; and high-heeled, white patent-leather boots.

"You look . . . 'groovy!' " Felice whooped.

"Yeah, yeah," I muttered. "Currency? Identification, please? I've got a job to do."

"Oh, of course, John," she guffawed, handing me one thousand dollars in 1966 dollars and a driver's license listing my birthdate as 19 July 1931.

"John, I think we've found your look," Felice said.

"Great," I said, stepping into the Zoom Room. "Let's get this over with."

"Peace, love, psychedelia!" Felice called. A moment later, I was back in the past.

The Sunset Boulevard of 1966 was far more familiar to me than that of 1940. The biggest difference was the absence of certain landmarks like Nicky Blair's and Spago. There were no yuppie coffeehouses that I could see, but a lot more hamburger stands and bars. The cars were all different; but in California, a '66 Mustang is not a particularly rare artifact even in my time. Perhaps I was getting used to the differences.

It was a typical Saturday night on Sunset. Traffic was pretty much backed up in both directions and the sidewalks were crowded with people. Two levels of people, as always: the ordinary date-night crowd; and the hookers, pimps, hustlers, and bums. Real bums—winos and dirtbags, not the tragic figures we have come to refer to as "the homeless."

There was no line in front of the Whiskey, which surprised me, but it was still early. From inside, I could hear

Morrison's distinctive voice singing about riding a snake. I was supposed to have caught him as he entered the club, but apparently I had been zoomed in a little too late. That was okay with me—I figured I'd watch the show and soak up a little 1966 culture. I paid the cover and went in.

The smell of marijuana was overpowering. Someone handed me a joint and I absently began smoking it. To tell you the truth, I felt right at home. My outfit, it seemed, wasn't as outlandish as I had thought, if everyone else's clothes were any indication. One guy was even wearing the American flag for pants.

The girls all wore very heavy eye makeup and colorless frosted lipstick, and many, although very young, were bleached blondes. They all wore miniskirts or very tight jeans that rode low on the waist, and were held up by belts as wide as my hand. The natural look was definitely out, but a lot of them were extraordinarily pretty nonetheless.

Most of the audience were zonked out of their minds. The room was hot, close, and smoky; and everybody seemed to just be standing there with their eyes closed, nodding from side to side with the music's insistent beat.

Morrison was pretty wasted himself. His eyes held that half-lidded, everybody's-a-joke cast to them that lots of good pot seems to engender. The rest of The Doors, however—a drummer, lead guitarist, and an organ player— seemed a lot more businesslike. From time to time, I noticed the guitarist and the organist look at Morrison, and then at each other with slightly worried glances.

I stood there, smoking my little joint as I watched him perform. I smoked it until it got too small, and I was about to drop it into an ashtray when a young girl gently took it out of my hand. She attached a metal clip to the end and took deep puffs from it. She offered it back to me, but I refused it, motioning in the noise for her to keep it. Another girl, older but very pretty, passed me a fresh joint, which I again puffed and then kept between my teeth.

"Hey, man!" she yelled in my ear above the music, "Don't Bogart it!"

"Don't what?" I shouted back.

"Don't Bogart it! Gimme a toke!"

"Oh," I said. "Sorry." I still didn't know what the hell it meant to "Bogart" a joint, but I stifled a giggle as I tried to imagine Bogie puffing a cigarette loaded with weed.

"Hey, man," the girl shouted in my ear, "wanna ball?"

"Excuse me?"

"You're cute. Wanna make it?"

Well, the idea had merit. This was, of course, pre-AIDS, although not pre-venereal disease. I was also still in mourning for Althea, and quite honestly sex was far from my mind—a rare happenstance in my life. "Sorry," I said. "I'm spoken for."

She shrugged. "It's cool," she replied. "Here, man. Shotgun."

"What's that?"

For an answer, she completely flabbergasted me by sticking the lit end of the joint in her mouth, leaving the other end slightly protruding between her teeth. Then she put her arms around me and put her lips up to mine so close that I could feel her mouth almost touching mine. Then she blew softly, and a powerful jet of smoke shot into my mouth.

"Wow!" I breathed, eyes tearing. She grabbed me and did it again.

"Lemme know if you change your mind," she said, and handing me the joint, danced away. I puffed the joint again and looked up at Morrison. He was staring straight at me, a lopsided smile playing across his face.

I felt my own face going slack and a slight vibration—not the music—coursing through my body. So this was what it was like to be stoned. What the hell, I thought, it's all in the name of research.

The Doors finished their set to thunderous applause, a lot of the girls screaming for Morrison. As he left the stage, I caught his eye and he nodded, motioning with his head for me to follow him backstage. I followed the band back to a series of mildew-smelling dressing rooms in a narrow hallway.

Morrison turned around as soon as we cleared the stage and entered the hallway.

"I know you, man," he said. He had spoken directly to me, but he was focused miles away.

"You do?" I said.

"I've seen you, man," he said. "On another plane."

"Another plane."

"Dig it, I know you." Someone handed him a bottle of Scotch and he took a good long pull from it. I companionably took a hit from the joint in my hand. I thought of this interesting, haunted young son of an admiral, who I knew would overdose in a Paris bathtub five years from now, and it saddened me. I felt guilty about writing him off as a lowlife without even knowing him.

"Death is a part of life, man," he said. "Don't be down, it happens. We just go to another plane of existence."

"How did you know I was thinking about death?" I whispered.

"I told you, man. I know you. You lost your love, man. I'm sorry."

"Jesus! How the hell—"

"I saw a family buy it on the road when I was a kid. They're still with me, man. You get to that plane, nobody's really gone."

I suddenly remembered my manners. "My name's—"

"John. I know, man. You're from the future. My friends told me you were coming."

I fell back against the wall, and not from the dope.

"Your secret's safe with me, John. What can I do you for?"

I fumbled in my pocket for a pen and a piece of paper.

"An autograph," he blew out his lips. "Shit, man. Guy comes from the future, all he wants is old J's Hancock. Shit."

"Could you make it out 'To Cornelia?' " I asked, feeling stupid.

He placed the paper up against the wall and wrote pretty well, considering that he was probably twelve times as shitfaced as I was. " 'To Cornelia with love, Jim Morrison,

Whiskey A Go-Go, 5-18-66.' Is that okay? I figure, where you come from, I'm probably dead, so maybe it'll be worth something.''

''Jim,'' I asked him as he handed back the pen and paper, ''how the hell did you know I was from . . . you know.''

He threw back is head and laughed. ''Oh, Johnny,'' he chuckled, ''do I look dumb? Anybody can tell if he knows what to look for.''

''But how did you know?''

''Some people do, man. It's either acid or peyote, or maybe they just fuckin' know. They used to burn chicks as witches for knowing shit like that.'' His half-lidded doper-eyes widened, making him seem almost straight for a moment. ''I look at you, John, and I know you. I also know you don't belong here. I don't know how I know. How do you look at some dude and tell he's French or English or German before he opens his mouth? Same thing with you, John.''

''Incredible,'' I said.

''Nah. It's nothin'. Who gives a shit, anyway?''

''Jim,'' the guitarist called from down the hallway. ''Guy wants to talk to us. I think he's an agent or something.''

''Comin', Robbie,'' he called. ''I wish those guys would relax. We're fucking gonna make it, man.'' He stuck out his hand and we shook, arm-wrestling style. ''Take care, John. Smoke a few more Js, maybe let one a these chicks in here slide on you, then get on back. We'll meet again. And say how-do to Cornelia for me.''

With that, he turned and walked down the hall.

Well, there wasn't much to do after that except go back into the bar, smoke another joint, and have a couple of drinks. Another pretty girl hit on me as I finished my third watered-down Jameson's on the rocks. It occurred to me that in a very silly way, I was holding my own private wake for Althea. I had had enough.

''Wanna see somethin' bitchen,'' I asked the girl, barely conscious.

''Sure,'' she replied.

"Okay," I said, "stand back." I reached into my pocket and hit the red button on my Decacom.

I wish I could have seen her face.

"Hellfire!" Doc Harvey exclaimed as I stumbled down from the zoom chamber. "He's assholed!"

"I know," I waved him off. "Very politically incorrect of me. Very un-00s of me. But I don't think I have to enroll in a twelve-step program just yet." I withdrew Morrison's autograph from my pocket and handed it to Cornelia. "Jim sends his love," I told her.

She looked at the autograph as if it were a diamond necklace. Then she looked at me as if I were something a dog left on a white rug.

"You idiot," she said. "You moron." She stared into my eyes. "How much pot *did* you smoke?"

"An entire hemp field," I replied. "Oh, man. I'm so horny all of a sudden. What do you say, Cornelia?"

"Oh, *God*!" she groaned. "Doc, take him home. Get him out of my sight."

"Come on, John," Doc Harvey said, taking my arm.

"Debrief at ten tomorrow morning, John," Cornelia said. "You'd better be there."

"Anything for you, my sweet."

"Come on, John," Doc said, prodding me out of the Zoom Room. "We'd better get you out of here before you wind up in PC Court."

I awoke the next morning feeling predictably awful, but I bulled my way through it and felt better after a shower and about a gallon of non-decaf coffee. By the time I got to work I was feeling pretty idiotic about the whole thing— except for the way Morrison had said he recognized me.

"And what have we learned from this valuable lesson, John?" Cornelia greeted me.

" 'I will not smoke anymore dope or drink anymore booze when I go back in time,' " I recited. "Do you want me to write it on the blackboard a hundred times?"

"No, that'll do, for now. So what happened? Oh, thank

you for the autograph," she said. "I've already framed it."

"What's next?" I asked her.

"That's what we have to decide. John, I want to secure a few periods that we know are safe. I don't want to give our future customers too much of a choice, and I want to be able to guarantee their safety."

"Okay," I replied. "Here's what I suggest: One year per decade. At least to start off with. No earlier than the 1920s, since L.A. was pretty much of a small, boring town before then. We also want to provide a certain amount of comfort, so we can't take them too far back.

"Finally, I think there ought to be a hook for each trip. Let's say the 1959 World Series, the first for the Dodgers in L.A. The opening of *Gone With the Wind* in 1939."

"How will we get them into a premiere like that?" Felice wondered.

"Not the premiere in Hollywood," I said. "The sneak preview in Riverside."

"*I'd* like to see that," Cornelia remarked.

"I think a lot of people would."

"We'd need a lot of close supervision," Corny said. "You might have to act as tour guide the first few times, and after that, a loose tail, keep them out of trouble. Okay, that's enough to think about for now. John, I meant to ask you. What was it like to meet Jim Morrison?"

"He knew me," I said.

Cornelia and Felice looked at each other in surprise. "What do you mean, he knew you?"

"He knew me. He knew my name. He knew I had come from the future. He also knew," I swallowed a little painfully, "that I had lost someone."

"How did he know your name?"

"He said he'd seen me before, 'on another plane.' "

"Why is it," Felice wondered, "that coming from anyone else it'd be nonsense, but from him I'll buy it?"

"We can't worry about it now," Corny decided. "What we do have to worry about is what we are in business for in the first place."

"Let the vacations begin," I declared.

FIFTEEN

AND SO THEY DID, BUT NOT RIGHT AWAY. I MADE NO LESS than ten subsequent reconnaissance trips—brief and simple ones this time. On the last trip, Corny sent me back into 1939, to make reservations at the Beverly Hills Hotel for our first paying customers. Just how much they paid wasn't something to which I was privy, but I would imagine that exorbitant only begins to describe it. We must have been operating at a loss until that time, with payroll and set-up costs eating through Corny and Felice's capital like a hungry Saint Bernard.

I do know that I was asked to reserve one of the bungalows at the hotel, which meant that these fine people could afford to travel in style. I also rented them a Rolls-Royce, a vehicle in which you could safely cruise back then without worrying about car-jacking.

Bob and Tiffany Lewison were so glowing with good looks and fitness that it almost hurt my eyes to look at them. Bob was six-five and weighed about two-twenty, all of it health-club muscle. He was an entertainment lawyer in Century City, and he wasted no time in letting everyone know that his client list began with a capital *A*. He packed a cellular phone on his hip and was quicker on the draw than Duke Wayne with a .44. Tiffany, at least fifteen years

younger than Bob, didn't have much to say for herself—
her looks did that for her. A perfect ash-blonde with enormous blue eyes, she had a figure that would have landed
her in *Playboy* if it still existed.

We sat in the briefing room for our introductory briefing.
We almost lost them immediately when I let Bob know that
he couldn't take his phone back to 1939. I had to bust a
gut convincing him that he and Tiffany would be returned
to almost the exact time of their departure.

He also bitched about the fact that I couldn't reserve him
a no-smoking bungalow at the hotel. Once again, I had to
talk myself cross-eyed explaining to him that just about the
only place you couldn't smoke in 1939 was on top of an
oil tank.

I was just about to tell him to take his business to Club
Med, when Corny ended the interview and sent the two
along to wardrobe.

"Christ," I groaned after the door closed behind them.
"Where the hell did you dig them up? They're going into
1939, for Christ's sake, not La Costa."

"Bob's a pompous jerk," Felice agreed. "But if he likes
what he sees, there's a lot of business he can get for us.
Discreetly, of course."

"Discreet? Him?"

"He's a pain in the ass, but he's good at what he does,"
Corny said. "But I want you to keep a close eye on them.
Okay?"

"They're gonna hate 1939," I said. "No tofu."

It occurred to me then that my job description would
include yet another task: I would have to brief each Tourist
on the customs and mores of the period they were to visit.
There had been many cultural and social changes in our
society over the years, and it was up to us to prevent any
unpleasantness that might come about. We had to bear in
mind that our customers were observers; and it was part of
the protection—the guarantee of their personal safety—to
arm them with whatever knowledge of the time that would
head off any conflicts. The Lewisons would be a good test
case; they had culture clash written all over them. I could

all too easily imagine Bob Lewison creating a scene because a 1939 waiter brought him regular coffee instead of decaf.

Now, it may sound to many that as I gave the Lewisons their final briefing, I was talking down to them a bit. This is entirely true. I could never understand how a well-educated man such as Bob Lewison, or an even moderately educated woman like Tiffany Lewison, might need constant reminding that in 1939 the world was an entirely different place; but they did. Bob was outraged that 1939 Angelenos did not live the same kind of life or hold the same values and mores that he did. Tiffany was extremely upset that she wasn't allowed to bring her Rollerblades with her.

"Look, Bob," I said, "think of it as a foreign country, where you don't particularly care for the government, but you mind your own business and do your best to enjoy the trip. It's 1939, Bob. People worked hard, they drank alcohol with their lunches, they drove without shoulder restraints or airbags, far more than half of all Americans smoked, people preferred red meat to anything else. Nothing in the world was considered healthier than dairy products. You may not like it, I may not like it, but we can't change it."

"Well, I don't like it," he said, miffed.

"Bob," Tiffany pouted. "I want to see *Gone With the Wind*."

"All right," I said, thinking that the 1980s would be a more suitable time for this couple than the 1930s. "Now, I'm going to be your personal Tour guide. I'll be staying in the hotel with you—"

"In our room!"

"No, Bob." No thank you, I thought. They both looked like screamers to me. "I won't even be in the bungalows. But I will be at the hotel, and I will be showing you around, if you like. And I will drive you out to Riverside for the sneak preview."

"Can't we spend *any* time alone?"

Not on your life, putz. "Of course you can," I lied heartily. "But you've got to remember, you are our first guests. You're entitled to special attention."

"For what we're paying, we deserve special attention."

•   •   •

And special attention they got—at least in the beginning. Bob Lewison was your basic bellman's and waiter's nightmare: a difficult, high-maintenance customer. But I came prepared. I explained to the desk clerk at the Beverly Hills that my client was "under a great deal of strain," that "overwork may cause him to be slightly irritable and unreasonable at times"; the staff was not to take any of it personally, and they would be amply compensated for any mental anguish. The desk clerk—obviously used to dealing with pains in the ass—nonchalantly accepted the hundred dollar bill I slid across counter and assured me that the staff was indeed highly professional and, in fact, prided itself upon dealing with every sort of challenge.

At first, the Lewisons were bored. There was no television, and therefore no cable or laser videos. There was no state-of-the-art health spa. They had to content themselves the first day by playing tennis and accepting a driving tour from me. I showed them the undeveloped San Fernando Valley, which left them unimpressed; neither of them cared too much for the Valley even in their own time. The Lewisons were not stop-and-smell-the-roses sort of people. But it kept them busy and helped to tire them out a bit. I needed some time to myself this trip, for I had a master plan of my own to bring into action.

For it was on that trip that I first engaged the services of the financial planning firm of Walker, Bernbaum, Schiff, and O'Leary, an investment company which thrives to this day and now has branch offices throughout the world.

They were an interesting group. Bud Walker, the eldest son of a family of dispossessed, dirt-poor Okies, had literally shoveled shit to pay his way through UCLA business school. Bernbaum and Schiff had grown up in humiliating poverty in Boyle Heights, the sons of Russian-Jewish immigrants. O'Leary was the son of a Chicago cop whose mother had died bringing him into the world, and whose father had left him orphaned, penniless, and alone after a shootout with the Genna gang in the 1920s. O'Leary drifted across the country and settled in Los Angeles, ending up as a janitor at USC, where he realized that an education was the only thing that separated him from the rich students and the lives they led. Walker, Bernbaum, Schiff, and O'Leary: they were all tough, hungry guys who had taken all the hard knocks life had to offer, and now had teamed up to give some of it back.

It had taken me weeks of research to find them. Walker would become governor of California in 1950. Eddie Schiff would make millions in the next two years, leaving behind a large, loving family when he helplessly parachuted into a murderous crossfire at St. Mere–Eglise in 1944. Irwin Bernbaum, who would serve with distinction on Saipan and Okinawa, would become one of the richest men in America and one of its most dedicated philanthropists. Pat O'Leary, future ambassador to Ireland, would never marry, but millions of orphaned children in a thousand deserted corners of the earth would benefit from his kindness.

Good guys. My kind of guys. I arranged to meet the four of them at their office downtown at nine o'clock on my first night back. Pat O'Leary found nothing odd about my request to meet them at that late hour. In fact, it seemed to pique his interest.

The Lewisons were safely tucked in for the night when I taxied down to Flower Street. It was an old building, past its prime and not long for this world. When a groaning, caged elevator arrived at the fourth floor, I saw furniture stacked up in the hall. I followed the furniture trail to a smoked-glass door with the legend WALKER, BERNBAUM, SCHIFF, & O'LEARY stenciled in gold. The door was wide open, and the place was a mess.

Four men in shirtsleeves were moving files and other belongings toward the door. But there was a lightness to their labor. You could tell that this was a firm that was moving up, not just out.

A huge man with red hair poked his head out the door. "Mr. Surrey? Eddie Schiff. Come on in." He extended a giant paw and shook my hand, revealing incredible strength. "Excuse the mess, but we're finally moving out of this dump. Next week, Beverly Hills!"

He led me into a cluttered room with a conference table. His partners drifted in. They were all young, intelligent-looking, and energetic; their eyes held the gleam of starving tigers. They had all come far, but they were nowhere near their goals.

Pat O'Leary, the smallest of them, probably from his years on the road without a clue of where his next meal was coming from, spoke first.

"Pat O'Leary, Mr. Surrey. I'm from Chicago, but no relation to the cow lady. What can we do for you?"

"A great deal, Mr. O'Leary."

"Pat, please."

"John. I'm going to be making some investments in the coming years," I began. "I need a responsible team to handle the management of my portfolio."

"Bud Walker, John." The clear, resonant Oklahoma voice came from across the table. "What kind of investments?"

"A little bit of everything. Land. Commodities. Stocks, bonds, even a Broadway show or two. I won't be in town too often. I want to know that everything is being well taken care of in my absence. I've heard you're the best."

Irwin Bernbaum studied me intently. They were all tough guys, but he was obviously the toughest. And, I was willing to bet, the lady-killer among them, as well. Naturally, I thought with pride, he would become a Marine when the war broke out.

"How much of this is legal, Mr. Surrey?" Bernbaum asked me.

"All of it," I replied. "It's just not . . . orthodox."

"Don't get us wrong, John," said Eddie Schiff. "Whether it's legal or not, we don't give a rat's ass. You bring us your money and we make more of it. Just like Merrill, Lynch, Pierce, Fenner, and Smith. We just have to do it by different means for one or the other. But even there, we do draw the line."

"How?"

"If you made money dodging the taxman, more power to you," Pat O'Leary said. "If you run a little bookmaking ring, who the hell cares? But if you're a pimp, or you do anything that hurts children or cons old people out of their life savings, we don't want anything to do with you. If you hurt poor people . . .'' he trailed off.

"We've all been poor," Bud Walker said. "My parents were kicked off the farm my grandfather staked in the Land Rush. Eddie and Irwin's parents had their villages burned by Cossacks, came here and sweated in a shirt factory. Eddie's mom jumped to her death in the Triangle Fire in New York. Pat was a rachitic orphan nobody wanted, almost starved to death a dozen times before he was fifteen.

"We don't hurt the poor," Walker declared.

"Neither do I," I said. "My money is legal. It's just not . . .''

"Orthodox?" Pat asked.

"Right."

The four looked at each other and nodded. "Okay," Bud said. "Where is it?"

I swung the attaché case I had been carrying onto the table and opened it. It was the good part of my savings, converted into 1939 currency. The cost had been outrageous, but the rewards would more than make up for it.

The money did not impress them. It wasn't anything they hadn't seen before.

"The investments I have in mind are long-term. Very long-term."

"That's okay," Eddie said. "We'll be here." Because I knew what his future held, a flash of sadness came and went.

"I want to start with land purchases," I said. "Wilshire and Sunset, any available lots to the west of Beverly. Anything up to forty percent of my total assets."

"Okay," Irwin shrugged. "That'll go."

"Anything at all in the San Fernando Valley, to the extent of an additional twenty-five percent of my total assets."

"The San Fernando Valley!" Bud exclaimed. "Are you sure?"

"Yes."

"It's worthless."

"Yeah. Now. But not after the w——not for too much longer."

Irwin Bernbaum's gaze drilled a hole through me. "Just how did you make your money, Mr. Surrey?"

"You'd never believe it."

"Try me."

"No. But it's clean. You'll just have to believe me."

"What do you do for a living, Mr. Surrey?"

"I'm an investor, obviously. Look, Mr. Bernbaum, I'm clean. If you don't want my business, fine, I'll go elsewhere. But I don't really want to go elsewhere. I like you guys. I like your style. I like it that you all grew up in poverty and haven't forgotten where you came from. I like the fact that you're hungry and you'll always stay hungry. Someday I'll tell you everything, but for now, you'll just have to trust me."

"Okay," Pat O'Leary said. "Let's vote on it."

He raised his hand, as did Walker and Schiff. Bernbaum drilled another hole through me, and then a slow smile crossed his face, completely transforming him from killer to charmer. He raised his hand.

"Just wanted to see if you'd stick to your guns," he said. "Welcome aboard. The San Fernando Valley, huh? I should live so long."

"Don't worry," I replied. "You will."

Because the San Bernardino Freeway did not yet exist, it took more than two hours to get to Riverside. The movie theater was reminiscent of the set of *The Last Picture Show*. But the December night was cool and the theater was comfortable.

"Everybody's smoking," Tiffany complained.

"This whole time period smells like cigarette smoke," Bob agreed. "It's disgusting."

"Oh, well," I said ambiguously. They were right, after all.

I managed to find us seats near some abstinent-looking

elderly people, but the smoke still wafted across the theater to their sensitive nostrils.

A newsreel showed French soldiers drilling at the Maginot Line, while quite visibly a few hundred yards away, German soldiers punted a soccer ball around. The newsreel stressed the invincibility of the French position. I knew better, but tried hard not to snort in derision.

"Is there like a war or something?" Tiffany wanted to know.

"I'm not sure," Bob replied. "I think so."

I rolled my eyes, showing enough white to light up the dark theater.

The newsreel ended and the lights came up. The manager, wearing a uniform and bow tie, stepped to the front of the theater.

"Ladies and gentlemen," he announced, "that's our show for this evening. However, it is my pleasure to invite you all to stay on for a special sneak preview of a new motion picture. You will be the very first to ever see this movie."

There were oohs and ahhs from the audience, and someone called out, asking which picture it was. The manager, clearly enjoying himself, replied that it was a big surprise.

His voice lowered. "Folks, if any of you want to leave, do it now. This is so secret, ladies and gentlemen, that we've been asked by the film studio to lock the doors once the film starts."

The audience oohed again. They were having as much fun as the manager. This was a wonderful surprise, and the manager, to his credit, was making it as exciting for them as possible.

"So, folks," he continued, "we're going to start the movie in ten minutes. The concession stand will be open, and if you need to leave the room for any reason, do it now. Thank you, and I hope you enjoy yourselves. I know I will."

It was the manager's finest hour, and it ended with enthusiastic applause. He was making it fun for the audience, milking it to the limit, and they loved him for it.

There was a mad rush for the rest rooms, candy stand, and cigarette machine. It took a bit more than ten minutes for everyone to get settled, but the lights went down only after that last stragglers returned to their seats.

For myself, I wasn't that interested in the movie. I'd only seen it about forty billion times. The treat for me was going to be the audience's initial reaction.

I wasn't disappointed. The Selznick logo came on the screen, followed by unfamiliar music.

"That's not the theme," Tiffany said. "It's the wrong music."

"Sssh!" came from the person in front of us.

"The movie hasn't been scored yet," I whispered to Tiffany.

"Oh," she whispered back.

"Sssh!"

The title came on the screen, and the audience exploded. There was wild applause, laughter, whistles, and cheers. No one here would ever receive a surprise gift like tonight's. I had never seen an audience have such good time, so fully appreciating a show, and I doubt I'll ever see it again.

What followed was pure and simple joy. To say the audience loved it would hardly do their reaction justice. They hung on every word, reacted to every scene. When the lights came up for intermission, right after Vivian Leigh declared for all the world that she would never go hungry again, the faces in the crowd were glowing.

Bob Lewison snored lightly beside me. Tiffany was filing her nails.

"I like it better on video," she said.

"God, I hate the 00s," I groaned.

If I were a vindictive man, I would have had some satisfaction in knowing that Bob and Tiffany were suffering from severe cases of diarrhea upon our return. The second we zoomed back, Bob made a mad dash for the men's room, and Tiffany shot straight toward the ladies'. Doc Harvey began assembling stomach remedies from his medical bag.

"What the happened?" Cornelia demanded.

"It's the food," I replied. "Their systems just weren't up for it."

"Great!" she snapped. "We're sunk! 'Apart from that, Mrs. Lincoln, how'd you like the show?' "

"Don't worry about it," I said. "It was like giving a teetotaler a bottle of Rothschild '26. No matter what they say about it, it'll sell us. Not everybody's as dull as they are."

"I hope you're right."

I *was* right. Bob and Tiffany hated 1939, and they told everyone just that. But as I suspected, no one gave a damn what they thought. The idea of going back in time was something no one wanted to miss out on. In less than two days, we were booked solid. Corny and Felice went from the red to pure profit in less than a week.

Timeshare Unlimited was a hit, and I was busier than ever. And a phone call to the firm of Walker, Bernbaum, Schiff, and O'Leary, long since renamed the International Investment Group (IIG), almost gave me a heart attack. There was enough money in my account to bail out a small country if it went belly-up.

We were busy. I worked seven days a week, and Doc Harvey warned me to slow down and have a little fun. After all, my body still aged whether I was in the past or present. In that first year, I lived two. But work was important to me. It kept my mind off Althea—at least, some of the time.

SIXTEEN

SENATE INTELLIGENCE COMMITTEE 4.2.07
Q: Mr. Surrey, we have now established that your actions led to—excuse me, sir.
(MUFFLED CONVERSATION)
Q: This session is now closed. You're excused, Mr. Surrey.

SEVENTEEN

HAVING BEEN MYSTERIOUSLY EXTRICATED FROM THE claws of the Senate Intelligence Committee, I decided that I had earned a small vacation. I had no idea why the hearings were suddenly canceled, but I was sure that the whole thing would return to haunt me later. Things usually do.

It had been my intention to have a long talk with Cornelia about the proceedings; and, in general, to complain about having been selected for membership to the chump-of-the-month club. But duty called. Fortunately, it was a no-brainer: just a couple who had met at Hollywood High fifty years before and wanted to go back and view themselves falling in love. This was not always a good idea, as it was usually a disappointment—not at all the momentous occasion created by warm, powerful, and highly selective memories. For many of our clients, the reality of young love revisited—or any milestone in life—was simply an unremarkable result of a surprisingly monotonous chain of ordinary events. Clients often searched for their own personal epiphanies, but rarely ever found them.

Still, I looked forward to going back to 1957. I had traveled in time often enough by then to know that every period, no matter how wonderful it seemed in hindsight, had plenty of warts. But the present was becoming increasingly trying, and I needed a break. We would put our couple up at the Beverly Hills as usual, but I would stay elsewhere, hang out by the pool, and maybe rent a Corvette or a Chevy Bel Air with a three-on-the-tree gearshift. I'd cruise Van Nuys Boulevard on a Saturday night, back when kids could do that without worrying about nine-millimeter bullets riddling their windshields. Just a sort of retreat, with no connections or complications. It was my own personal therapy. I needed a time that I could delude myself into thinking was childlike. I needed a dose of some sort of innocence. Even the Seventies, as much fun as they were, were beginning to wear thin. The casual sex of that era, which at first acted as a balm on my ravaged psyche, was beginning to inspire guilt on my part. It relaxed me, but it didn't calm me. It was like going to Disneyland and staying too long.

The Fifties, I decided, might provide the emotional R&R I so desperately needed, which the Seventies no longer offered. I would just be an overgrown kid, cruising past the auto lots with their fluttering, multicolored pennants on Van Nuys Boulevard, with Bill Haley and the Comets blasting from a tinny AM car radio. I would eat charbroiled hamburgers and french fries served in red-checkered containers until they were coming out of my ears. I would go bowling and listen to snatches of excited conversations about the Brooklyn Dodgers moving to L.A. I would go to the movies and for the first time, view Alec Guiness's Oscar-winning performance in *Bridge on the River Kwai* on the big screen.

The Kosicks were a nice couple, warm and enthusiastic, and I knew right away that they would give me no trouble whatsoever. They got a kick out of everything, from the clothes we provided to the actual check-in at the Beverly Hills. They viewed everything with the wide-eyed enthusiasm of small children, and for the first time in quite a while I took great pleasure in my work, much like a good cook providing a meal to a gourmet.

I left the Kosicks at their hotel, and decided to do a little progress check on the Haases, the family I had permitted to remain in 1949 Redondo Beach. I was interested in their status eight years later.

My contacts at IIG provided me with an address and credit history for the Haases. Not surprisingly, they had moved in the ensuing years, first to Highland Park and then to Bel Air. Walter Haas had done well for himself without being a total hog about it. He had invested in various stocks and land—much of the same investments I had made—and his net worth had risen from a few thousand to a little over ten million. Nothing to sneeze at, of course, but a lot less than he could have done if he were really money-hungry.

Still, the house in Bel Air was a mansion—a good twenty rooms, a pool, and a tennis court. All paid off, according to IIG's credit report. Ten million went a lot further in 1957 than fifty years later.

A uniformed maid answered the doorbell, closing it again while she went to fetch Julie Haas. While I waited, I watched a team of gardeners hard at work on the meticulously kept lawn.

The door opened. Julie Haas looked at me questioningly, as though she knew we had met before but couldn't quite place me. Not only had the years been kind to her, they had been downright magnanimous. Eight years ago, she had been attractive but careworn—she was now happy and had even become beautiful. No doubt she had plenty of help from Elizabeth Arden, but that wasn't the whole reason. Her face had the look of a woman who had done well, very well, but had never stopped appreciating it. If I was in some way responsible for putting that look on her face, then I'd've let the Haases stay a hundred times over, and bankrolled them in the bargain.

A slow, becoming smile of recognition crossed her face. She embraced me wordlessly.

"This is not a come-on in any way," I said to Julie Haas as we sipped a poolside lemonade, "but you look utterly gorgeous."

"I *feel* utterly gorgeous," she replied. "I never thought I'd say this, but money *does* make a difference."

"Did it solve all of your problems?"

"In a word—yes. Because our only problems were

money-related. We loved each other, we had wonderful
children, and no neuroses to speak of. But the financial
burden was ruining everything. Now that it's gone, we've
had nothing but good times—knock on wood.''

''Where are Walter and the boys?''

''Oh, they're at the club,'' she said with mock-snobbery.
''Ryan will be starting his junior year at Harvard in the fall,
and Jeremy will join him there as a freshman. I can't begin
to thank you, and I won't even try.''

''All in a day's work.''

''How long has it been—for you, I mean.''

''Just a few months.''

A look of concern crossed her features. ''John. You look
awful.''

''Thanks,'' I replied.

She blushed. ''Oh, come on, you're still a handsome devil. That's not what I mean. You don't seem happy.''

'' 'I have of late—wherefore I know not—lost all my
mirth,' '' I quoted.

''*Hamlet*,'' she nodded. ''That much I know, although
it's beyond me how some people can remember the act and
the scene. To tell the truth, John, even eight years ago, there
was a certain sense of melancholy that surrounded you.
You've brought so much happiness to us—and to others,
I'd bet—why are you so sad?''

She said it with such genuine concern that I opened up
and spilled my guts to her. I told her about 1940, Althea,
the Duke, and Bogie; and then about 1966 and Jim Morrison.

''I'm sorry,'' I said suddenly, ''I didn't mean to unload
all of that on you.''

''Oh, no,'' she said gently. ''*I'm* sorry. I didn't mean to
pry.''

''Pry away. There aren't a lot of people with our shared
experience.''

''I think, John, as long as you ask, that it's time you did
something for yourself. You've already given so much.''

''Mommy!'' A little boy ran out to us suddenly. A maid
was at his heels. The boy jumped into his mother's lap.

"Who are you?" the child demanded, pointing a little finger at me.

"This is our dear friend, John Surrey," Julie told him.

"Is that who I'm named after?" the boy asked.

Julie blushed again. "Yes, it is, Johnny."

"I'm six years old tomorrow," he said gravely. "I'm going into the first grade."

"I'm glad to meet you, John," I said. "Julie," I said, "remember what you said before about my bringing happiness to people?"

"Yes."

"Well, I think you've just paid me back a hundred times over."

So I felt a little better about things after that.

It was eight-thirty on Saturday night, and as I'd promised myself, I was slowly cruising down Van Nuys Boulevard in a red 1956 Corvette convertible—top down, of course. On the radio was *How High the Moon* by Les Paul and Mary Ford. Looking around me at the traffic, I saw that I was the oldest person on the Boulevard by a good fifteen years. I was surrounded by kids, some with dates in the middle of the front seat; some alone, looking for action; some cars filled with boys, some with girls. It was scene so clichéd and innocent that I had to laugh with the pleasure of it.

The aroma of charcoal-broiled burgers, a smell that has all but vanished in my time, permeated the air and made me hungry. I pulled into a Bob's and took a seat in a large semicircular booth. I ordered a deluxe cheeseburger plate from a gum-chewing, flirtatious waitress and sat back to enjoy the atmosphere.

Now, having been a detective—and a damned good one, at that—there is one word that has all but disappeared from my vocabulary, since any detective who uses it is considered incompetent, unimaginative, and ill-suited for the job at the least, or more often, a dumb fuck who belongs back in the bag—and even then, only on probation.

That word is *coincidence*.

Any cop knows, or should know, that there is no such thing, and the more serious and involved the case, the more miniscule the chances are for coincidences to occur.

Yet, as I tucked into my burger, and heard the conversation in the next booth, coincidence was the only explanation that I could find.

"You kids, you can't imagine what it was like," a strong storyteller's voice carried from the next booth. "I got one engine out, another one givin' me fits. I'm tryna gain a little altitude, but the goddamn control cables're almost shot. I got more bulletholes than I can count, goddamn plane looks like a . . . a—what's that thing your mother uses to drain spaghetti?"

"A sieve," said an adolescent voice.

"A colander," piped up a younger voice.

"That's it, a damn sieve, colander, whatever. I got FW190s above me, and them damn 88s openin' up from the ground. I gotta climb up to drop the friggin' bombs. I'm workin' the rudders like a damn bicycle, and I finally get up to fifteen hundred. Toby lets 'em go, and then we turn around and *BAM*! It's like King Kong didn't like my attitude and punched my plane in the nose. Them fuckin' 88s!"

"Well, you didn't get killed," the older boy said.

"And you weren't shot down," added the younger boy.

And *I* knew what was coming. Cornstalks in the bomb doors.

"Nah, we were luckier than a lotta guys. But we flew so low on the way back that we had cornstalks in the bomb-bay doors! Can you believe that crap? Ain't that a bitch?"

I dared to turn my head in the direction of the neighboring booth. A strapping blond-haired man of about my age was regaling two boys, obviously his sons, with his most terrifying war story. Not a rare occurrence in the Fifties, when most veterans were still young and the memories were still vivid.

The difference here was that the man telling the story looked like me. Almost exactly like me. As he should have, because he was my Grandpa Joe. And his two sons were my father and my Uncle Jack.

Joe noticed my glance in his direction. He gave me a puzzled look, shook it off, and then grinned.

"Ploesti, right?" I asked conversationally.

"You ain't kiddin', brother. You in the war?"

"I had my war," I replied, unable to lie completely. "Marines."

"My hat's off to you pal," Joe said. "You guys could sure take it. And dish it out."

"Wasn't exactly a cakewalk for you guys. You were a B-24 pilot?"

"Thirty-two missions. Sometimes I can't believe I'm still here to talk about it. Whyn't you come on over?"

"I'd like that," I replied. Grandpa had died when I was ten years old. He had gone into a decline during the six years that Uncle Jack was missing, but he had recovered somewhat upon his return. Still, the bad years had taken their toll, and I had bitterly missed growing up without him.

My twelve-year-old uncle and my fourteen-year-old father stared at me with great curiosity. My father, never one to keep his opinions to himself, looked at me frankly.

"He looks like you, Pop," Dad said.

"Freddy," Joe cautioned.

"Well, he *does*," Fred insisted. He nudged Jack. "Doesn't he?"

Jack stared at me wide-eyed. "Are you our uncle or something?" he asked.

"No," I replied, and then, only half-kidding, "you're my uncle."

"What's your name, stranger?" Joe asked.

"John."

"Well, I'm Joe Surrey, and these two men-about-town are my boys, Fred and Jack."

"We were just in Dad's plane," Jack told me.

"I got a little Cessna I tool around in," Joe said. "You fly?"

"As a matter of fact, I do. I have a Cessna of my own."

"I'm gonna be a pilot when I grow up," Jack announced.

"I'm sure you will," I said.

"He probably will," Joe said. "He's got the gift."

"I get airsick," Fred said apologetically.

That'll never change, I thought. My father must have been miserable on the interminable flight to New Zealand. Even short hops to Vegas or San Francisco were agony for him.

"That's okay, son," Joe said soothingly. "You do about a million other things better than anyone else." Which was also true. My father could do just about any other thing brilliantly. He had been a three-letter athlete and made the All-City baseball team in high school. He could play six instruments and draw a perfect portrait with little more than a golf pencil and a cocktail napkin. He turned a failed greeting-card shop into a wildly successful chain of ten stores. And he could make the dumbest joke funny enough to make half the people in the room scream for mercy. But it always bothered him that he could never share the one abiding passion of my grandfather and uncle—flying.

"I'm gonna be a Navy pilot," Jack said.

"Christ, I hope not," Joe said. "Those guys're nuts. You know what a carrier looks like from a plane? It looks like a matchstick. Go to work for Pan Am, or something."

I could hardly imagine Jack as anything but an admiral, certainly not a commercial pilot.

"Sissy stuff," said the future Chief of Naval Operations, pulling a face that was so out of character that I had to laugh. My father, deep into adolescence and big for his age, was beginning to take on some of the appearance that he would later carry into manhood. But my polished and distinguished uncle was still a kid. I had never realized that he had been dark-haired like my grandmother—his incarceration had turned him completely and prematurely gray.

There was also the dynamic of the relationship between the three. My dad was independent and very much his own man, and Joe treated him almost like an equal. Jack was the baby of the family, doted upon, indulged, and protected by one and all. When he was reported missing in action, it must have torn the family apart.

I do know that my father and uncle shared a closeness of almost mythical proportions. On the very day that Uncle Jack punched out of his A-6 over North Vietnam, my father was struck by neck spasms so intense he could barely move. And in total opposition to the grief and resignation of the rest of the family, my father never entertained the slightest doubt that Jack was still alive, insisting that he would "feel different" if the opposite were true.

Meanwhile, Grandpa was looking at me quizzically. "What's your last name, John?" he asked me.

I considered that for a moment. "Kent," I replied. Kent, Surrey, Sussex, Wiltshire, what the hell.

"Like Superboy's father!" Jack exclaimed.

"Right," I said. "Not the same guy."

"What do you do, John?" Joe asked me.

"I'm a travel agent." Which was sort of true.

"My dad's a plumber," Jack said proudly.

"Just a simple tradesman," Joe said with mock-humility and we both laughed. For me, there was a private side to this joke. The San Fernando Valley was growing like a healthy teenager, and Joe was on his way to becoming a wealthy man. Later on, when I was still too young to understand, he would explain the secret of his success: "You got thousands of people and hundreds of businesses moving into the Valley," he would say. "And what do they all have in common? They all take leaks and dumps, nearly every one."

Grandpa Joe was a contented man. His easy ways and generosity of spirit were something I would always miss, but fortunately, both his sons would inherit the best aspects of his character.

"Are we gonna play miniature golf?" Jack asked.

"Sure," Joe said. He fished into his pocket and drew out a five-dollar bill, which he handed to Fred. "You boys go on ahead. I'll be along."

"Nice meeting you, John," Jack said, sliding out of the booth.

"Glad to know you, John," Fred said, a little more gravely. He looked back at me twice as the two boys headed for the miniature golf course next door.

Joe slid a Camel from a pack on the table and fired it up with an Army Air Corps Zippo. "When I was in the war," he began, "I started believing in some really strange shit." He glanced at me to see if I were puzzled by this non sequitur, but my expression was one of interest. "Not religious, or anything like that. I mean, there's either a God or there isn't; either way, with so many guys buyin' the farm, He wasn't gonna take out time from His busy day to listen to *my* bullshit."

I simply nodded.

"It would only happen when I was in the air, on a combat mission," he continued. "But everything would get really weird. You get that eerie feeling that you're not exactly there."

"I know," I replied truthfully. It had also happened to me, in both the Gulf and on the streets of Los Angeles.

"The only way I can describe it," Joe said, "is that all of a sudden, you start thinkin' that a lot of stuff that maybe you'd write off as crap in the real world, well, maybe it ain't so far-fetched, after all. I mean, so many guys die. You're having breakfast in the mess, ten guys at your table—next day, half of them are gone. But just gone. Poof.

"What happens to them? You got a guy, he's born, he goes to school, his parents worry about him because maybe he's a fuckup or something, he meets a girl, gets laid, maybe even gets married. Then one day, he's in a plane over enemy territory and in one second he's dust. What happens to him? What happens to all those hopes and fears and desires?"

"I know what you mean," I said.

"He can't just go away, can he? He has to leave *something* behind, doesn't he?"

"I don't know," I replied.

"Ah, neither do I. But what I'm tryna say is, I'm more . . . receptive to weird shit than I used to be. Maybe because

I felt like I had one foot in the grave so many times, maybe I was closer to that stuff than I thought.''

I chewed on that for a moment. ''What're you trying to tell me, Joe?''

''What I'm tryna tell you, John, is maybe I'll believe your story more than you think I will.''

I choked on my coffee.

''You do have a story, don't you,'' he insisted, grinning triumphantly.

''Yes, Joe, I have a story. And no, I don't think you'll believe it.''

''Try me.''

''Okay,'' I said. ''First of all, the kids were right. We *are* related.''

''Well, all right,'' he exclaimed happily. ''I knew that. Are you a long-lost cousin or something?''

''Not quite. Joe, I'm from the future. The year 2007.''

''Hah! Okay. Who's gonna win the AL pennant this year?''

''The Yankees.''

''Aw, shit.'' He sounded disappointed. ''I don't need a crystal ball to know that. Who'll take the National League pennant?''

''Milwaukee.''

He shrugged. ''Yeah, I could see that. They came close enough last year. Who takes the Series?''

''The Braves.''

''Okay.''

''You don't believe me, do you?''

''Let's put it this way. I'm skeptical. But I'm willing to listen. How are we related?''

''I'm your grandson.''

''Really? Whose kid are you—no, don't tell me. Fred's. Don't ask me how I know. Fred seems like he'll find the right girl really early—he'll waste no time turning into a pipe-and-slippers kind of guy. Jack'll shape up to be a real swordsman.''

''You're right on the nose,'' I said.

"Yeah, I could see that. You do resemble Fred more than Jack. What happens to them?"

"Fred will become a successful businessman, a pillar-of-the-community sort of guy."

"And Jack? Not a delinquent, I hope?"

"Jack *will* become a pilot. And he will then become the highest-ranking officer in the United States Navy."

"I did good then," he nodded.

"You did real good."

He leaned back. "So I'm your grampa, huh? Do we go fishin' and shit like that?"

"Yes."

"Did I take you to your first ballgame? Me and Fred and Jack?"

"You and Fred. Jack was . . . away."

"Away?"

"At sea. We went to Dodger Stadium—I still have the scorecard. We beat the Reds—"

"Dodger Stadium?"

"Yes."

"Then it's true! They are gonna move here! Hallelujah! Where is this 'Dodger Stadium?' "

"In the Chavez Ravine."

"Where the hell is that?"

"Near Elysian Park. Across from the Police Academy."

He made a face, looking almost exactly like Jack when he did it. "Oh, yeah. That's a goddamn Hooverville, all those poor Mexican bastards livin' in shanties. Where are they gonna go?"

"I don't know."

"So, what brings you back here?"

"I work for a company that sends people back in time, you know, for vacations. To get away."

"Why would people want to get away from their own time? You couldn't pay me to go back to the Thirties. Or the war."

"You live in a nice time," I replied. "The nation is prosperous, you live in a place where there's no crime, your kids are getting a good education, growing up happy and without scars.''

Joe nodded and lit another cigarette. "What's your time like?''

I paused for a moment. "Not so good," I said.

"Then I don't want to hear about it. But my boys—they're happy?''

"Yes."

"Then I'm happy. So you're a kind of travel agent? How did you get into that?''

"I was a cop first, and then I just sort of lucked into this.''

"You were a cop? Here in Los Angeles?''

"Yes. Detective.''

"Ugh," he winced. "What a bunch of assholes. A grandkid of mine couldn't get a real job?''

"Well, I was in the Marines after high school. I joined the Reserves and then I got called up during college for the Gulf War.''

"The what war?''

"It's not important. We won it pretty quickly.''

"Shit. I was kinda hoping that no kid of mine would ever have to fight a war. But you came out okay?''

"I won a bronze star. I joined the cops because . . . Well, I always wanted to be a cop. It was tough at first, because in the Nineties we went through a pretty traumatic period in the LAPD's history. There were riots, the LAPD was labeled racist, called thugs—''

"Well, *there*'s a shock," he interrupted. "I always thought the L.A. cops were a goon squad.''

"Not all of them, Joe. Not even most of them. But enough, I guess.''

"You don't seem like a goon to me," he said sympathetically. "It must have been rough on you.''

"It wasn't easy, but I loved the job," I said.

"Well, anyway," Joe said, "here you are. You're not married, are you? You don't have any kids.''

"No. How could you tell?''

"I've been married since 1940. That's a long time in

anybody's book. You just don't look married.''

"Well, I was, but only for a few years.''

"Nice girl?''

"Very nice girl. It just didn't work out.''

"I'm sorry.''

"I almost got married again. Also in 1940, as a matter of fact.''

"That must've been a little complicated,'' Joe remarked.

"It was.''

"She died, huh?''

"How did you know that?''

"Your voice got a little smaller. You don't have to tell me about it.''

I shook my head. "But I want to, Gramps.''

He laughed. "Sorry. But I'm forty years old, and someone's callin' me 'Gramps.' What was she like?''

"She was an actress. She was killed in the war.''

"That's awful. An actress? Like in the movies?''

"Yeah.''

"Well, hell, boy, who was she?''

"Althea Rowland,'' I replied painfully.

"Althea Rowland? Holy shit! She was gorgeous!''

"That she was.''

"Well, hell, son, don't be bashful. Tell your grampa all about it! If Althea Rowland was almost my grand-daughter-in-law, I sure as hell want to hear about it.''

So I told him everything, just like I had related it to Julie Haas earlier in the day. I still wasn't sure if he believed me or not. As receptive as he might have been to "strange shit,'' my story had to have been over the top. But no one could deny our striking resemblance to each other, or the fact that the small traps he laid in our conversation—innocent questions to gauge what I knew about our family history, never stumped me even for a moment. We joined the kids as they finished the last hole on the miniature golf course.

"Why don't we all go for an ice cream?'' I offered.

"All rigggghhhht!'' cheered young Jack.

"You kids do your homework?" Joe cautioned.

"Heh-lo," Jack replied. "You know better than that."

"All done, Pop," Fred replied, a little more politely.

I knew for a fact that Fred was a Corvette fanatic, so I offered to let him drive over to the Carvel stand. Even though he was only fourteen, it was a matter of family record that Joe had already taught him to drive, and he handled the Corvette carefully, like a mature driver.

"So, how do you like the car, Fred?" I asked conversationally.

"It's great," he replied, keeping his eyes on the road. "I sure hope I can own one someday."

"You will," I replied. In fact, he would own three. My earliest memories were of Dad pulling into the driveway in a 1966 Stingray.

"How are you related to us?" Fred asked.

"What makes you think we're related?" That's my papa—never misses a thing.

"It *feels* like we're related. You look like Daddy. You look like . . . like me."

My dad is not the most spiritual guy in the world, but whenever he has a gut instinct on anything, the smart play is to mortgage your house and borrow from the Mafia to bet on it.

"Yeah," I said. "We're related. Distant relatives, but the same family."

We stopped at a red light. He turned and faced me. "Are you going to be here for awhile? Are we going to see more of you?"

"I'll be here for a little while," I said. "In fact, why don't you guys come down to my motel for a swim tomorrow?"

"Neat! I'll ask Dad."

We pulled into the Carvel stand and I parked next to Joe's Buick. I went up to the window and ordered without asking the kids what they wanted.

"Let me have a Brown Bonnet and a vanilla in a cup with chocolate sprinkles," I told the server.

"Hey!" Jack exclaimed. "How'd he know that?"

"Yeah," Joe said, a smile playing at the corner of his mouth. "How'd he know that?"

Each item cost fifteen cents. In my time, you couldn't even get the sprinkles for that price. I ordered a cone for myself, marveling at the taste. I, of course, grew up on frozen yogurt, and had never realized how good real soft ice cream could be. I swore off yogurt forever from then on.

I noticed that Fred was looking at a few teenaged girls out of the corner of his eye. Blood will tell, after all.

"Got a girl, Fred?" I asked him.

"No, not yet," he replied, blushing.

"Well, don't worry about it. I predict that you'll marry a beautiful, smart, and funny girl. And you'll have a beautiful, smart, and funny daughter and a dashing and debonair son."

He gave me a bewildered look. It was a rare expression, because nothing ever puzzled my Dad. "Are you kidding me? Or do you really know this stuff?"

"Someday, I'll tell you all about it."

"He's a physic," Joe said.   "I mean a psychic. A fortune-teller."

"Do you really know the future?" Jack asked.

"No," I said. "I'm just having fun." But not that much fun. From the look on Fred's face, I took the cue to knock it off about the future. He was a good kid, and would grow up to be a great dad. I didn't like the idea of messing with his head.

"Well, I think it's time these cowpokes headed for the corral," Joe said.

"Would you guys like to come over to my motel for a swim tomorrow, after school?" I repeated my invitation for Jack's benefit.

"Oh, yeah!" cried Jack. "Can we, Pop? Can we, huh, huh?"

"I don't see why not," Joe said. "Call us tomorrow afternoon. You know the number," he added with a smirk.

The next morning, after checking up on the Kosicks and finding them enthralled with the Fifties, I popped unannounced into the IIG offices, where I opened two $100,000 trust funds. My father and uncle would each have a decent head start on life, accruing compounded interest every day. A stroke of a pen and two boys were already men of substance and property. I enjoyed it immensely and looked forward to telling Joe about it.

I drove back to my motel. It was a hot-sheet hole-in-the-wall in my time, and the neighborhood was a nightmare. I might have even kicked open a door or two there during my years as a cop. But in the Fifties it was still a pretty nice place, the westernmost lodging for families on cross-country trips.

I had had trouble sleeping the night before, so I decided to take a nap before having the kids over. As it turned out, I didn't have any problems at all falling asleep this time. As I turned the key in the lock, something heavy struck the back of my neck and I was in dreamland before I hit the ground.

EIGHTEEN

WHEN I CAME TO, MY FIRST THOUGHT WAS THAT I WAS going to have to change professions if I was going to keep getting knocked around like this. I hadn't taken this many thumps as a cop. My second thought was, *Who the hell hit me?* How could I, of all people, get mugged? I felt in my pocket for my wallet. It was still there. Then I felt for my Decacom and Taser. They *weren't* there.

"Oh, *shit*!" I muttered.

"Still as eloquent as ever, Mr. Surrey," a familiar voice jeered.

I looked up and saw my captor. He was heavyset, gray-haired and in his late fifties.

"*Lorenz!*" I gasped.

"The same."

"Karl, you've gotta stop whacking me on the head all the time. It's beginning to piss me off."

"It's incredible, John. It's been what? Seventeen years? You haven't aged a day! How do you do it?"

"Clean living," I grunted, getting up and moving myself over to the bed, while Karl covered me with a pistol. He drew my Decacom and Taser out of his pocket. "Later on, you must tell me all about these wonderful toys. But first, we simply must talk. You wouldn't have anything to drink, would you?''

''There's a soda machine right outside. Pepsi, Orange Fanta. I could go get you one, if you give me a dime.''

''No, I'll do without, thank you.''

''So, Karl, how did you find me?''

''Pure chance. I saw you coming out of an office building on Wilshire Boulevard, not far from our consulate. I couldn't believe it. I followed you, and here we are. I was sorry to hear of Miss Rowland's death,'' he added. ''You didn't have much time together, did you?''

''Fuck you,'' I snapped.

''May I remind you,'' he said, ''that the circumstances are somewhat . . . reversed from our last meeting?''

''Yeah, yeah. Karl, what are you *doing* here?''

He drew himself up proudly. He still cut a pretty imposing figure, I had to admit it. ''I'll have you know,'' he said, ''that I am the Los Angeles Consul General of the Federal Republic of Germany.''

''And how in the hell did you swing that?''

He took a chair and sat down opposite me. ''Well, it's a long story, but it has its moments. I was brought to England, questioned, imprisoned in Scotland. They really didn't know what to do with me. After the Battle of Britain, I knew we were going to lose the war. It was just a matter of time before the Americans got into it. So I began to change my tune. I gave the British a few of our agents in America, small potatoes, but it went over well. I started to distance myself from the Nazis. By the time the war was over, I was completely white-listed.''

''Oh, yeah? What about the camps, the genocide of the Jews?''

''I was truly horrified.''

''Bullshit.''

''No, I'm quite serious. I never thought it would come to that. I thought we'd treat the Jews and the Poles and others the way you treat your Negroes, that's all.''

''Come on, dickhead, you called me a Jew-lover.''

''I'm not a good man, but I am not evil,'' he insisted.

"I'm just an opportunist. I knew in 1930 the only way to survive was to join the Party. If the target of the Fuhrer's wrath had been Methodists or Buddhists, I would have gone along with it."

"Well, Karl, no one could say that you're dishonest, I'll give you that."

"Just so. After the war, there was a critical need for white-listed Germans in the new government. My captors had become my friends, for the most part, and it was a simple matter to get into the foreign service.

"I've got quite a reputation, John. Do you know that before I received this assignment, I was First Secretary in our embassy in Tel Aviv? I have lots of Israeli friends. I even learned to speak passable Hebrew. To be truthful, I was quite angry when your government forced them to break off the action in the Sinai last year."

"Yeah, you're a real citizen of the world, Karl. I'll bet you've got lots of old pals in Argentina and Paraguay, too. Speaking of old pals, whatever happened to those two who were with you?"

He chuckled. "Heinrich, you remember, the large fellow, he endured his captivity with his usual stoicism. He is now a machinist in Frankfurt, with a round hausfrau and three children. Dieter is much more interesting. He remained in England, married an English girl and now runs his father-in-law's pub in Hackney. You should hear him—you'd never believe the man was once a German. He speaks with a cockney accent! Oh, it's hilarious! 'Aw don' dew nuffink 'gainst the Queen,' he says. 'If the Queen sez it's awright wiv 'er, it's awright wiv me.' "

Karl's own cockney imitation was perfect, and funny. I laughed in spite of the situation.

"So, why are you here, Karl? Everything worked out. I actually did you a favor. Would you rather have been in Germany when Götterdämmerung came crashing down on your head?"

He absently picked up the Decacom. "Is this the thing you fired at me?"

"Uh, I'd be really careful with that, Karl. Watch that red button."

"Is this the trigger?"

There was a knock on the door. "John? Are you there?"

"Who is that?" Lorenz whispered.

"Opa," I replied, using the German term for grandfather.

"Be quiet!" he hissed.

"Coming, Gramps!" I called.

"Goddamnit!" Karl barked. He pointed the Decacom at me and pushed the red button. He disappeared in an instant.

I got up, strolled to the door, and opened it to admit Grampa.

"Are you all right?" He looked worried.

"What makes you think I'm not? Where're the boys?"

"I made them wait in the car. You sure you're okay? You don't look so hot. Are you in any trouble?"

"Why did you think I was in trouble?"

"I didn't. Fred did. He just started worrying about you, out of the blue."

"Aw, he's a wonderful father, isn't he?" I said, half-kidding, half-moved.

Terry Rappaport materialized in the room. Joe's eyes bugged. "Keep this to yourself, Joe," I said.

"Who the hell would believe me?"

"John!" Terry put an arm on my shoulder. "Are you all right, kiddo?"

"I've got a headache, but I'm okay. Terry Rappaport, meet Joe Surrey. My grandfather."

Terry extended his hand. "Hiya, Joe. You've got a good grandson here." He looked around the room. "So this is 1957, huh? Black-and-white TV, wall unit air conditioner . . . Where's Elvis?"

"In the Army? I'm not sure. Anyway, he really is alive. What've you done with our guest?"

"Cuffed him to a chair in the conference room. I got his piece—It'll make a nice addition to my collection. Here's your Decacom and Taser. Who is that guy?"

"Lorenz . . . that Nazi asshole from 1940 I told you about."

Terry grinned wickedly. "You don't say?"

"Not so fast, old buddy. The son-of-a-bitch is the West German Consul General here in L.A."

"Crap! Those pricks always land on their feet, don't they? Okay, we'll hold him until you get back."

"Okay. I'll see you later."

"Much later. Nice meeting you, Grampa." He pushed the red button and was gone.

"I've gotta sit down," Joe said, dropping into a chair. "This is all too much for my poor addled brain." He fished into his shirt pocket for a cigarette.

"You shouldn't smoke so much," I said.

He put it back in the pack. "That's what my wife says— sorry, that's what your gramma says. Hah! Lee as a grand-mother. That's a good one."

My grandmother, now a great-grandmother, lived in New Zealand with my parents. I had seen plenty of pictures of her taken in the 1950s, however, and it *was* hard to believe she would ever get old. Even in her late eighties, she still carried herself like the beautiful woman she had once been.

"Joe," I said. "I need you to do me a big favor."

"Name it, kid. After all, you are my grandson."

"I don't want you to worry, that's all."

"Worry about what?"

"The kids. They're going to be fine."

"Why would I worry? They're great kids."

"Because you're a father. No matter what happens, I want you to remember that they're okay. Fred is going to marry early and run a successful business. Jack is going to be an admiral."

"Hah! Jack, an admiral! God, I'd love to see that."

"Listen to me, Joe. Remember what I said: Jack is going to be an admiral. He's going to be fine. In fact, even now, he's my best friend. He's sixty-two years old, tall, hand-some, muscles out to here. Will you promise me you'll always remember that?"

Joe's eyes narrowed. "What're you tryna tell me? What happens to Jack?"

"He's going to be *fine*. Okay?"
He shook his head. "Okay," he sighed.

Joe and Jack were wrestling in the shallow end of the pool.
I noticed that Joe was being particularly attentive to his
younger son.

I sat on the edge of the deep end, with my feet in the
water. Fred swam up to me, lifted himself out of the pool,
and sat next to me.

"When are you leaving?" he asked me.

"Tomorrow."

"Why?"

"I have to go back. I'm a workin' man."

He paused, obviously searching for a way to phrase his
next, probably awkward question. I suddenly felt glad that
this kid would grow up to be my father.

"Do you ever . . . feel stuff?"

"Sure," I said. "You walk into a room and you feel like
you've been there already—"

"No, not like that. Sorry to interrupt," he added quickly.

"No, it's okay, Fred. Tell me about it."

"It's hard. But I feel like I can talk to you."

"Well, we *are* related."

"That's what I mean. Look, Jack's my brother, right?
And that's my dad, and my mom is out shopping. I know
they're my family. And that's how I know you're my family."

"Then what's wrong, Fred?"

"I'm just worried that we're not gonna see you again
for a long time."

I whistled softly. My father had always had good instincts, but I had never realized that he was this perceptive.

"I *am* away a lot," I said. "But don't worry, I'll see
you all again. I promise."

"You'll be okay?"

"Of course, Fred. Why wouldn't I be?"

"I don't know. I just get worried sometimes. And I'm
usually right."

I put my arm around his shoulder. "You're a good kid,"

I said. "And I don't mean that in a full-of-crap grown-up kind of way, either. I promise, you, I'll be fine. And so will you. So will everyone."

I saw them off later on in the parking lot. I hugged each of the kids, Jack a little sad to see me go, Fred much more so.

"Joe," I said motioning him aside and handing him a slip of paper.

"What's this?" he asked, glancing at it.

"It's two numbered accounts. I've set up two one hundred thousand dollar trust funds, one for each of the boys."

"Well, it's the least you could do, you cheap bastard," he said sternly, and then broke into a grin. "Are you sure you can afford this?"

"Quite sure. You're the only person who can touch this money until they're twenty-one, and even then, only for college."

"I can afford their college," he said. "This'll be a hell of a graduation present, though."

I hugged him, realizing that this was the last time I would ever see him alive. I was dry-eyed, but not by much.

"Remember what I said, Joe."

"I know, I know. Jack's okay. He's an admiral."

"Don't forget."

"I won't. Don't be a stranger."

"I'll . . . try."

I stood in the parking lot long after they drove from sight.

I had a slight, unforeseen problem when I picked up the Kosicks at the Beverly Hills. They weren't speaking to each other—that was the problem. I didn't know why, but I knew I had to get them back and sort it out in debriefing. It was bad policy to let clients go away mad, even if it wasn't our fault.

It was hard to believe they were the same couple. The expression on Mrs. Kosick's face whenever she had to glance in her husband's direction was one of pure disgust. Mr. Kosick's response was one of outraged innocence, as though he were constantly demanding, "What'd I do, for Christ's sake? What? What?"

This was all I needed, a damned domestic quarrel to settle, as if I were a patrol rookie fresh out of the academy. But something had to be done, I thought as we stepped out of the Zoom Room and I saw Mr. Kosick's hurt expression when his wife shook his helpful hand off her shoulder.

I met Terry's eye and nodded to him to join me in an empty office.

"Terry, I need your help on this one."

"What's the problem? What's with the Kosicks? She looks about ready to spit in his eye."

"She is. The question is why."

Terry nodded in mild annoyance. "Oh, God. Shades of uniform patrol. That's what I hated the most about being in the bag—domestics. Who do you want me to take, the husband or the wife?"

"The wife. Don't ask her anything about it. Just do a routine debrief. I have a feeling she'll blow when she's ready, so just wait for it. I'll talk to Mr. Kosick. Then we'll compare notes and see if their stories add up."

It didn't take long. Mr. Kosick was very forthcoming with me, feeling extremely foolish but insisting that after fifty years, the statute of limitations should definitely apply.

Mrs. Kosick's anger was already beginning to dissipate, Terry said later, but she was having trouble letting go of it completely. Needless to say, the explanation of the entire contretemps was given in more detail by Mr. Kosick. But their stories gelled.

Fifty years before, at the beginning of their senior year at Hollywood High, the Kosicks met and were instantly attracted to one another. It was one of those rare events when a couple meets and knows right away that they have found the missing piece.

They met in an English class, where they were assigned seats next to each other. After class, they walked across the campus to their next class, gym, and that was where they agreed to go out on their first date, that night.

All this was observed by the Kosicks themselves, and it

was heartwarming, not so different from the way they had remembered it.

That night they went to the movies and then out for a burger, after which they drove up to Mulholland and parked. All of this, observed at a discreet distance by themselves fifty years older.

Parked at Mulholland, looking out over the sprawling lights of the Valley, they talked of many things. It was the kind of conversation where new couples unconsciously probe for weaknesses; if they find strength, the result is the possibility of a relationship.

For the Kosicks, the more they talked, the more they found to like about one another. And even though their conversation concerned a multitude of topics that had nothing to do with romance, they found themselves drawing closer and closer to each other—both figuratively and literally.

Finally, all of their pent-up passion exploded, resulting in an intense necking session of mammoth proportions. That was it. They were officially an item; and would be for the next fifty years, four kids, and six grandchildren.

What then was the problem? Two simple words: *high school*.

The next morning, they observed themselves as each arrived at school. First was the future Mrs. Kosick, still glowing from the night before, flanked by two envious girlfriends to whom she breathlessly and repeatedly described the events of the night before.

Then came the young Mr. Kosick, surrounded by his pals. Apparently, young Mrs. Kosick was a new girl in school, extraordinarily pretty, and the unconscious target of the lust of many of her male classmates.

At first, young Kosick tried to shake off the congratulations and demands for details with a few modest shrugs. But as the challenge of "Wudja get?" became more and more insistent, his resistance weakened and finally collapsed.

"Second base," he had replied, unable to keep the braggadocio out of his voice; and fifty years of respect went up in smoke. For in their new found delight and passion, he *had* copped a feel off of his future wife, and she had allowed it—even on a first date—because she trusted him and knew they were serious about one another. What she hadn't foreseen was that he would tell anyone about it. As it was, it had taken her fifty years to find out.

For Kosick's part, he told me that he recalled feeling ashamed for a brief time, and then he had forgotten about it. It would have gone unnoticed and unremarked upon, if not for Timeshare.

"Well," said Terry, "I can understand how she feels. But it was fifty years ago, and they've had a life together that most people would kill for. I know I would. What do we do about it?"

"I think it's time we let them kiss and make up," I said.

We escorted the Kosicks into one of the small rooms we keep for those times when we are required to work around the clock. It was the equivalent of a good hotel room, with a bed, a sitting area, bar, and bathroom: Very often, we'd have our clients "depressurize" there after a return from a trip, using it as a temporal transition area.

The Kosicks said not a word as I led them into the room. I could tell from the uneasy silence that they were ready to patch things up; all that had to happen was for Mrs. Kosick to decide that she wasn't angry anymore—that, and for Mr. Kosick to say just the right things.

"Okay, folks," I said. "We've found—I know I have— that after a trip you need a nap before hitting the road. Being back there takes more out of you than you'd think. There's a fully stocked bar and some snacks in the fridge, so help yourselves. Take as long as you like."

"Is this really necessary?" asked Mrs. Kosick.

"I'm afraid so," I lied. "It's for your own protection. Otherwise, it'd be the equivalent of letting you drink and drive."

I closed the door and joined Terry in an office nearby. We turned on the audio, but prudently left the video monitor off. We weren't really busybodies—we were just dying of curiosity.

It took a while before either of them said anything.

"I'm sorry," Kosick said finally. Judging from his voice, they were seated across the room from one another.

"It's not enough," Mrs. Kosick answered stiffly.

"Aw, come on, honey. I was a kid, for Christ's sake!"

". . . So humiliated!"

"Look, they were good guys. Nobody ever said anything to you about it, did they? Of course not! Why? Because they probably thought I was fulla crap, that's why!"

"That was really tacky, Len."

"I know! I know. But, gimme a break, you saw how they busted my balls. It just—popped out—before I could take it back. Come on, we've had four kids. You know what teenagers are like."

"I know. But it doesn't excuse . . ." She trailed off. He was already getting to her.

"Look, you wanna know how I really felt that day?"

No answer.

"It was the first best day of my life. I say 'the first' because they just kept getting better after that. But you know what I thought? I couldn't believe my luck, that's what. And you know what else? After fifty years, I *still* can't."

"Oh, Len. You still think you can get around me."

"Because I can," he chuckled.

"Len! Here?"

"Well, there's a bed, isn't there?"

Terry reached up and flicked off the audio switch. "Lucky bastard," he said.

We still had one more guest who needed our attention. Terry followed me into the conference room where Lorenz was being held.

He sat at the head of the long table, one arm extended downward where it was cuffed to the chair leg.

"Karl, baby," I said. "Long time, no see."

"Where am I? I demand to be released at once!"

"No prob, old pal. Karl, I want you to meet my associate, Terry Rappaport, formerly of the New York City Po-

lice Department. Terry, Karl Lorenz, West German Consul
General. Formerly a *sturmbannfuhrer* in the SS. That's a
major to you, Terry.''

"No kidding," Terry replied. "A major? Highest I ever
got during my hitch in the Army was E-5 sergeant. You
must be some kinda guy, Karl.''

"You two have a lot in common," I continued to Karl.
"His family came from Germany. Well, half of them *didn't*
come from Germany. They stayed there, because, well, hell,
they were Germans, after all. Like, for example, Terry's
great-grandfather, boy, there was a kraut for you. Won the
Iron Cross, first-class, in World War One. Where was it,
Ter? Ypres?''

"Paeschendaele," Terry replied. "He was a real kick-
ass soldier.''

"A real kick-ass soldier," I repeated. "Kind of guy,
well, if he were American, we wouldn't waste him on the
Army—sorry, Ter, Terry was Airborne—we'd make sure
he was in the Marine Corps, a guy like him.

"But we'd never get the chance. Why? Because he'd
never leave Germany. That was his country, after all. He
loved it. That's where he wanted to live. And that's where
he wanted to die. Right, Ter?''

"Right," murmured Terry.

"Well, Karl. He never got his wish. Because in 1941, he
was deported to Poland. They took away his citizenship—
an acknowledged war hero, whose family was German to
their bone marrow—and they took away his citizenship.
You want to guess *where* in Poland they sent him?''

Karl looked fearfully at Terry. "I wasn't ... you must
believe that I had nothing to ...''

Terry patted his shoulder in an exaggeratedly soothing
manner. "Of course you didn't," he cooed, like a mother
to a small, injured child. "It's all right.''

"Well, you two have will have lots to talk about." I got
up and went to the door, then turned back abruptly. "Hey,
Terry, I just remembered. Karl said he speaks Hebrew.
Maybe you guys could—''

"I forgot all mine about five minutes into my bar mitzvah reception," Terry said. "That stuff just goes if you don't use it."

"Oh, that's a shame," I clucked. "I'll be back. I gotta make an important phone call. I gotta call New Zealand. There's a birthday in the family over there. My Grampa Joe is ninety years old today . . . Can you believe that?"

"Tell him *mazel tov* for me, willya?" Terry said. He smacked Karl lightly on the back of the head.

"Mazel tov," croaked Karl.

NINETEEN

I LET TERRY PLAY A FEW MORE MIND GAMES, SCARING THE crap out of Karl, before bringing in Doc Harvey. We had the Doc give Karl a drug-induced form of hypnosis before zooming him back to 1957. He would wake up in my motel room and not remember a thing.

Meanwhile, I did something hadn't done in a quite a while. I spent a quiet evening at home. I worked out for a couple of hours and then settled back to read a good book. I had dug up a copy of Thomas Hardy's *The Mayor of Casterbridge*, a book I thought I had read a long time ago and which delighted me when I discovered that I hadn't.

It was therefore with great annoyance that I went to answer my doorbell. My irritation turned to elation when I opened it and was greeted with a blast from the past—my own.

Standing before me were two cops in full uniform, my closest friends on the force: Captain Jeannie Silvera and Deputy Chief Randolph Dickinson.

''Out of my way, white boy,'' Dickinson growled in his booming basso profundo voice, shoving his way past me, before turning around and sweeping me into a bear hug.

''Let me get a piece of this,'' said Jeannie, shoving the blue giant away from me and giving me a hug and a kiss.

"You don't call, you bastard? Almost two years, just a lousy Christmas card? I'm gonna have to drag you down to the alley and beat the shit out of you."

"I missed you too," I said. "Come on in."

"Martha has been worried sick about you," Dickinson said, plopping into the chair I had just vacated. "You don't call, you haven't been over to dinner. We're just about to give up on you." He picked up my book and flipped it over to read the cover. "I much preferred *Tess of the D'Urbervilles*. But that's neither here nor there. Do you have anything to drink?"

"What would you like?"

"Do you have any champagne? That is to say, sparkling wine from the Champagne region of La Belle France? If so, get thee to the scullery."

I got me to the scullery, wondering as I did so why my two old friends had dropped in. I hadn't seen either of them since leaving the department, even though I had promised to keep in touch.

Jeannie Silvera had been my classmate at the Academy. She came from a family of cops, although none of them had ever gone higher than Senior Lead Officer. She had been the outstanding cadet in our class, and the most popular, as well. We had been close friends since the beginning of training. And although our paths never crossed much on the job, we had kept in contact throughout our careers—always ready to help each other with unowed favors. Unlike me, she had remained in uniform, taking the exams and rising swiftly to the rank she now held. And in case you're wondering why, since we hit it off so well, we never got involved, the answer is simple: She had gotten married just before coming on the job. Her husband, a successful insurance executive, adored her and supported and respected her completely.

Randy Dickinson was my watch commander during my rookie year in Devonshire division. He was a good boss, easy to work for as long as you did your job well. He was also the consummate empire-builder, and was constantly on the lookout for protégés who could make him look good and help his own career. In return, he offered his unshakable and total support, career guidance, and occasional dinners at his home. The latter was the most important benefit; his wife Martha was the best cook in the civilized world. Half the cops in the division would have gladly put up a month's pay each to back her if she ever opened a restaurant. It was Dickinson's good luck that he was over six-and-a-half feet tall and large-framed; a smaller man would have turned into a blimp after a few years in that marriage.

It was Dickinson who was in command of the Fugitive Squad when I made detective, and he wasted no time in bringing me over more senior cops, rescuing me from the usual entry-level dead end of Business Burglary or Vice. Since then he had gone on to greater things, rising through the ranks to Captain, Commander, and now Deputy Chief.

As I brought in the bottle of Piper and three glasses, I wondered what was up. They were still in uniform this late at night, which meant that they had just come from a high-level meeting. If I had still followed local news, I might have known which meeting, but my concern of late had been old news.

I popped the cork and filled the glasses.

"To old friends," I toasted. Dickinson winked at Jeannie and said, "To the future," which handed me a private laugh of my own.

"All right, kids," I said as we leaned back and sipped. "What's the story?"

"Don't you read the papers?" Jeannie asked me in disbelief.

"Not if I can help it," I said.

"Well, for God's sake, didn't you vote in the last election?"

"I wasn't in town," I replied, not adding that I wasn't even in this century. "Did I miss something?"

"Proposition 224. More cops? Twelve *hundred* more cops? *If* we could get matching federal funds?"

"So?"

"Well, we got it, John. The good citizens of Los Angeles have had it with crime, and they're finally willing to go into their pocketbooks to do something about it.''

I shrugged. ''Oh. Well, that's good.''

''Jesus,'' Jeannie breathed, rolling her eyes. ''Curb your enthusiasm.''

''Patience, Jeannie,'' Dickinson said, looking at his champagne flute appraisingly. ''Baccarat. Our boy has done well. He may not be interested in the fact that effective thirty days from today all promotions will be unfreezed. Or is it unfrozen? No matter. Which means that our dear Jeannie will proudly don a star and become a commander. And certain other officers, like those who have been inactive for just under the two-year cutoff, may still return to active duty with their standing on the lieutenants list very much intact.''

''And you, Randy?'' I asked. ''What about you?''

He refilled his glass. ''We've just come from an emergency session of the police commission. Chief Spier, our fearful leader, has just tendered his resignation. Assistant Chief Blaine, a numbnuts equally lacking in fortitude, will succeed him, but only in the interim. The commissioners made that quite clear. Ergo, the game's afoot.''

''They won't go outside the department for a chief, will they?'' I asked.

''I should think not. After all, we have a few good prospects right here at home. And the fact that the best prospect is a brother, is all to the good.''

''Namely you.''

''Namely me.''

''Will you please come back, John?'' Jeannie pleaded. ''You've only got a few months left to decide.''

I shook my head. ''For what? Look, Randy, I think it's great. The least you'll do is assistant chief. Jeannie, you'll get your star, make deputy chief in a few years and then, congratulations, you might even go out as the first female chief. I mean it, hon, I think it's wonderful. Hell, I knew back at the academy you'd go higher than anyone else in our class. But what do *I* do? Great, I come back in and make lieutenant. That means one of two things: I either start out on the graveyard shift at Seventy-seventh Street—in uniform—or they put me back in Juvey. No, thank you. Not in this life."

"Did I neglect to mention . . ." Dickinson began.

"Mention what?"

"During the interim, while Numbnuts is having his fifteen minutes of fame, I will be in command of the Administrative Bureau?"

"Yeah, so?"

"Well, my boy, that will allow me to make certain . . . administrative . . . decisions. And one of those decisions will be to bring back the Fugitive Squad. Jeannie, that is a lieutenant's command, is it not?"

"It is," Jeannie nodded. "Of course, it would have to be the right kind of lieutenant."

"One with experience in the Squad."

"A proven leader."

"A cop with ability who has shown himself to possess intelligence and ingenuity. Also, one who is cunningly and charmingly just one oar short of a full galley. Do we know of anyone like that, Commander?"

"I think we can dig one up. Come on, John, don't be a wuss. You do the usual eighteen months on your favorite duty, but this time, in command of the Squad. And during that time, you'd damn well better study for the captain's exam."

It was all too much. To have a purpose again. To be back on the Fugitive Squad . . . to *command* it! To have a future in the department brighter than anything I could have imagined during the gritty patrol days at Newton Street. Eighteen months ago, it would have given me wings. Today, weighed against Timeshare, what was it?

It was a moral dilemma, that's what it was. For who was I? An ex-cop with a good corporate job. And where had it left me? Like Evelyn Waugh's Charles Rider, I was loveless, childless, and middle-aged. I had helped make a great discovery, but what was I really doing with it—besides making hotel reservations and getting rich betting on sure things? I had had some wonderful times, but the woman I loved was more than half a century dead and my life was spinning itself out in a routine of solitude. I had almost been sacrificed by my own employer, who threw me to the wolves of the Senate Intelligence Committee, from which my escape was too narrow for comfort. Where was my purpose? My raison d'être?

"I don't know," I said finally. "You can't imagine what you're asking."

"John," Jeannie began, but Dickinson cut her off.

"Let him think about it," he said. "I sense inner turmoil." He nodded to Jeannie and they both got up.

"Randy?"

"Yes, John."

"If I do decide to come back, can I ask a favor?"

"Of course."

"I have a good friend. We work together. He was a detective in New York. A damned good one. He worked undercover for two years and busted the Mob wide open. Could I bring him in with me? Say as a Sergeant Two?"

"I don't see why not, if he's as good as you say."

"He's got a bum leg. Metal shinbone. But I think it'd be a waste to leave him behind. He gets around okay."

He patted my shoulder. "We'll see. Let's work on you first."

After they left, I tried to sit down and think, but I couldn't keep still. I was constantly jumping up and prowling around the apartment. I tried to watch a movie, but it was just too awful to capture my attention for very long. The other eighty channels all had infomercials for the same stomach flattener.

Finally, I sat down and did what I should have done in the first place. I picked up the phone.

"Mom? Is that you? Is Dad around?"

"John! Are you all right?" Her old mommy-radar was kicking in right on schedule.

"I'm fine. Is Dad there, too?"

"I think he's out in the lower forty," she said, putting on an old farmer's voice. "Wait, here he is."

"Is that you, John?" Dad came on the line.

"All right, I'll let the two of you talk," Mom said.

"No, no, I need both of you," I said.

For the next fifteen minutes, I gave them the details of my dilemma. They listened attentively and without interruption, but even in their silence, I could tell that they were not thinking too hard on what I was saying. They knew that whatever was bothering me was much deeper than a simple occupational decision.

"No one ever liked the idea of your becoming a cop, John," Mom said when I was finished. "But if that's what makes you truly happy . . . And you *do* need to be happy."

"Maybe we should discuss this when we get to town," my father said.

"You're coming to L.A.?" I exclaimed. "When?"

"Next month," Mom said. "All of us. We found a nice place in Beverly Canyon and—"

"You're moving back?"

"Only part-time," Dad said. "Half the year. But we all need it. Your mother misses the social whirl, and quite frankly, so do I. Not to mention the food. We miss you. And if I may be so bold, you need us."

"I can't argue that," I said. "It's wonderful! I can't wait to see you. What made you decide?"

Mom said, "We just wanted to stop running, John. You should keep that in mind, because isn't that what your problem is really all about?"

"Your mother's right, John. It's time to stop running. There's something bothering you—it has been for awhile. I don't know what it is exactly, and you don't have to tell me. But for the past few years you've been hiding yourself away, and it has your mother and me worried. She's right, John. It's time to stop running."

"You know me like a book, Pop."

"Have since I was fourteen, kiddo."

I hung up feeling a lot better, as is so often the case after talking to the folks. I felt flush with a new sense of purpose, and I picked up the phone again.

"Hello, Cornelia? I want to see you in fifteen minutes. No, not in that yuppie restaurant. Meet me at Van Nuys

Airport, at my tiedown. You know where it is. Fifteen minutes.''

The most important decision of the rest of my life would take place on my own turf—in the sky.

TWENTY

"YOU'D BETTER BE ONE HELL OF A PILOT," CORNELIA warned me as I sideslipped the aircraft and then raised the nose to bleed off airspeed. "Are you sure there's an airfield down there?"

"Uncle Jack taught me how to fly when I was twelve. I know every inch of the map between L.A. and Vegas."

"Well, I can't see a thing down there."

"Trust me," I said, as I cut the throttle and greased us in sweetly on all three points. We were at an uncontrolled desert airstrip outside of Victorville that had been used by the Air Force for emergency landings in the days before the base was closed down. I shut off the engine and we climbed out. The night was moonless but full of stars.

"All right," Cornelia demanded, striding around the aircraft to where I was checking the control surfaces. "What's all this about? Why did you bring me here?"

"I wanted to be sure we were alone," I said, not adding that I also wanted every advantage I could muster.

She shivered. "Are there rattlesnakes around here?"

"Probably. Don't worry. I've got a gun in the plane. Okay, Cornelia, I've done more than my share of bowing; now it's your turn to curtsy. I want to know what the hell is going on, and I want to know now."

"I don't know what you're talking about," she answered huffily.

"Fine," I retorted. "Then this is my official notice. I quit!"

"You can't quit."

"The hell I can't. I'm going back to the police force. I've had it."

"I thought you'd had it with the police force."

"Things have changed. Chief Dickinson wants to recall me to duty and hand me my lieutenant's shield. He's going to re-form the Fugitive Squad and give it to me. What's *your* offer?"

"What's *my* offer? You've got your nerve! I've given you adventure, made you rich—"

"I don't give a good goddamn about money, anymore than you do. And you know it. I'm tired of being your pratboy, Cornelia. I want my life back. Randy can give it to me. What can *you* do?"

She sighed and sat down on the tarmac. "All right, John. Go ahead. Tell me what you want."

"First of all, I want to know what you've been doing every night."

She looked startled. "What do you mean?"

"Oh, come on. You've got two brilliant detectives working for you. We wiped the apparatus clean one night, and the next morning, we lifted fingerprints off the controls— *your* fingerprints. A twenty-point match. What's the future like, Cornelia?"

"I can't tell you that."

"All right," I said agreeably. "Tell me about the past. What happened with the Senate hearings?"

"I called in a favor."

"A favor? From where?"

"I think you know where."

"The President? How'd he get involved?"

"We go way back," Cornelia said. "I first met him when he was a congressman on one of the scientific oversight committees. I had to appear to help justify a raise in my department's budget. After the meeting, he hit on me."

"Can't blame a guy for trying, can you?"

"No, and I didn't. We became friends after that. And we helped each other's careers."

"I see. And how'd you manage that?"

"John—"

"Come on, Cornelia, this is getting good."

"I was able to help him to . . . look ahead."

"Wait a minute. Are you saying . . . you invented the Zoomer a long time ago?"

She smiled. "I had the theory down when I was still an undergrad at Caltech. I was even close to the technology. The only thing that gave me any problem at all was the temporal equalizer."

"The what?"

"Look, the principle of the machine is simple. It's not exactly 'time travel' per se. What is really involved is the reversal or acceleration of the aging process, by placing the subject in a vacuum. That was the only problem. I had to protect the subject from the aging process reversal, keep it isolated."

"And you discovered this when?"

"Oh, years ago. It was much cruder then, but serviceable."

"Don't tell me. You gave our future prez a certain insight. He knew who was going to be on the way up, and who wouldn't amount to anything. He could befriend the movers before they became important enough to be suspicious of his motives. He could also predict crises before they actually occurred."

"Right. He was a good man, why shouldn't he have had the advantage? Coming from a small state, he never would have had a chance otherwise."

"Hey, I voted for the guy, Cornelia. He's doing a pretty good job, considering, and I'll probably vote for him again. So you're still working for him, huh? Well, hey, I think it's a good idea. The President can stop something bad from happening while it's still in an embryonic stage. But why the hearings?"

"One of our clients shot his mouth off to the wrong

person. I knew you'd never get in any real trouble, and the President would've bailed you out if it had come to that."

"Boy," I said. "I do run in lofty circles, don't I?"

She was silent for awhile. "John," she said finally, "you can't quit."

"Oh? And why not?"

"You're still going to be unhappy. And going back on the force won't help much."

"Why not?"

"I'm not you, John. I can't really say, although I might have an idea. But it'll affect the way you do your job. You'll take more chances than you should. And, John . . . you'll die."

I gasped. "What do you mean, I'll die? And where have I heard this before?"

"All right, John, I'll tell you exactly, because it'll be in all the papers a year-and-a-half from now. You'll kick in a door, and because you always insist on going first, you'll catch the full load of buckshot waiting on the other side."

I stood up walked slowly around the Cessna, placing my forehead against the tailplane. I felt Cornelia's hand on my shoulder.

"I'm sorry, John."

I spun around. "You know what? I don't care. I always figured I'd go out like that, anyway. There are worse ways to die."

"John . . . all right, you asked me for a better offer. Here goes. Felice and I want to expand our operations. We also want to retire from the day-to-day running of the place. We'll make you CEO and give you twenty percent of Timeshare Unlimited."

"That's a start," I said, "but it's not what I want."

"I've been working on the machine, John. I've installed the latest technology. Do you know what that means?"

"I haven't the foggiest."

"We're portable, John. We're not restricted to Los Angeles anymore. We can bring the machine anywhere in the world. Can you imagine the possibilities?"

"Actually, I can."

She put a hand on each of my shoulders. "You told me that what I've offered isn't enough. Very well. I know what *will* be enough. And this will be my final offer. I think you'll take it."

"And what might that be?"

"You'll know. Now let's get the hell out of this godforsaken place. We've got work to do."

Terry and I stepped out of the British Airways terminal at Heathrow and were struck in the face by a driving wet wind.

"English weather," Terry grunted. "Almost as rotten as English cooking. Where's our ride?"

We had just deplaned from an interminable flight out of L.A., and both of us were feeling cranky. I had agreed to make this trip before deciding whether I was going to quit or not. "There're some limos down there," I said. "Let's go take a look. At least we got to go first-class."

Our first overseas customer, an Englishman of minor nobility but major wealth, wanted to visit the early 1930s and see for himself if they were as much fun as they seemed in Granada television productions. I imagined that they probably were, unless you happened not to have a private income.

We walked by three skinheads, who were having good old time shoving a Pakistani woman around. They were brawny young guys with crosses in their ears, missing teeth, and steel-toed boots on their feet.

"Welcome to Merrie Olde England," Terry said, grabbing the first skinhead and rendering him unconscious with his sap. Although he couldn't carry a gun overseas, he wasn't going anywhere completely unarmed.

"Kids just don't seem to have the right kind of values these days," I remarked, punching the second dirtbag in the solar plexus, and ramming his head against the bullet-proof terminal window.

"I weep for the future," Terry said, as the last one flicked open a switchblade. "I can't believe cops don't carry guns in this country. What can they be thinking of?"

he added as he caught the skinhead's knifehand, karate-chopped the weapon to the ground and pushed him toward me.

"Well, you try not to let it ruin your day," I replied, bitch-slapping the lowlife a few times before shoving him back to Terry, who bid him night-night with his trusty sap.

The Pakistani woman fled. Behind us, a skycap whistled serenely and pushed our luggage in the rain.

Terry had never been to England before, and the traffic coming at us from the wrong side unsettled him a bit. But we both became a bit more enthusiastic when the limo left the city for the rolling green countryside of Kent. Even in the rain, its beauty made us forget our discomfort—and our inherent chauvinism.

We were somewhat disappointed, however, when the limo pulled into a modern hotel owned by an American chain. I suppose we had expected a castle, or at least a baronial estate right out of the pages of *Country Life*. Still, there wasn't much to complain about as we checked into our sumptuous two-bedroom suite.

"I'm going to shower off the grit, order some room service, and sleep the clock around," Terry said.

"I wholeheartedly concur," I replied. The telephone chirped and I picked it up.

"I'm glad you two got in all right," Cornelia said. "Did you have a nice flight?"

I put the phone on speaker. "A little overlong," I replied. "But pleasant enough. Is everything assembled?"

Portable as the apparatus might have become, it still required a large portion of the cargo plane on which it had been shipped.

"Yes. We're on for tomorrow, if the weather clears."

"What does the weather have to do anything?" Terry wanted to know. "It won't matter where our guy's going."

"It matters," Cornelia said firmly. "The limo will call for you at nine. Get some sleep. We've got a busy day ahead."

• • •

Nothing in the world is more exhausting to me than sitting on my ass in an airplane for ten hours, so I fell asleep instantly and was roused only by our wake-up call. After I showered and dressed, I went into the living room and found that Terry had had the same idea. A full breakfast spread had been rolled in, and Terry was already tucking in.

"Well," he remarked, buttering a brioche, "it ain't the Donut Hole in TriBeCa, but it'll do."

"You sleep okay?" I asked as I sat down at the table.

He poured me a cup of coffee. "Only for awhile. Then I woke up and couldn't get back to sleep. I've got a strange feeling that something big is gonna happen today."

I shrugged. "Just another job," I said. "Same shit, different accents."

"I don't know," he replied. "Maybe it's because I've never been to England before. After we're done, I hope the Boss'll give me some time off. I'd like to see all the touristy stuff, take in some of the museums, Shakespeare's birthplace."

"I'm sure we can arrange it," I said. "I'll talk to Cornelia and set it up."

"Thanks, John. I'd like that."

"Terry? You ever miss it? Being a cop?"

"All the time. It's worse for me, I think, because I didn't just put in my twenty and pull the pin. I put everything I had into it for fourteen years, and then they gave me my three-quarters on a medical. Most cops I knew would kill for that three-quarters—tax-free for life. Not me. I belonged on the job."

"Would you go back, if you could?"

"I don't know. It wouldn't be the same. It's like starting over with an old girlfriend after a long time. You expect things to be the same, but they can't be. You're both different. You've both adjusted to life without each other. Now you can get back together, and it might even work, but only if you both understand that you're not picking up where you left off—you're starting over from scratch.''

"I never looked at it that way," I said. "Is that how you'd really feel about going back?"

"I don't know, kid. No one's asked me."

TWENTY-ONE

THE LIMO TURNED OFF THE MAIN AVENUE AND ONTO A narrow tree-lined road. As we cleared the trees, I saw a few rusted Quonset huts and several large hangars that seemed to have been recently restored. There was a runway that was overgrown with weeds.

"This is an old airfield," I said, "I'll bet this place hasn't been used if fifty years. I wonder what we're doing here."

"Maybe the client owns the place," Terry replied. "Anyway, we'll soon find out."

We were dropped off at the nearest hangar, next to an ambulance parked just outside the giant doors. They were partially opened, and Felice stepped out and greeted us.

"Good morning," she chirped. "Welcome to the Mother Country." She surprised us by kissing both of us on the cheek.

"Well!" I said. "There's an unexpectedly pleasant beginning of our working day."

"I'm certainly ready to go to work now," added Terry with a smile.

"Come on in," Felice said. "So we can get started."

"Felice," I asked her, "what's with the ambulance? Is someone sick?"

"No, that's just there for emergencies. You never know what could happen in a foreign country."

"Yeah, somebody might eat some of the food," Terry cracked, and Felice responded with her likable trademark laugh.

Cornelia stood by the control console making calculations. The equipment may have been miniaturized, but not the zooming area. It was gigantic, at least ten thousand square feet.

"Good morning, John. Terry."

"What's with the Zoom Room? It's huge."

"We might need the extra space," Corny said.

"Where's our client?"

Corny smiled mysteriously. "We have to talk."

"Why?"

"*You're* our client."

"Me?"

"It's part of my final offer. I'm giving you a trip, on the house. A perk. The ultimate company benefit."

"A trip? To where? I mean, when?"

"Felice?" Felice reached into a van parked in the hangar and took out two suits covered in black plastic bags.

"Here are your costumes, boys," she said.

"I'm going, too?" exclaimed Terry.

"Of course. Even the best cops need backup once in a while, don't they?"

We removed the plastic. Each of us had been given the uniform of an RAF wing commander.

"Cornelia . . ." I began.

"Save it, John. We're not going to lose you, and if this is what it takes, then so be it."

"I don't know what to say," I told her, choking up a bit.

"Forget it, John. Besides, I'm being selfish. I've got a company to run. Timeshare is only the beginning. I need you—and you, Terry—to help keep things running, and to make sure the new divisions succeed."

"New divisions?" I asked. "What new divisions?"

"Right now, there are two in the works. Both of them

just waiting for you and Terry to launch. *MedEvac Central*—Doc Harvey over there will be a big part of that one, but we're going to need your historical expertise, John. And Terry, your file says you're an enthusiast of the Old West.''

''That's right, ma'am. Someday I may even write a book about it.''

''Then you'll be just the man for *Cimarron Central*.''

''Oh, I like that. This may well be the very first bribe I've ever accepted.''

''This all sounds wonderful,'' I said. ''But first we've got to get through this.''

I took Terry aside. ''Ter, this isn't going to be any walk in the park. It's going to be damned dangerous.''

He didn't even blink. ''Yeah,'' he said. ''So what's the downside?''

''Terry—'' I began.

''John, I'm not sure what you call it in L.A., but I know a ten-thirteen when I hear one.''

''A ten-thirteen?''

''Officer needs help. I've never turned one down yet. I don't intend to start now. Now, come on. It's showtime.''

Cornelia broke with tradition and issued us Colt government model .45s with the rest of our gear. Neither of us had any idea what a use a pistol would be against a Messerschmitt Me-110, but we were zooming back into a war, after all.

We looked pretty snazzy in our RAF uniforms. ''Wing commander is a pretty high rank,'' Terry said, pointing to the three rings on his sleeve. ''It's like a lieutenant colonel. Isn't that a bit much? And not that I mean to nitpick, but neither of us have wings.''

''I understand,'' I nodded. ''The high rank is to scare off any busybodies we might come across. With no wings, we look like staff pukes from the Air Ministry. No one'll give us any trouble. Pretty slick, Cornelia.''

''I knew you'd approve, John.'' She glanced at her watch. ''Are you two ready?''

''My, you seem to be in a hurry this morning, Cornelia.''

"Let's just say we've got a schedule to keep."

She handed us two small radio units. "I want the two of you in radio contact at all times. Keep it on the set frequency."

I extended my hand to Terry. "Thanks, old buddy."

"It's an honor, John. Come on. Let's go get your girl."

Manston Airfield on August 14, 1940, was a hive of activity. There were three squadrons of obsolescent twin-engined Blenheim bombers dispersed near the east end of the runway. At the west end, a squadron of Hurricane fighters were hurriedly swinging onto the tarmac. Apparently, radar had already spotted the incoming Luftwaffe raid.

Terry and I materialized on the far side of the airfield, near the middle of the runway.

"How're we going to find her," he shouted over the roar of two Hurricanes in their takeoff run.

"Let's split up," I shouted back. "You take the east end, I'll take the west. Keep your radio on."

"It won't be much use off," he yelled.

"Terry! Your leg! Can you get around okay?"

"I'm the fastest gimp in Britain," he shouted back, and took off limping as the last pair of Hurricanes became airborne.

The air-raid siren began to wail. Personnel began diving for cover, jumping into foxholes and diving into buildings. Antiaircraft crews swung into action, pulling back bolts and swinging the guns in the direction of the impending raid.

The drone of engines became audible. A lone figure emerged from an automobile and began running for cover. I ran toward the figure. As I got closer, I saw that it was a woman, and I knew right away that it was Althea.

My first thought was, *Damn, she runs fast.* In 1940, couples didn't make a habit of jumping out of bed and going for a morning run together, so I had never been aware of her ability in outdoor sports. But she ran with a light, quick step, even in the old-lady shoes that were a part of her uniform.

She had lost a good deal of weight, a result, no doubt,

of British wartime rationing. But even as I sprinted toward
her at top speed, with only seconds before German bombs
began to fall around us, I was on fire, because there she
was, alive again.

The antiaircraft guns began firing, although the enemy
planes were still out of range.

"Althea!" I screamed, but she couldn't hear me over the
guns. She was hopelessly exposed, with far too much
ground to cover before reaching shelter. "Althea!" This
time, she heard me, and stopped. She saw me and put her
hand to her cheek. "Keep going!" I shouted. I looked up;
there was a mass of black dots in the sky. They would grow
larger soon enough. Like objects in a rearview mirror, the
enemy was much closer than they appeared.

Neither of us could make it now.

I put on a final burst of speed, my heart banging away
against my chest, my lungs burning. I caught up to Althea
and threw myself on top of her just as a Blenheim parked
at the runway's end exploded.

"John! Is it—what are you—"

"Keep your head down!" I shouted into her ear.

At least we would die together, I thought grimly, and
that's the way it's supposed to be.

I covered her entire body with my own, even though I
knew that my flesh would be an ineffective shield. I dared
to look up.

A squadron of Me-110s—fast, heavy, twin-engined ter-
rors with plenty of forward-firing armament—were bearing
down on the airfield like a swarm of vengeful bees. An
antiaircraft emplacement exploded, with pieces of guns and
men flying outward. Blenheims were on fire. From treetop
height at the end of the runway, a stream of bullets stitched
the ground in our direction in a swift, perfect line.

I screwed my eyes shut, waiting for the inevitable hail
of lead that would end our lives in the next moment.

KA-BOOM! KA-BOOM! KA-BOOM!

I looked up. The three leading 110s, the ones whose machine guns had marked us for death, had exploded in
midair, with their broken pieces cartwheeling into the trees.

KA-BOOM! KA-BOOM! KA-BOOM!

The next rank disappeared in flames. The rest of the planes broke formation and went skittering across the sky, doing anything to escape the fate of their comrades.

VRRRROOOOOOOOMMMM!

Two blue Royal Navy Sea Harrier jet fighters shrieked over the runway at twenty feet, dipping their wings to show their blue-and-orange roundels.

"Shit-hot mamma, you Nazi fuck-errrrs!" A jubilant voice crackled over my radio.

I fumbled for the transmit switch. "JACK! Is that you?"

"It ain't Wendell Wilkie, kiddo. Stay down, sports fan, I got another raid comin' in. Futureboy Two, let's come on back to zero-eight-zero."

"Got you, Futureboy Leader," came a measured English accent.

The Sea Harriers roared over the airfield again, firing Sidewinder missiles as they passed overhead. I heard more explosions, this time in the distance.

"That's enough for today, Futureboy Two," Jack's voice crackled over the radio. "Let's head for the barn."

"Right, Futureboy Leader. I suppose all good things must come to an end."

"Is Althea okay?" Jack asked.

I rolled off of her. She was dazed, but uninjured and alive. "Nothing a few weeks in Maui won't cure," I said.

"Good. See you in oh-seven," he called. "We're out of here."

"Are you all right?" I said, helping Althea to sit up.

"John! Oh, John, is it really you?"

I kissed her. Happiness flooded through me like an electrical current. "It's me. Is it you?"

Terry came running up to us. "Are you guys okay—whoops!" he said, pulling out his Decacom. "Somebody's a third wheel here, and I have a feeling it's me."

"Darling, this is my good friend, Terry."

She tried to smile. "I've heard so much about you, Terry. Forgive me for not getting up."

"That's okay." We each took one of her arms and helped her to her feet slowly.

"Let's blow this war," Terry said. I nodded and he hit the red button.

Doc Harvey and the medical team rushed the Zoom Room as we returned to the present. "I'm okay," Terry said. "Check the lady."

Doc Harvey and another technician attacked her with stethoscopes and other diagnostic equipment. I looked past them to the control panel. Cornelia stood with Felice, an arm across her shoulder. Both of them had tears streaming down their faces. I gave them both a thumbs-up and a silent thank-you.

The zoom area sparked and boomed, and the two Sea Harriers slowly materialized before us. Both canopies lifted, and technicians ran forward with portable ladders. Climbing down from the planes, the two pilots shot each other a salute of success. Uncle Jack then jumped down from the ladder, rushed up to me and pulled me into his arms.

"You're okay? We were in time?"

"We're fine. Jack . . . I don't know how to thank you."

"Hey, it was great to be back in action after all these years. Even if it was a turkey shoot. Besides, we had a stake in this, too."

" 'We?' "

The other pilot pulled off his helmet and ran a hand through a thick mane of white hair.

"May I present," Jack said, "Admiral Sir Anthony Rowland, Royal Navy Fleet Air Arm (Retired)?"

"Tony? Althea's little brother?"

He smiled and threw an arm around my shoulder. "I told you I wanted to fight the Germans," he chuckled. "Well, I finally got my chance."

He hurried over to where Doc was working on Althea.

"I've got to see this," I said. Jack and I followed him to where Althea was being poked and prodded by the medical team.

Tony stood behind Althea and tapped her on the shoulder. "Excuse me, Miss," he said. "Could you tell me how to get to Lancaster Gate?"

Althea turned around slowly. She looked searchingly at Tony, until a sob of recognition escaped her. "Little brother," she whispered to the old man.

"I've missed you so terribly," he murmured as he took her in his arms. "It's so good to have you back."

Jack and I turned away to give them the private moment that had been so long in coming.

"Jack, how the hell did you swing the Harriers?"

"It's a P.R. deal," he shrugged. "Tony handled it, with some help from Cornelia. Oh, and a call from the President to the Prime Minister, who put a word in the ear of the First Sea Lord. Just a couple of old admirals showing off. Matter of fact, we've got to get these planes back to the *Invincible*."

"You're amazing, Jack!"

"There's the one who's amazing," he said. I turned and saw Cornelia standing off by herself. I walked over and gently embraced her.

"So that's why you needed the extra space in the Zoom Room," I said, gesturing toward the Harriers. "And that's why you needed a window of good weather."

"You deserve the right to be happy, John. I told you not so long ago that you were part of our family. I meant it."

"I know," I said. "So, you were saying CEO and twenty percent?"

"We'll talk later," she said. "Go and debrief the love of your life, in your own inimitable style."

The planes were towed outside the hangar. Althea walked out with her brother, holding his arm. I helped Uncle Jack up the ladder into the cockpit.

"You're some uncle," I said.

He began to put on his helmet and stopped, looking frankly into my eyes. "All those years in a POW camp, and later on during my career, one thing I always dreamed about—besides Janine—was having a son. Then it occurred to me. I don't need one. I have you."

"And I have two terrific dads."

"We always knew it, kiddo. Back in 1957, I suspected it, and Fred was positive about it. We grew up arguing about it—just kidding, you know? We couldn't explain it, but we knew you were one of ours. And when I punched out over Nam, it was my big regret—you would be Fred's kid and not mine. Only Dad knew for sure, but he wasn't talking."

"It doesn't matter a damn, Jack."

"I know. But that didn't stop me from doing everything I could to put you back in the land of the living. Including this."

"Jack . . ."

"Forget it. That's what I'm here for." He put on his helmet and gave me a thumbs-up. Althea hugged Tony a last time and he climbed into his plane.

The two Sea Harriers ran up their engines and turned out onto the runway. In perfect concert, the Harriers began their incredibly short takeoff run and lifted into the air.

Althea and I walked slowly toward each other.

"Well, that was an adventure," Althea said.

"How do you feel?" I asked, taking her hands.

"Strange. Disoriented—" she put her hand to her mouth. "Oh my God!" she giggled, "I'm AWOL!"

"I don't think it matters too much now," I said. I pulled her close to me.

"You didn't honestly think I could live the rest of my life without you, did you, Althea?"

"I didn't think either of us had a choice," she replied, kissing me.

"That's the beauty of what I do," I said. "I mean—of what *we* do. No matter what happens, we'll always have choices."

"We? We'll be doing this together from now on?"

"We'll be doing everything together from now on," I said. "We've been apart for sixty-seven years. That's long enough."

"I like the sound of that," she said, kissing me.

Overhead, the two Sea Harriers boomed their approval.